BROTHERS & SISTERS

Edited by Charlotte Wood

Tegan Bennett Daylight

ALLEN&UNWIN

Some of the stories in this collection use real events as their settings, but they are stories, and the characters and all their actions are works of fiction.

First published in 2009

Allen & Unwin
83 Alexander Street
Crows Nest NSW 2065
Australia
Phone: (61 2) 8425 0100
Fax: (61 2) 9906 2218
Email: info@allenandunwin.com
Web: www.allenandunwin.com

Cataloguing-in-Publication details are available from the National Library of Australia
www.librariesaustralia.nla.gov.au

ISBN 978 1 74175 822 1

Set in 12/16 pt Filosophia by Bookhouse, Sydney
Printed and bound in Australia by Griffin Press

10 9 8 7 6 5 4 3 2 1

CONTENTS

INTRODUCTION

Your brother or sister, it might be said, is your other self—your grander, sadder, braver, shrewder, uglier, slenderer self.

Your sibling is your most severe judge, and your fiercest defender. You must always rescue them. They always abandon you. They abandoned you only once, and you will never forget it. They are a pain in the arse. They save you. They will not be conquered. They never leave you alone. They always leave you to pick up the pieces. They won't grow up, won't let you grow up. They are a gang, and you its weary leader, its exhausted captive. They still get off scot-free. They protect you from evil, from yourself. They are the stone in your shoe, the thorn in your side, the one who remembers things you won't. They are the special one, your ugly mirror. They will not be fooled by your nonsense. They are the only one who makes you wake and worry in the stark, dark night. They make you laugh more and cry harder than anyone ever has, or will. They withhold things: little, silly things; bad secrets. They will never stop banging on about the *past*. They don't care about you. They see through your bullshit. They are an unfillable well of need. They give you everything, and you take it all. They are still angry; you wish they would let it go. They are always telling you to let it go. A certain piece of music makes you lock eyes. You hate what they do to your parents. Your parents love them, not you, and always have. You have not touched each other since you were children. You can destroy their precious, hard-won idea with one glance. When calamity befalls you, they are first through the door. In a crisis they disappear. You only notice them when they're gone. They will never be gone. They steal your clothes, it doesn't matter; you own each other. Your friends think they are weird; they don't understand. Your friends think they are great; they don't understand. Your sibling is the only person who has ever hit you. You have never really hurt anyone but them. They are the loop, the circle of your life, and you can never break free. They have spent their life trying to break free from you, and it has broken your heart. They make you wish you were an only child. They are the reason you have an only child. They never speak to you directly, nor you to them: your lives are lived sidelong, desperate or tender or both, but you feel your shoulders touching at weddings or christenings or funerals; more and more, at funerals. One day it will be yours. They never mention your childhood. You recognise one another, this is your relief and your ruin. They are your duty. They stun you with the sudden presence and force of their goodness. They give you Christmas presents that show you are strangers. You are strangers. You love them; it cannot be explained why, or how. You can never forgive them, and you will die wanting their forgiveness.

The writers in this collection are as obstinately different from one another as your brothers and sisters are from you. They have written in surprising ways about the deep bonds—bad, beautiful or broken—between brothers and sisters, and, in one piece, about our abiding suspicion of that happy, foreign creature, the only child. Twelve stories speaking of love and fear, separation and tenderness, confusion and—sometimes—reunion.

When Patrick White's sister Suzanne died, he wrote that he and she had nothing in common 'beyond blood and a childhood'. But for so many, of course, blood and childhood is what haunts us, and always will. This book is for you.

Charlotte Wood

ABOUT THE OTHERS

Virginia Peters

I like the kitchen best because it's the smallest and darkest room in the house. The little windows are overshadowed by a large pohutukawa tree, its knotted branches peering in through the window, tapping as the wind blows. Inside there is the soft orange glow of the oven light, the hum of the element as the meat cooks.

I'm sitting on the bench, watching my mother. I can see her hands—large brown hands, the skin slightly loose like a glove, the nails strong and oval, the polish, fading, in a shade called ginger jam.

She cups a potato and, sliding the knife beneath her palm, she chops four ways then takes another. Once the basin is full of quarters, she starts on the carrots. I watch the rings wheel across the board. She talks to me while she works—or rather I talk to her, coaxing responses from her. She gets into a rhythm with the knife, the soft flow of her voice punctuated by the chop-chop-chop as her arm cranks. Every so often she stops what she is doing, and with a sigh lifts a crystal glass to her lips. I watch the lump in her throat draw back like a syringe and the dark liquid disappearing. I can smell sweet fumes atomising in the warm air as she exhales: dry sherry and Oil of Ulan.

'Tell me more,' I say.

'Well,' she begins, 'your father's mother was a lady. Very elegant, despite the fact she'd given birth to eleven children.'

I'm impatient. 'Just get to the swimming bit,' I tell her.

'*Well*,' she says, luxuriating in the vowel as she thinks. 'Your grandma went to Point Chevalier one day. And once there, she took her clothes off, folded them neatly and placed them on a rock near the water's edge.'

I lean forward on the bench. 'Was it winter?' I ask, though I already know the answer.

'Yes, it was winter. A cool day, quite blustery on the point. That's why they knew she was not just cooling off, as you might in the middle of summer.'

'*And?*'

'Well, once in the water she swam as far as she could, all the way over the low mudflats until the water deepened; and she kept going, and going, and going until the sea dragged over her like a silver blanket.' She puts her knife down and looks at me. 'And from that day onwards, Grandma was never seen again.'

'Why do you think she did it?'

'Probably because she'd had enough,' she says, placing the potatoes around the meat.

It's always the same unsatisfying response, but it doesn't stop me from pressing her, as though one day something new might be added, something she'd not thought of before, that will make things so much clearer.

By the time she is spooning the juices around the pan I've moved her on to the story of my father's brother, Jack.

'How could you cut your own throat?' I ask, fingering the corrugations in my oesophagus.

'I suppose it would require some effort,' she says.

'But *why* would you do it?'

She makes a line with her lips as she looks at me. 'Depression. It runs in the family.'

'And what about Aunty Shona?' I ask. 'What does pulverised mean again?'

And when she tells me, I ask her, 'What about her bones? Would they be pulverised?'

'I'm not sure about the bones,' she says, and for a moment I picture Aunty Shona's bones, snapped like branches on the train tracks.

We hear the door open, my father clearing his throat. So often we forget he's here. Most of the time he's not; he's up-country, travelling between doctors' waiting rooms with his bag of promotional pills.

'Hello, Mummy,' he says as he steps into the kitchen. His voice is grave, and has been since he lost his job in management. I would never know the man she married, my mother tells me, for he is certainly not the one she has now.

'Hello, Daddy.' Her voice is brisk as she dries the chopping board, completely disguising the macabre conversation we've just had.

Turning to me, my father nods. 'Girl,' he says in a frowning voice, and I turn my head, showing him the edge of my jaw.

'What's going on in here, then?' His voice is a tremolo of suspicion.

'Nothing much, Daddy.' My mother turns to smile at me. 'Just chatting with Bubba,' she says. Her voice is bright, and although I'm just a little girl, I know well enough that it's a game. I'm inside the circle with her, and my father is on the outside. He's not got the slightest idea what she's thinking right now, but I know. I know everything about her.

•

My mother has no friends. She says she doesn't have time for 'that sort of thing', as though friendship is a modern fad that won't last. I am her friend. The best companion any mother could have. A little girl who loves her.

It seems her other children, years older than me, have amalgamated into one, joined together by their proximity in age and their ordinariness. Boy, boy, girl, boy. I arrived six years later, followed by the announcement there would be no family holiday until Bubba was old enough to travel. My mother tells me they'd not been on a family holiday before, and rightfully suspect that now they never will.

Rather than dote on me like any decent older siblings might, mine ignore me. When they do speak to me, it's only to torment. In the early evening, when they arrive home from high school, they barge into the tiny kitchen where I sit quietly with my mother, talking or playing teacher with her as I run through the lessons I learned that day at school.

I watch as, with her back still turned to the bench, she throws her voice over her shoulder.

'How was your day, boys?'

'That's good. Tell me all about it,' she says when they grunt back, but I can tell by the thoroughness of her tone that she is only pretending to be interested in what they have to say.

I wait as they bang cupboards looking for food, noticing the way the corners of their eyes seem to snag each time they pass me. Sometimes they can't resist it and they have to say something—the words don't matter, it's the gruff jeering voices I can't bear. When I put my hands over my ears and sing, sure enough they raise their fists and pretend to jab me. I have to scream and scream until my mother is treading on the spot. *I can't stand it, I can't stand it. I'll end up in a mental home,* she cries.

'Why don't they like me?' I ask her when she is calm.

The answer is always the same: they are jealous of me.

'You're a very special little girl,' she explains. 'Quite different to the others. I can sit and talk to you about anything.'

The more she tells me this, the more I embody her words, and the more unremarkable my siblings appear to me.

Although they are bigger and taller, I cannot look up to them. They don't excel in any area of study at school, not even sport. Neither do they appear to be unique in any way at all, except for the simple fact one is a girl.

I can't complain about her. When my father is home and I can't sleep with my mother, I share a room with my sister. On the whole I find her an inoffensive roommate, mostly because she is barely here. She spends most of her time working at the dog kennels after school. And when she is here, her face is hidden behind two lengths of hair that are slightly parted, like curtains.

Sometimes when she is sleeping she opens her lids to find me looking at her from my pillow on the other side of the room.

'Whaddayu want, face-ache?' she growls.

I screw up my nose. 'You're a real mole,' I say, and she curls her lip in a way that makes me laugh.

'Shurrup,' she says, not *shut* up, like me. My sister has poor elocution. I speak like my mother, who won first prize when she was a little girl for her recital of 'Daffodils' by William Wordsworth.

'She's a funny little thing,' my mother says, as though it is my sister who is smaller than me. 'She really has no conversation. I never know what to say to her. Does she talk to you?'

'Sometimes she barks at me,' I say to amuse her.

'Oh, you've got a sharp wit, Bubba,' she says, ruffling my hair. 'You'll go far.'

•

Every so often my mother surprises me with the declaration that there will be no school today. Instead, we are going on an excursion. We sit on the train, our shoulders touching as we rock from side to side, looking out the window at the milky bays and inlets, and the oat-coloured sheep on the hills. Once in the city we disappear among the old government buildings, passing ministries, police headquarters, legal chambers, until we arrive at the criminal courts.

My mother examines the list with her fingernail for the best case. She has a preference for sexual assaults.

'Nothing like that will ever happen to you, Bubba,' she reassures me later.

And I tell her I already know that, for I will hardly have anything to do with such rough types as the Mongrel Mob or Black Power.

Other times we drop in to see the Prime Minister in the Houses of Parliament, as though he is a personal friend, or we take a tour of a radio studio or newspaper printing press. I am guided around by a staff member like a visiting dignitary, while my mother stands back, her two hands shyly clasping the handle of her bag.

I have the impression with all these visits she is grooming me for a bigger life than the one she has—one in the outside world of politics, communications and justice.

'You can be anything you want,' she shouts in my hair as the train roars through the tunnel towards home.

'What about the others? Can they be anything they want?' I yell back, fisting popcorn into my mouth. I'm testing her theory, for surely if she believes those hopeless lumps can be anything, she is not a reliable source of information.

I wait as she thinks for a moment, and by the time we have exited the dingy light of the tunnel for the outer world of sky and space, she says, 'I'm not so sure about the others.' The disappointment in her voice is reassuring.

'Why?' I ask, encouraging her.

'Well, they don't have the same interest in the world as you and me. We're different. And I suppose I didn't have the time to give them as I do to you. There were four of them under five. What was I to do? Take them all with me? I couldn't possibly.'

She's off track. I don't want to hear about her or *we*, I want to hear about *me*, how different I am from them, from her too, for surely she does not think I will ever be like her, cooking, washing and ironing.

'A mother can only do her best,' she is saying. 'No one is ever satisfied. Never.'

'But I'm satisfied, Mumma.'

Her eyes cast down her shoulder at me, sadly.

'You're the best mumma in the world,' I say, looking up at her.

As we face forward again, I see our heads tilting together in the glass at the end of the carriage.

'One day you'll grow up and leave me,' I hear her say. It's spoken lightly, but my response is firm.

'No I won't. Never. I will always need you to look after me.'

•

I like to go into my brothers' bedrooms when they are out, to check their pockets for coins. I also like to go through their drawers and feel about for things. Sometimes I find copies of the same magazines I find under my father's side of the bed, ones with large glossy pictures of girls. Their arms and legs are folded up in the creases of the pages, and I like to stretch them out like a picture book, then fold them up again. I know these are the sort of girls my brothers like. Pretty ones. Not the slags and dogs I hear them snicker about.

I look to the place they split open with their scissor fingers, then their bosoms, and finally I look at their faces. I spend a lot of time peering at their big soft eyes and kind smiles, noticing the way they seem to be looking at men like they love them. I never even look at my brothers, or my father, without turning my head away, just as they, too, avoid looking at me. One day I put my wall mirror on the floor and try to smile just like the girls with my legs open wide, but my forehead looks stern and my tummy thick and white—also I have a birthmark on my thigh that looks like dirt.

'Don't worry. Everything will grow. You have nothing to worry about,' my mother says when I show her the pictures. 'You're your mother's daughter, and men *love* me, I can *assure* you,' she adds with a sneaky laugh. 'But you're right, Bubba. You must learn to smile more.' She rubs my cheek with the backs of her fingers. 'You must learn to look happy and bright. Men like that most of all.'

•

I don't eat what the others eat. My mother makes me all my favourite foods. Chippie and Vegemite sandwiches, pancakes, ginger crunch, butterfly cakes and biscuits made with chopped-up chocolate. I have taken to shattering the biscuits and sorting through the broken pieces like a palaeontologist, brushing away the crumbs until I am left with the dark brown lumps. I toss the remaining pieces back into the tin for the others. I've found that the same pleasure is to be had in a new tub of hokey-pokey ice-cream. I pick out all the tiny pieces of golden sweet, as small as babies' teeth, using my large spoon like a gardening trowel.

For dinner, my preference is potato. My mother cuts through the roasted skins, making a lumpy grid into which the gravy soaks. I like to have my dinner on the Goldilocks stool. I call it that because it has a broken back. It's just the right height for me to sit at the open oven door with my plate on my lap, enjoying the remnant heat, free from the clattering of knives and forks of the others, who are hunching in front of the TV.

'This girl is not getting proper nutrition,' my father tells my mother. He has left his job to become a sickness beneficiary these days and is hanging around the house.

'I know, I know,' she says. 'She eats what she likes.' And I can tell from her tone he's got her flustered.

'Well it's not good enough,' he says.

I'm indignant at the gruffness of his response and I inform him in a loud voice from my corner of the bench that he doesn't have any control over me. Not surprisingly, he doesn't respond, just gives me a dark, resentful glare.

I watch as his face gradually becomes monochromatic, the only hint of colour about him the sallow shade of windbreaker he wears for his long walks on the grey beach below our house, a long stick for a companion, seagulls crying in his wake.

'Will he kill himself like the others?'

'No, darling. He's perfectly alright,' my mother says.

'But he's had a heart attack, hasn't he?'

'Yes, but lots of men have heart attacks. Most even continue to work.'

We're disappointed in him. We often have to share the kitchen with him now, and when he's not in the kitchen, we hear him as he creeps around the house, as though he knows he's not meant to be here, creaking on loose boards, shutting doors so quietly that the latches barely click. We're unnerved. We can't stand it. He makes our shoulders stiffen, our throats dry as the air thins around us and the space shrinks.

My mother makes a shuddering sound, like someone bracing themselves after a cold dive. 'My *God*, he's changed, Bubba. You have no idea,' she says, banging her crystal glass back down on the bench.

'He had the big company car, the big salary. He was going to be the general manager, then poof.' She clicks her fingers. 'It was all snatched away. Just like that. Lives can change without a moment's notice.' She puts a cigarette in her mouth and strikes a match, and for a moment I enjoy the strange smell of gunpowder.

•

'You've utterly *ruined* her,' I overhear him say one day as I crouch low at the kitchen door.

'I don't know what to do with her,' my mother responds. 'She's well and truly beyond me. She wears me down.'

I know she doesn't mean it. It's awful. My poor mother has to say these things to defend herself. I can hear the exasperation in her voice. She's tired. Worn down by his constant lurking presence, his grey shroud of a face. And now, to shut him up, I hear her rattling metal in the utensils drawer, then the sound of her whisking something, frantically beating the sides of the bowl.

'Divorce him,' I tell her when the kitchen is ours. 'He doesn't make you happy.'

She laughs. 'Oh, Bubba, you are such a funny little girl.'

'Am I?' I say, frowning at her, for I certainly don't feel very funny. I miss not waking up next to her. I miss not seeing the sheers at her windows blowing in like veils.

'I love your daddy,' she is saying as she picks up her crystal glass. 'He's my husband. He's the father of my children.'

'*Children?*' I say. 'The others are hardly children. They're old enough to look after themselves.'

•

'This girl's scalp is yellow,' he says to my mother as I loll around on the carpet after a long day at school, twisting and stretching like a cat. 'When on earth did she last have a bath?'

When on earth . . . I'm astounded by his melodrama.

'I have no idea,' I hear my mother say. She's hesitating at the entrance to the lounge, her wet hands frisking guiltily over her apron.

'Well she needs a bath—*now*,' he says, with such confidence.

'I will not have a bath,' I say. I've developed an aversion to water since my failed attempts to swim and I will not put my face beneath its surface. 'I will not!' I shout at him. 'I will not!'

'You will have a bath,' he says. 'Mother, look at her scalp,' he commands. I'm appalled by this sudden authority over my being, this late arrival, this johnny-come-lately, and it seems my mother is too, for she won't look at my scalp.

She says she knows nothing about it, 'Nothing at all.' And she turns her back, and disappears into the dull light of the kitchen, her hands flapping at the sides of her head.

My brothers, who ran wild during my father's trips away up-country, have since found a sense of purpose and unity in his presence. Hearing the rising tension, two of them arrive like henchmen to lend a hand.

'We'll take her feet,' they offer, leering at me as they drop into a wide-legged stance. They inch towards me with stalking movements, haka-style, their raised palms shifting erratically in an attempt to bamboozle me.

'She's like a wild pig,' one offers excitedly as I ram my heels back and forth into the carpet. My kick is wild and off the mark, the childish limb flailing hopelessly in the air.

I hear my father breathing hard above my head now; his hands hook under my armpits, he's struggling to restrain me.

'Come on now,' he's saying. 'Come on.'

'It's not easy, mate. She's a bloody mental case.' The reference is more loaded than they realise, for only I know the family history. They wouldn't understand it, my mother has told me—it's not their thing.

I grow frightened as the muscles in their jaws jut forward in a grim overbite. Determination is taking them over. In the uplift, one of them swipes at my calf and finally grabs hold. Now I have one leg free, heel hammering the floor like a mallet.

My mother's crashing pans in the kitchen.

'Mum,' I cry. 'Don't let them do this to me. Please don't let them do this to me.'

'Stop it,' she cries back. 'Stop it, stop it, stop it. I'll have nothing to do with it. Nothing. You can all go to hell. I hate you. I hate the lot of you.'

She's increased the stakes.

'You little bitch,' spits the one with the softer flesh. Humiliated by his fear of being hit by my shoe, he finally chops my calf with the side of his fist. 'Got her,' he says.

I can smell them as they cart my body down the hall. Sharp smells of meat and urine—or is it me? My legs split apart, my dress gathered around my waist; I'm slumped like kill. I wrench my head from side to side—like a lunatic, I imagine—but I can't tell if it's really me or just an attempt to summon the family demons I'm sure I must carry inside me.

Someone has turned the water on for the bath. It beats against the enamel like a torrent as we approach. Too small for four in here, they don't know what to do with me.

'Do we take her clothes off?' one enquires.

'No, no,' I beg, writhing my hips in mid-air.

'Throw her in as is,' my father says. 'Just pull off her shoes.'

I feel them yank at my feet. I hear my school shoes fall like clods of earth onto the tiles.

'Okay, boys.'

They have to fold me between them to fit around the door, and now with our bodies all drawn together in a grisly show of unity, I gather my spit and fire at the cheek closest to mine.

'Bitch,' a voice snarls, and I'm let go, falling into the pounding water.

I'm surprised by the soft landing. My clothes seem to expand to catch me. Looking down I see my smart school tunic rising to the surface, the wide green pleats swaying like leaves, brushed cotton ballooning on my arms, long white socks still standing stiff to attention. And now, surrounded by defeat and wetness, I sob for my loss of dignity.

Quietly, like a final word on the matter, one of the boys looks down on me. His lips fat with contempt, he says, 'Who will marry that? No man will ever want her.'

Of everything that has been said and done in the last five to ten minutes, this is what makes my breath stop, for I realise he doesn't see a little girl dumped in a tub of water, but rather the beginnings of a madwoman. I take a breath into my belly and let out a long and final cry into wilted air.

•

As usual, it pains me to see my eighty-five-year-old mother waiting for me on the pavement outside the cafe. We meet most days, out of habit. She knows I'm never on time but she refuses to take a table on her own. A rational side of me realises that if I was a better daughter

I'd be on time, but I can't bring myself to do it. Part of me wants to make her wait.

She's wearing her little red shoes. They are flat with round toes and straps that button on the side—like Clarks for five-year-olds. Around her neck, I see the gleam of her Good Conduct medal, awarded to her by the Sisters of Mercy in 1937—medallions are in fashion, she says, and it's gold, something of value. Unlike me, she has little of value.

The golden curls are long gone. Her hair is white these days, shaped like a basin and cut square around her eyes. As she spots me, she rises up onto the balls of her feet like a little girl in her cotton plus-fours, flexing her surprisingly shapely calves.

We sit at one of the small round tables, my mother taking the padded bench against the wall. She pats the vinyl for me to sit next to her, *all the better to hear me*, but I decide on the bentwood chair opposite, placing the large sack of washing I am carrying between my feet.

We now live in a little town on the east coast of Australia. It's been years since we left New Zealand, shortly after my father died at sixty-two. Not by his own hand. They called it *heart failure*, but I'm more inclined to think it was a general sense of failure. They were sad times, my mother says on reflection, but then on other days she says they weren't sad at all, we were all perfectly happy.

I often feel like we blend in with the locals in our straw hats and shorts, as though both of us being here was part of some grand plan, but in truth my arrival was pure coincidence. The others, of course, think it was destiny. You'd think I'd taken her hostage, reading the cards on her mantelpiece: *Is she being good to you Ma? Come and visit us, if she'll let you.*

'It's all in good fun,' my mother says, when I read these lines out loud. 'You know they like to tease.'

I watch her now as she lowers a globule of honey into her coffee and twirls the spoon. 'How are the children?' she says, smiling up at me.

'They're fine.'

'That's good, darling. You look a little tired. Are you tired? I *do* worry about you. You run around after them far too much.'

'I don't run around after them too much,' I say. We've been through this so many times before. 'I just want the best for them. Like you did for me. Remember? You took me everywhere.'

She smiles weakly.

'You did do it for me, didn't you? You weren't just bored?'

'Of course I did it for you,' she says, smiling as she lowers her lips to the cup. She's looking up over the rim now—I can see dark smudges in the crumpled hollows beneath her eyes, irises milky green with failing sight. Today she's applied a fish-scale shimmer above her eyelid, too much on one side. Her lashes, just a few, are like broken stitches, and her eyebrows have completely disappeared apart from a couple of in-grown hairs. Lately she's been talking about having them tattooed back on, but she says it costs too much. And besides, she's too old, she'll be dead soon. I've noticed she's since invested in a pencil from Woolworths, approaching her brow bone like a landscape artist with impressionistic flair. I've seen the pencil in her pink make-up bag in the bathroom when I've looked through her things, curiously examining the facial fluff collected on its worn stub where she's dragged it savagely across her skin.

I say to her, 'I think you need to rub your eyebrows in a bit. Just lick your finger and give them a rub.'

She tosses her head, taps the table with her nail as she observes the room with a critical stare.

'Don't look like that, now. I didn't draw those barbs on you. *You* did,' I tease.

But the nail keeps tapping, slowly, like the tail on a cat.

'You're mocking me,' she says in a leaden tone.

I seem to be very good at mocking her. My siblings, on the other hand, I've noticed treat her with special reverence, as I suppose a mother should be treated, honouring her as it says offspring should in the Ten Commandments. *We wish for her twilight years to be as free from pain as possible*, one wrote to me in a rare email last year. *Please take good care of her.*

'What's that supposed to mean?' I ask her. 'What have you been saying I do to you?'

My mother often tells me my siblings actually look up to me these days.

'And why would that be?' I say, disbelieving.

'Because you've traversed the world, you've done big things.' She is flattering me.

'*Big things!*' I say. 'You mean because I have a university degree. *Oh please.* That's not *big things*.'

'Well it is to some,' she says, and then she goes on about them being good, simple people over there, earthy, with their hearts in the right place, as though that's got something to do with me having a degree.

'Where exactly are you going with this?' I say, and she says she doesn't know, she has no idea at all.

'They have their own lives now,' my mother says when I ask if she misses them. 'They have their own families and partners. You don't keep your children forever.'

'But they're all still there, aren't they? Sharing their lives. And we're not.'

'Oh, I don't know,' she says with a shrug. 'I don't know how much time they actually spend together. Birthdays, maybe. Christmas or New Year, perhaps.'

I often find myself thinking about them all when I'm out jogging. It's usually towards the end when I'm tiring and I need that extra boost to get me home. I square my shoulders and look straight ahead, but on the sides of the road I can hear them calling to me, whipping their fists. *Go, Bubba, go*, they cry. *You can do it, Bubba.* And it's then I feel my heart bursting and my legs breaking into a gallop, as though I'm heading for the finish line, the gold medal.

My mother is staring into space now, her jaw quite set when she's not remembering to smile.

'What are you looking at?' she says with a start.

'Nothing,' I say.

'You were looking at me. Very critically. I know you were.'

'You weren't even on my mind,' I say drolly.

'Hmmm. Charming,' she says, and she pistol-grips her chin and looks narrowly down her nose at me.

'Don't even try to look intelligent,' I say. 'You look like some D-grade actor.'

She laughs. 'Oh. Am I *so* transparent?' And she throws her head back like Marilyn, her mouth wide open as she smiles. It would be impressive if she was thirty years old and I was a man.

Now she's raising her finger. 'Ahhh,' she says, her head back on straight. 'I knew I had something to tell you. I got a lovely call from your eldest brother last night. We had a nice long chat.'

'That's nice,' I say. 'Did he ask after me?'

She lengthens her neck to think. 'No, actually, he didn't mention you at all.'

'And I suppose *you* didn't mention me either?'

I wait, impassive, as she smiles. 'Hmmmm. Let me think. No, I don't think I did mention you. Not everything revolves around you, you know.' She looks at me shrewdly.

'I wasn't for a moment suggesting that it does. I just would have thought my name might have popped up, in passing, as it was a long call. And I live here. I see you every day. None of them ever call me.'

She shakes her head. 'I'm not getting into this.'

'Into *what*?' I say.

'Come on now. You know very well they're funny about you.'

'What do you mean, *funny*? In what way?' I ask.

'Oh goodness. I don't know. They're probably jealous,' she says.

'Jealous of *what*?'

'Oh, your big house. Your flash car. You're big-time to them. You know what they're like over there. They can be very small-minded.'

'Why are you talking like this?'

But she's waving her hands now. 'Oh no. I'm not going back over it. I've had enough of all that.'

'Of what?'

'Nothing. Nothing. I wipe my hands of it.'

'That's not fair,' I say, leaning across the table. 'You mustn't say things like that without explaining yourself.'

'For goodness' sake, it's all in the past. Leave it alone,' she drawls.

'It's not in the past. It's still *here*,' I hiss. 'And I don't know what I've done. Tell me what I've done. *Please,* would you just tell me what I've done?'

'I won't. You're nothing but a bully. I know it's my fault. I know I ruined you. But even as a baby you ruled me with a rod of iron . . . that *roar* of yours. My God you could bring the house down. It's no wonder the others didn't like you.'

'That's an awful thing to say. You really are becoming a very nasty old woman.'

She looks over her shoulder, her arms clamped tightly across her chest. When she turns back, I see she's become calm and dignified.

'I'm not nasty,' she says, her voice high in her throat. 'All I've ever wanted in my life is peace and quiet. I'm a simple person. I'm a Swede. I'm a pacifist.'

'You're only a quarter Swede,' I say impatiently. 'Now tell me what I've done to them. I saw them only a short while ago and they were perfectly nice to me. Please tell me what I've done.'

She shakes her head. 'I don't know. I really don't know. Maybe it's because I'm here with *you*. And not there with them. I really don't know. Oh dear *God* I've had enough of it all.' She crumples. 'I really have. I could die. I could die right now.'

This is what I do to her. *And soon you will be dead*, I think. *You really will be dead and I'll be alone*. And I'll feel slightly responsible, perhaps even more than slightly responsible—who can tell until it happens.

'I'll get going now,' I say, and I stand up, noisily scraping my chair across the floor. I wait as her brown fingers burrow into her purse for coins—they look far too big for such a small purse.

'I'll get it,' I say, and her catch snaps shut.

'Thank you,' she breathes, exhausted.

When I come back from the counter I see she is on her feet, my wretched sack of washing bulging inches off the ground, its tie twisted around her brown knuckles. For just a moment she looks eighty-five years old.

'I'll take that,' I say.

'No, you won't. I'm quite capable, thank you very much.'

So I walk on, out of the cafe, her following behind.

It's so sunny outside. Our squints have the effect of smiles as we stand facing each other on the hot concrete of the car park.

'I've got yesterday's washing in the car. It's all beautifully clean and pressed.' She looks rueful. 'I'm really very good, aren't I?' Then she tilts her head so that her hair shines. 'What would you do without me?'

'I really don't know,' I say as I pull her to my chest. I close my eyes tightly, squeezing the moisture from them. 'I'm sorry,' I say as I kiss the top of her head. Her hair feels as soft as duck feathers as I stay there, resting my nose and lips upon her crown.

PALEFACE AND THE PANTHER

Robert Drewe

Anthony's skin was so white, almost translucent, you could see the veins fanning out from his temples into his rusty curls. The vulnerability of those electric-blue wires shocked me; sometimes his skull looked like a physiology poster. At the same time, the eggshell frailty of an orphanage or illness seemed to cling to his body. When he had his shirt off for the bath or beach there were those eerie neon veins again, beaming out from inside his chest.

I tried to paint him a few times but I find children difficult. They come out either too sentimentally cherubic or Hollywood demonic. In oils Anthony looked like a changeling, with a wily old face. And I couldn't resist the veins—maybe I overdid the cobalt. Anyway, the paintings met with strong disapproval from the Miller sisters, pale redheads too, who maybe had Renoir and innocence and velvet suits in mind, and they were destroyed before I could reuse the canvases.

Even in real life he didn't appear a normal West Australian boy, neither tanned nor sunburnt, not freckled or peeling, more like a vitamin D-and-protein-deprived European waif from yesteryear.

Just off the boat, as they used to say. Dickensian poorhouse. But he wasn't sick or poor, just pallid and thin. And he was actually a fourth-generation Sandgroper, and only half orphaned, and now that a temperamental flush masked his veins, and his curls were unravelling in the summer humidity, he was the image of my father.

It was Anthony's birthday party, and in the cricket game taking place in a municipal park of buffalo grass sloping down to the river, a match he had insisted on, he'd just been clean bowled for the third time in a row.

It was torture to watch. He was trying out his new Slazenger cricket set, my present to him: a cricket bat, ball, pads, gloves, stumps and bails which came in a nifty PVC bag with the Slazenger panther emblem leaping in full horizontal stretch the length of the bag. It was expensive but I'd wanted to give him something sporty and manly, something we could do together and maybe shift the gender balance a little. Make him not so milky-pale and veiny. He was always surrounded by women and I felt guilty for not paying more attention to him in the past couple of years when I was living it up. Painting hard, yes, but also playing hard. The usual recreational activities. Anyway, if his flushed cheeks and boisterous eagerness to test the cricket set this afternoon were anything to go by, he loved the gift.

But now he was clean bowled again, and he refused to leave the crease. Even as he flailed around, his glowering, determined face—my father again—seemed to say, *Are you all mad?* Why should he go out? What idiot would swap batting for bowling or, even more ludicrously, fielding? Batting was the whole point, wasn't it? It was *his* birthday and *his* new cricket set and he was the most important person here, especially today of all days.

Not surprisingly, the fifteen party guests fielding in the park this January afternoon were losing concentration and patience. Of course the birthday boy had been allowed to bat first. Uncle Brian was bowling underarm, and had substituted a tennis ball for the hard cricket ball—and, what's more, had bowled him out three times already.

All over the park, young fielders were flopping down on the ground and sucking twigs and peering longingly towards the river or the party table that Anthony's mother and aunts were setting up under the peppermint trees. The kids had given up on having a turn with the bat and now they wanted to swim or eat; at this rate there'd soon be an uprising. Oblivious to the general restiveness the three Miller sisters were drinking their customary spritzers and laughing while they blew up balloons and tied them to the trees' branches, special balloons that said *Happy 8th Birthday Anthony!*

I was wicket-keeping. Because I wanted him to succeed, and I wanted the cricket set to be an appreciated gift, I was torn. But eventually I said, 'You're really out, my man. Give someone else a turn.'

He swung at another slow underarm ball from Brian, and missed again. I trudged uphill after the ball while he thumped the grass in frustration. But he still didn't give up the bat.

Unusually for a Perth summer afternoon the sea breeze hadn't arrived and the day gave off a sullen chalky glare that stung the eyes. In the river below us, other shrieking children were bombing and diving off the jetty—non-party guests having a better time than us—and becalmed yachts lolled in a deepwater bay as smooth as oily glass. Ageless impressionist subject matter. You've also spotted the scene in a hundred atmospheric summer photographs: skinny show-off boys caught mid-air, spread-eagled between jetty and water. Even at my age I envied them. Already my shirt was sticking to me from all that trudging after the missed balls. The buffalo runners had an annoying way of gripping the ball and stopping it from rolling back down to me.

'Don't be a bad sport,' I told him. I was feeling disheartened as well as hot. Anthony was ruining the party mood. As I threw the ball back to Brian, I said, 'Don't bowl any more until the spoilsport walks.'

Brian looked for direction to the women with the spritzers and balloons. In the shade of the peppermint trees the Miller sisters had taken off their sunhats, revealing three different hues of red hair in gradations from vivid orange-peel to mercuric-sulphide pigment to dark rust. They had cigarettes going, too, which interfered with their balloon-blowing efforts, and every now and then one of the women would gasp and giggle and her half-inflated balloon would escape, spinning, blurting and farting crazily over their heads.

The dark-rusty one, Liz, Anthony's mother and my stepmother, glanced at us. 'I hope you've got sunscreen on, Ant,' she said.

Brian looked back at me uncertainly. 'Show him again how to hold the bat.'

Jesus, Brian was being *avuncular*. He was twenty-eight, married to the youngest Miller sister, Jeanette, and in our occasional dealings the seven years he had over me seemed to give him the advantage.

But in the matter of Anthony, I felt I had the upper hand. Brian was only Anthony's uncle by marriage, and even less related to me, not my family at all. Anyway, I had deaths on my side. Two deaths gave me the edge.

'Here we go again,' I said. I gripped Anthony's narrow shoulders and spun him side-on to the bowler. The panther emblem was stamped on the bat as well. I twisted the bat handle around in his hands. 'This is your last ball,' I said. 'Keep a straight bat. See that panther on the bat? It should face your right leg. Defend your wicket. Take it easy. Don't swing like a dunny door.'

He squirmed free of my hands and shuffled back to his incorrect stance. If he swung the bat from there he'd not only miss the ball again but knock his wicket over. His eyes had an oddly familiar shine. My father's old Dewar's glint, his Johnnie Walker midnight-aggressive glint. 'Go shit-fuck-shit away!' Anthony growled. 'I don't have to take any notice of you!'

My God, he needed a smack. 'That's not even proper swearing, Paleface,' I said as I walked off.

•

When I arrived at the restaurant, an outdoor seafood place in the Fremantle fishing harbour, he was already seated. An unusual choice for Anthony, I thought; not fashionable, overly marine-themed, with a table of bluff Yorkshire accents and porky pink skins on one side of us, a tidy arrangement of Japanese on the other. There was the usual network of wires strung above the tables to discourage seagulls, and several pleading *Please Don't Feed the Birds* signs. The tourists were ignoring these deterrents and hurling their chips into the harbour, where diving and wheeling gulls enjoyed uninterrupted and raucous access.

I'd suggested the lunch at my stepmother's behest. 'What's he doing with his life?' Liz moaned. 'Can you find out and give him some advice, put him right?' According to her, Anthony had abruptly left Angela and their two children, tossed in his partnership with Fairhall Burns Corrie, turned vegetarian, and was 'living with some hippie witch in a mud hut up in the hills'.

I think she thought I was more in tune with low-life ways. Painting and bohemia and all that. It sounded like an early midlife crisis to me, a middle-class cliché, but at this stage Liz was phoning me in tears every night with news of Anthony's latest New Age transgression. 'He's killing me. I don't understand him anymore. He's acting all superior to everyone, angry and touchy-feely at the same time. The hippie witch must have some eerie power over him.'

I heard deep raspy breaths; she was drawing heavily on a cigarette and even over the phone she sounded old and needy. I pictured the almost-empty bottle of white wine close by. 'What's all this guru stuff anyway?' she went on. 'Numerology, astrology, holistic blah-blah, tantric mumbo-jumbo. A thirty-seven-year-old lawyer doesn't need all this *hoo-ha*. *I* certainly don't need all this *hoo-ha*! Bruce would be rolling in his grave. What are we going to do?'

We? I didn't need any *hoo-ha* either. But I felt sorry for Liz. She was no storybook evil stepmother. Sally and I had hardly begrudged her marrying our father. She hadn't pinched him from Monica, our mother; Bruce had been a widower, after all. And for a few years we were still sort of numb, and kept to ourselves while Dad grieved alone and left us to our own devices. Then, as a widowed parent herself—after *his* death five years later—she'd always been amiably haphazard and not the least bit maternal. I think that's why we didn't overly resent her when we were younger: she wasn't vying for our love. Sally and I had each other and it suited us that she was affectionately distant, not in competition with our mother over anything, and allowed our sad reverence for her to remain undisturbed.

Her focus was completely on Bruce, her husband whether living or dead. As soon as Anthony was seven, she'd sent him off to boarding school, to far-off Guildford Grammar. She'd married late, at forty, the eldest Miller sister and the last to go, and for the fact of being married at all she was grateful to Bruce every day. If he was no longer there, she wanted to be alone with his memory; his memory and the remains of his wine cellar.

But *we*? What could I do? Anthony was a grown man and, by Perth's standards, already a successful one: a commercial lawyer, yachtsman, weekend tennis player (of minimum ability), and the owner of two storeys of heritage sandstone, a pool, a tennis court behind a disciplined plumbago hedge and, from the second-floor bedrooms at least, three river glimpses and a misty view of the Darling Ranges. He was responsible for his own actions.

Anyway, maybe he was doing the right thing. I was sorry for his kids, but Angela was a provincial Anglophile snob with a cleanliness obsession. The sort who washed your beer glass the minute you set it down, who made you feel unkempt and grubby in her company. Maybe Anthony had seen the light.

How would I describe our half-brotherly relationship? We were like long-time acquaintances. Beyond our father we had little in common. Our political views collided. Anthony was conservative and well-off, and I was neither. He was a law graduate and I was basically self-educated. There was a thirteen-year age difference and no physical resemblance. Whenever we met up, at Christmas or other family gatherings, we didn't converse so much as banter and nod agreeably and earnestly top up each other's drinks.

'How's the art world?' he'd ask. 'Selling any?' He came to my exhibitions because he liked the business–social aspect, plus the chance to mingle safely with a few raffish characters.

Always we acted as brothers. But we were *acting*. We weren't exactly brothers, and we weren't exactly friends. We were something in between.

But this was an intriguing twist, being called on for advice. Until recently the role of the family bohemian, the black sheep, was mine.

•

Even his handshake was different now, loose and metallic. All those silver rings on his fingers. Another in his left ear. Silver bracelets on each wrist, a necklace of little beads and seeds and stones, and another thin chain with some sort of gemstone pendant banging portentously against his sternum. I'd never seen an ornamented

Anthony before—the Old Guildfordian cufflinks used to be his limit. Add the rumpled natural fibres, a collarless shirt, rubbery sandals (no leather in evidence), floppy drawstring trousers like pyjama pants that didn't reach his ankles, and he'd gone the whole hog, sartorially. Guru-wear, his mother called it. It looked more like grandpa-wear to me—if your grandpa was institutionalised and had got into grandma's jewellery box.

I'd dressed up in a shirt with a collar and, for the first time, I felt like the conservative brother. 'So, what's happening, Ant?' I said as I sat down. The *what's happening* came out more abruptly than I'd intended. I meant it more as *How are you going?* but it came out like *What the Christ are you doing with your life?*

'What do you mean?' he said, frowning. To be honest, he looked well. He'd lost the extra weight he'd stacked on. Of course those childhood veins had long since vanished into ruddy cheeks and freckled temples.

'How are things? What are you up to?'

That frown at least was familiar. Was he going to answer or not? His cutlery caught the sun as he was arranging his knife and fork at right angles to the table edge.

'I heard you'd gone vegetarian. So, you eat fish then?'

Yes, he ate fish. Apparently his new lifestyle didn't preclude alcohol either, or his liking for good wines, and once the bottle he'd ordered had arrived he began to open up. 'Look, I've embarked on a new journey,' he began, guardedly. His fingers were still fiddling with the tableware. 'Everything in my life has been leading me to this point.'

'Doesn't it always?' I said. But I was trying to be understanding. 'Tell me about your life changes. Who's the girlfriend? Do I know her?' There was a fair chance I did. My gravelly three acres of banksias and grass trees were also up in the hills. 'Are you sure you're doing the right thing?'

Part calming-Jesus, part-lawyer, he raised an admonishing hand. 'Let me show you something.' He held up the wine bottle, pointed to its label, read out its name: *Torbreck Roussane Marsanne. Barossa Valley.* Its design featured two concentric circles. He tapped them with a beringed finger. His expression, very legal and wisdom-of-the-ages, declared, *I rest my case.*

'What?'

'That label says it all,' he said. 'It's a personal message to me. It tells me I'm doing the right thing.'

'Really?' I toyed with the idea of the Torbreck wine people not only knowing of his existence but basing their graphic designs and marketing strategies around his changing emotions. 'I thought the label was saying, *Please buy this wine*.'

Anthony sighed and cast his eyes around the restaurant. 'The thing is, I can get confirmation anywhere,' he said. 'Okay, see those napkin rings on the buffet over there?' Two silver circles stood side by side, intersecting slightly. 'They're speaking to me. They're confirming the rightness of my journey.'

'Do the circles represent you and the new woman?'

He sighed. 'Among other things.'

'Are you going to tell me her name?'

'Does it matter? Sarita. Maya. Parissa. She goes by several names. She's the essential, fundamental woman.'

Fundamental woman. I got the picture. Cuntstruck.

He said, 'We don't have sex, if that's what you're thinking.'

Our plates of snapper arrived then, the fish engulfed by circles of beetroot and orange slices and onion and pineapple rings. Collage as much as meal. As I scraped the bright geometric toppings off my fish I almost asked whether all this round food was conveying wisdom to him.

I was running out of questions and Anthony, his cheeks already flushed from the alcohol and conversation, was still frowning. I swallowed another mouthful of wine. I was forced to raise my voice over the dour northern English voices and seagull squawks. So, this new life journey, one of tossed-in job and dumped family—a celibate journey, to boot—was being determined by serviette rings and wine labels.

'Ant, I think you need to see someone,' I said.

•

Charged with carbohydrates, the melee of eight-year-olds fled the debris of the party table. For several minutes Brian and I tried to exhaust them by organising a game of Red Rover under the peppermint trees, but the idea didn't take hold.

Weary of manners and adult directions, first one boy then another broke away from the game and began running up the hill and rolling down again. Soon all of them were rolling and shrieking and somersaulting down the slope. Late-afternoon shadows were stretching across the park but the day's clamminess seemed to have increased. In the heat, with the river so close, this fierce prickly game looked like madness. Over and over, hysterical, they rolled and climbed.

Behind the main clump of boys, Anthony, less quick and agile, dizzy and red-faced, grass sticking to his shirt, picked himself up and staggered up the incline once more. His legs were wobbly sticks. As he climbed he had to avoid the mob of boys tumbling down, and several times he was knocked over. He was no longer in charge of events and the rebellious horde ignored his angry protests and indignant arm-waving. That urgent noise he was making sounded somewhere between shouting and sobbing. Then he got to his feet halfway up the hill, beat his sides with his fists and started to scream.

•

Anthony drained his glass, leaned back in his chair, dropped his hands in his lap, breathed deeply—once, twice—as if willing the dangerous glimmer in his eyes to fade and a suitably serene expression to slide down his cheeks. 'See someone? You mean a shrink?'

'Well, a psychologist or counsellor or whatever.' It sounded lame. He'd lost his father at the age of five. I tended to forget that. I'd been twelve when Mum died and eighteen when Dad did. Being five was probably worse. But at least he still had a mother. 'You might find it very helpful, dealing with old emotional stuff.'

'I have my own spiritual mentors,' he declared. 'And I've never been more emotionally stable in my life. In fact, I'm so calm that I don't even resent your bloody gratuitous advice.'

'Just because you're calm doesn't mean you're not fucked up and don't need help.'

'And you'd be competent to judge that? With your background? A fucking painter who didn't even go to university?'

'Someone with more life experience and common sense than you, brother.'

He raised an eyebrow. The resemblance was extraordinary. It could have been our father, towards the end. When he was bitter and hitting the bottle late at night, and always giving Sally and me strange looks; when he realised he'd remarried too soon, the wrong woman; when he was still mourning my mother. '*Brother?* Are you sure?'

'*Jesus!* Well, half-brother then.'

He was running a finger round the rim of his wineglass so it made an irritating thin scream. Another bloody circle. 'You're sure of that?' he repeated.

I could have whacked his smug hippie-lawyer head. 'What are you getting at?'

Anthony wore a prim smile, as if an old score was finally settled. 'You never wondered why you're short and olive-skinned? How incurious can you be? I hate to be the one to pass on family secrets, but you know your mother couldn't have children?'

For a few seconds I couldn't see. The glare off the harbour, snowy tablecloths, the swirling white ruckus of the seagulls, blinded me. The whole scene was leached of tint and shade. Strangely, I recalled the faint watercolours of Lloyd Rees when his sight was fading at the end of his life. If it were me, I'd have chosen brighter and brighter colours. But his were pale, soft yet urgent paintings that paralleled his life force. Paintings needing to be quickly said before time ran out.

I remembered how stressful my sister always found those get-togethers of the gingery Millers. The insouciant ways of the Spritzer Sisters, as she called them, the blithe, patronising attitude of Liz's siblings towards 'Monica's kids' made Sally edgy and self-conscious in their presence, and savagely mocking later. My shy sister always got plenty of sardonic material from family gatherings but they wore her out and in the end she'd given up attending them. My older, smaller sister.

Anthony was rolling his napkin into a ball. 'Very commendable of them in the circumstances to take you both in. I guess it must have been spiritually fulfilling in its way to snatch you from the tribe. All Monica's doing, I've been told, and he went along with it because of her infertility problems. Complex legal processes involved, health and cultural risks. Made it easier you two being pale, I guess. God knows *that* community doesn't give up its waifs too readily.'

•

Some of the boys on the hill stopped surging and somersaulting to stare at Anthony and his noise. The sisters glanced up from their spritzers and cigarettes, shook their heads wearily and resumed chatting. Anthony bellowed on. Tired of the hubbub, a couple of boys made for the shade, brushed themselves down, drank some Coke and looked around for entertainment. Then they spotted the Slazenger bag, unzipped it, got out the bat and ball, set up the stumps and quietly began playing.

I joined the game behind the wicket. The bowler bowled properly overarm, using the regulation hard six-stitcher; the batsman struck the ball squarely back to him two, three times. The face of the bat and the panther emblem hit the ball correctly with sharp, efficient cracks.

Down the hill thundered Anthony. His pallor was gone and his curls were damp and stringy. Muddy tear streaks ran down his cheeks and spit frothed on his lips. 'Give everything to me!' he yelled. He raced up to the surprised batsman and snatched the bat from him; he took the ball from the bowler; he grabbed up the stumps. From the bitter ferocity of his glare, I could tell I had betrayed him.

'What are you doing?' I said.

From under the peppermint trees his mother sang out, 'Ant, play nicely.'

For a moment he stood there undecided, with the cricket gear clasped possessively to his chest. Then he stacked it back into the Slazenger bag, picked up the bag and marched off down the park. He'd gone maybe twenty metres when something apparently occurred to him and he stopped, returned to the party table, collected all his birthday presents—some gifts still unopened—and crammed them into the bag as well. It was a tight squeeze: the panther was stretched to bursting.

Very businesslike then, a grim smile fixed on his face, he strode down to the river. I watched him go, just as grimly. The sea breeze had finally arrived, sweeping through the peppermint trees, and snappy little waves began breaking on the shore. I followed him but I wasn't going to stop him. Surely this tantrum would soon play itself out.

Indeed, the bag must have become heavy because he had to haul it the last few metres across the sand and onto the jetty. Brushing aside skylarking wet children, curious onlookers, he dragged it the length of the jetty until he came to a pontoon just above the deep water. Then he heaved the bag into the river.

All that wood inside it, and the trapped air; it floated easily. A couple of children dived in and set off after it, then gave up. The tide was going out and the Slazenger bag sailed away into the bay and bobbed into the wide river estuary. I reached the pontoon, and sat down along from Anthony, and we watched the bag in silence until it was gone.

BEADS AND SHELLS AND TEETH

Cate Kennedy

When my sister was eight, I was almost seven and my precious long-awaited brother was only a couple of weeks old, my father left for a year's duty in Vietnam. A special car came to pick him up and we stood on the kerb outside the front fence to wave him off and, for reasons I couldn't fathom, laughter bubbled up in my throat, weird hysterical giggling. My mother looked across at me with disbelief, her own face blotchy and swollen with crying. Later, during that year of his absence, she would refer to the inappropriateness of my reaction. 'You were smiling when he left,' she would say with incontrovertible finality, when the topic of missing him came up. 'You were *laughing*.' I was, too—there was no denying it—laughing, while his face gazed with desperate pale sadness at us from the back seat of the car, as we watched him fasten his seatbelt and grope for his sunglasses, the occasion as solemn as a military funeral. Many times I would remember my laughter rising uncontrollably like the last silvery spheres of oxygen from a drowning mouth. In the moment that bubble rose and burst I became a mystery to myself, and the knowledge of how easily this slip could occur burned like an oozing skinned knee, stiff with the jarring impact of an ignominious, unexpected fall.

On the wall in the kitchen our mother hung a calendar of a fighter jet, with all the months of the year laid out beneath it. Each morning, after breakfast and before the school bus, my sister and I would cross out another day as it arrived. We had to take it in turns to avoid bickering, taking up the pen ritualistically and making a big solid X. We were scared to bicker, conscious that the smallest transgression in that house, tightly wound around our father's absence, might cause everything to fly apart. Still, that calendar began to mock us from the wall as we carried days away from it, crumb by crumb, like ants.

The airforce base sat on the flat baked-dry featureless plains west of Melbourne; the base itself and the aerodrome and fields and airmen's quarters and the mess all secured with cyclone fencing and guard gates at either end.

A man in a uniform would check your car and open the boom gate for you, and if your dad was driving the man would look ahead into the distance and salute smartly as you drove through. With the exception of the Group Captain's place at the end of the street, every house on the base was exactly the same. People tried, with different curtains and configurations of furniture, to express a little individuality in these houses stamped from identical prefabricated floor plans. They hung up carvings from their postings in Malaysia or displayed souvenirs and paintings they'd bought in Europe and the UK, but, ironically, because everyone had been to more or less the same few RAAF locations, even these ornaments gave the houses a familiar sameness. Everybody had a few carved wooden animals from Nairobi, and a set of watercolour prints of Paris street scenes. Everybody had lacquered raffia ottomans they'd bought from street vendors in quick onshore visits while crossing the Suez Canal on the boat on the way home, and a set of placemats depicting Britain's stately homes. The houses themselves were surrounded by square patches of lawn and neatly edged rows of shrubs, zinnias and pansies. People generally planted annuals rather than perennials, things that would bloom for the year or two you were there, flowers that weren't planted to last the duration, because they didn't need to be. There was nothing perennial about airforce life.

We always felt perfectly safe, with the guard gates there—it was a rare occasion we had a babysitter, although social life on the base for the adults seemed generally conducted at a punishing pace of cocktails, dinner parties and dining-in nights. Our parents had already undertaken a posting in England, and so the ornaments and furniture in our meticulously maintained house seemed to have been wrongly set down there from some other posher, bigger house in another era—Wedgwood jugs on spindly rosewood-varnished side tables, copper coal scuttles, an antique *chaise longue* we weren't meant to sit on, silver tea and coffee pots stored with dinner sets in the chiffonier. It always felt strange to sit on the lounge suite in the living room, like the cushions had somehow been plumped for someone more important than you, who might arrive at any time.

I loved my books, and pored over them like they were illuminated manuscripts. It was the stories in books which stayed clear and unchangeable; they were always exactly as I remembered them.

In our square prefab house on the base and in the 'portables', the shoddy demountable classrooms of our school, it was real life that had a temporary, illusory air, as if every building in our lives could be knocked down or transported elsewhere instantly on someone's whim. Stories were the constant—reliable and unwavering as a song learned by heart. You were allowed to keep some to put in your box when your dad got posted somewhere new, and even though everything would be strange and scary you could open that box and there were your dear beloved friends, waiting for you, still smelling exactly the same.

•

With a new baby in the house our mother required us to be good and helpful and not argue or drive her mad. We tried to stay under her radar and learn the complicated strategies required for survival. In this, like any kids, we were hopelessly outmanoeuvred, brilliantly kept in check—and, in fact, checkmated—by simple adult sophistication. There were eighteen months separating my sister and me in age, but our mother dressed us exactly the same, as if we were twins, although two more unlikely twins you'd never see—my sister was small and dark and pretty; I was fair, wore glasses and always looked untidy. Our childhood photos show us setting off for birthday parties in identical dresses, holding our presents under our arms, our fine hair scraped and coiffed with ribbons, cringing into the full sun for the camera. In others we sit with Santa in mirror-image outfits, smiling sheepish best-behaviour smiles, full of the sad, dutiful obedience of childhood. Our best dresses were squarish white-flecked pink, with a long thin bib of crimson ribbon edged in puffy lace. We looked, frankly, like a couple of Iced Vo-Vos.

We never questioned this, any more than we questioned the uniforms worn by all men on the base; it was as inviolable and irresistible as the weather. People who bought us gifts of clothes conceded to it as well, and purchased the same items, and our hearts would sink when we saw two presents predictably identical in size and shape appear. Other people seemed to have some instinctual understanding, though, that two sisters eternally dressed the same would nurture a secret longing for a splash of differentiation. They would buy the outfits in two different colours. My sister would receive the pink version, and I would get the blue. (Was I a tomboy? Was that it? Or just a bookish geek with glasses who meekly wore what she was given?) The clothes were always a little big, of course, so we could 'grow into them'.

We stood and looked at our acquired personas hanging in the wardrobe, the identities that we would grow into, taken care of on our behalf. We were siblings, and so we were rivals—for favour, for attention, for bitterly contested territories invisible to outsiders. Every assumption that we were keen to wear the same clothes, or be invited on outings together, or be treated, in fact, as a single entity, made this opposition more precise, more obsessive, more intricately maintained. We never mutinied—we barely spoke. Instead, we hunkered down to sit out our childhood with cold-war enmity flowing between us like two opposing magnets. We divided our bedroom and our property into two exact and scrupulous halves, with invisible boundaries separating the floor, the wardrobe space and the items on top of the dressing-table. It was a covert inch this way then a retaliatory inch back that way, like the Battle of the Somme.

'Don't they look lovely?' people said as we stood ready for photos, and we turned the corners of our mouths up obligingly, eyes front, neat in our identical dresses. Dreading the instruction *Put your arm around your sister*.

How could adults do this—ignore reality and manufacture an instamatic cosiness that existed nowhere else? Were they satisfied with it, content to see their children bare their teeth in such stiff pretence of exuberance and spontaneity? When I look at photo albums now—not just my own, but everyone's—I wonder about these moments summoned and preserved flat behind cellophane pages, this passing-out parade. I catch sight of an arm carefully around a shoulder, and I hear an adult voice behind the lens, instructing; I feel the duress, the prickling reluctance of skin-to-skin contact. *Over here, girls. Big smiles.*

As the weeks of that year turned into months and news of the Vietnam War was on the news every night, my sister and I began to up the ante with the calendar. It wasn't enough just to cross out a day; we needed more. We took to scoring the pen heavily and thoroughly through the whole week, blocking out the entire seven days with the grim satisfaction of defacement. We'd compete to see who got to make the X on the final day of the month, because that person would win the right to take down the calendar, turn the glossy page towards themselves, and methodically scribble through the whole month. We approached this task like acolytes undertaking the holiest rite allotted to them. The other sister would watch, mesmerised, as the lucky one would run the pen back and forth, scribbling vertically and horizontally, until the paper began to disintegrate under the ballpoint and the saturating ink.

I see what we were doing now, because that calendar still exists, with its blue-sky image of a fighter plane, black-nosed and camouflage-khaki, suspended over twelve solid scribbled chunks of misery. We were doing everything we could, with the puny tools at our disposal, to obliterate our enemy—traitorous, intolerable time. Through our vertical and horizontal lines we slashed big extra Xs in jagged diagonal crosses. I can see them there still, with a jolt of nausea, like annihilated targets, like a giant single negation.

With all that time came awful, belated realisations. I remembered the nights before our father had left, when my sister and I would be in the bath. He'd breeze in, bringing with him the intoxicating scent of the mess where he'd just had a beer or two, mingling with the smell of cigarette smoke and conversation, laughter and weather, exertion and oxygen. The door would open and fresh air would blow through the house with him as he entered, the smell of the outside world pouring through as he hung his hat on a chair and rolled up the sleeves of his powder-blue shirt to splash us clean in the bath. He would indulge us, making the soap jump from his hands like a fish while we laughed helplessly. Once he left for Vietnam, it was like he'd taken the keys to that door, and no afternoon breeze entered the house. The air felt short on oxygen. We lost our familiarity with that hinted-at outside world, or the faint, inchoate sense that we might one day come to live in it ourselves. We ceased to breathe it in, and, like breathing, we missed it with the shock of something taken purely for granted. The Clark's pool stayed folded in an aqua-blue pile in the garage instead of unfailingly set up there by the Hills hoist, and our school shoes remained just where we left them, scuffed and knotted under our beds, instead of side by side by the back door, dark with polish and the laces magically untied by morning. I couldn't recall ever thanking him for any of these things, of course; they'd just been there, reliable and unquestioned. Now my heart jumped guiltily like that soap from his cupped hands; recognising, too late, every one of these small things for what they were—gestures of love from an undemonstrative man.

•

A parcel arrived taped with limp, scuffed paper, and we knew it was from Dad. Inside were two cylinders wrapped in newspaper which was thin and smelled different and was in a different language. As soon as I saw it I imagined taking a few pages of it somewhere—a bus stop, a park bench, the school quadrangle, somewhere public—and sitting, pretending I could read it. As I hesitated, looking at the strange writing on it, my sister unwrapped one of the cylinders and it was a beautiful black-haired doll, with white skin and pink cheeks, a tall slender figure in the Vietnamese national costume fixed onto a black wooden stand. She was wearing a long dress with black velvety designs on it, and little slippers, and unbelievably, that dress was blue. When I saw this I began to unwrap my parcel very slowly, because I knew now, with a thrilled, suppressed delight, what would be inside—an identical doll only in a pink dress. Pink! The parcels hadn't been labelled with our names, so I'd scored.

I unwrapped my doll and looked her over carefully. It was immediately clear that she was superior on two counts. Not only was her dress pink, her hair was loose with a small bun on top, while my sister's doll's hair was in a cumbersome beehive. It was a red-letter day. I examined her lips and almond-shaped eyes, drawn in with the finest of black lines, and her skin as pale as a peeled egg. She was perfect in every way.

I couldn't stop thinking about how I would look if I had a dress like that, long and fitted with the white trousers underneath. That night, I wrapped my sheet tightly around myself, right down to my feet, and looked at myself in the dressing-table mirror, holding up my hair with one hand. Our mother sometimes put our hair up in a bun for special occasions, using a thing like a donut to pull our hair through, then she'd spray it and all day you'd smell that sticky flowery smell and the pins would push into your head. My sister looked great with her hair in a bun, as cute as Gidget, but I knew that with my glasses I looked stupid, the way librarians always looked in comics, like someone to make fun of. I could have a compromise bun, though, like my doll's. What I wanted most were her serenely uptilting, almond-shaped eyes.

When I took my glasses off and leaned into the dressing-table mirror and pulled my eyelids just slightly slanted, I looked totally different. It was hard keeping the sheet wrapped tight with both forefingers at the corners of my eyes, but I was oddly compelled towards this new, possible me.

After we turned out the bedroom light I lay with my fingers against the side of my head, pulling back my eyelids. I could stretch them into place, I thought. If I lay there all night and did it, it would work. My hands started to get tired and I began to experiment with positions where it wasn't so uncomfortable. It would be worth it, having those beautiful, unusual eyes.

'What are you doing?' my sister whispered from her bed. She'd learned the perfect modulation required for icy contempt.

'Nothing.' But somehow, she knew.

'That is so, so stupid,' she said. She turned over, in her pink pyjamas, and we lay there as stiff as boards in our beds, me with my fingers braced in place, furtive and embarrassed but still soothed, somehow. It was almost like having an important job to do, something special entrusted to me.

But in the morning, my hands were under the blankets, tucked between my knees, the way I always slept. And my eyes, I noted miserably, were still round. Behind my glasses, they looked exactly the same.

•

Our dolls lived on a high shelf in our room, our belongings placed into their designated halves, surveying all that went on below, never played with, never mussed or 'ruined'. They were too precious. I just had to smell their synthetic dresses and black, lacquered hair to conjure up the olfactory world of Vietnam—a world of women on tippytoes with pure white faces and eyebrows as fine as an upswept eyelash—it was warm and exotic there, and smelled like nylon and plastic and dust.

Our next presents arrived. Two square boxes this time, wrapped extensively in layers of protective paper and tape, with that same secret, spicy smell. We turned our backs to each other in tacit collusion so we wouldn't see the other's first. Under the layers were two identical black and red lacquered music boxes. When you wound up the brass key and turned the snib to open the lid, a tiny pink plastic ballerina pirouetted in front of a wall of mirrors to the tune 'On the Street Where You Live'. When I heard that song and recognised it from *My Fair Lady*, a film I'd actually seen down the road at the base cinema, I felt a sudden fierce squeeze of choked recognition, as if everything were momentarily connected—the music-box factory, my father in a market in Vung Tau, the Saturday matinee, Rodgers and Hammerstein, all of it.

'They're not to play with,' our mother said. 'Put them somewhere they won't get ruined. Imagine how Dad would feel if he came home and they were broken.'

She made sure that we didn't overwind them or touch the fragile ballerina on her tiny spring, and after a while the shining red and black music boxes did indeed seem too special to play with, and we put them solemnly on either side of the dressing table in our bedroom, which our mother had decorated with a frilled pink tulle valance. Inside, next to the ballerina, was the little hinged lacquer drawer.

'For all your precious things,' our mother said.

I'm sorry to say that, at first, even our precious things were pretty much identical. First to go in were the rosary beads Nanna had given us when we visited her in Adelaide, before Dad went away. She'd let us play with her glow-in-the-dark statue of the Virgin Mary and given us each a set of old silver rosaries. She'd told us why they were so special but I hadn't been listening; it was my turn after she'd gone to hide under the quilt again with the glowing lady, and in any case my rosaries were soon, inexplicably, broken.

Also in the drawer were our round discontinued fifty-cent coins, which we believed were very valuable.

Then I put in, secretly, some tiny pink shells Dad had sent me from a beach in Vietnam which he'd included in one of his weekly letters. Mum had told me he'd had to walk a very long way for these special shells, right to the end of a huge beach. It had been a hot day, she'd said, and yet that's what he'd done; that was the evidence that he was always thinking of us. The shells were no bigger than my little brother's delicate pink fingernails.

I imagined that beach; a long shining curve of it hazily disappearing into the distance. At the near end the shells were large and ordinary, scattered in their millions, but as you walked further and further towards the horizon, your feet crunching on nothing but shells, they began to shrink in size. It wasn't until you came to the very end of the sliver of beach, a place a little like heaven, that the tiny, truly precious shells lay, a reward for true devotion. They were the ones that I had, now.

Years later, when I came across my lacquered music box in a storage carton somewhere, I lifted the lid and checked inside the drawer. I was taken aback to see in there, alongside the shells and the tarnished rosary beads, some small pearly objects I recognised with a start as my own milk teeth. What perverse childlike conviction had possessed me to save my own teeth that year as they fell out? I'd believed them to be something uniquely valuable, something worth saving, to show Dad. They looked a little creepy now, jumbled there with their sharp red edge of root exposed, but I saw my seven-year-old reasoning: the teeth and the shells resembled each other; lustrous with nacre and enamel. They seemed to belong together, like something you could thread side by side onto a necklace, something to wear next to your skin that nobody else had.

•

Summer came and we wore our Chinese shortie pyjamas in pastel pink and blue, decorated with dragon embroidery. They were narrow-cut and uncomfortable, chafing our sunburnt skin, but we loved them because they'd come all the way from Vietnam. We pulled them over tight, sunburnt shoulders on Sunday nights to watch *Disneyland* as heat radiated from our scarlet legs, slick with Johnson's Vaseline Intensive Care Lotion, watching as Tinkerbell touched her wand to the Disney buildings and our favourite show started with animated fireworks. Adventureland! Fantasyland! Frontierland! We gazed, transfixed by all of them. Whichever land it was, we wanted it.

We waited our turn to pick up the pen and make the cross. We tried to entertain and look after our baby brother, bouncing his bassinette, tickling him, dipping his dummy into chocolate Quik or honey to stop him crying. One day Mum told us we had something special to look forward to—a trunk-call telephone conversation with

Dad. We learned about it weeks in advance and the night approached like Christmas.

'You'll have to think carefully about what you're going to say to him,' our mother warned us. 'You'll hardly have time for anything. I'll give you the phone and you'll just have time to say, "Hello, Dad, I'm missing you!" and not much else. Do you understand? Don't waste time, because it will be terribly expensive. Maybe you should write something down so you don't go blank.'

That night in bed I stared sightlessly at my library book, racking my brains. There was so much to say to Dad, about the presents he'd sent and the shells and how careful I was being, how hard we were trying to be well behaved all the time like he wanted and how our little brother had a new tooth, and the pool and the shoelaces. These were all things that had to be said, but I wouldn't be able to say them because Mum, not to mention my sister, would be hovering right behind me listening to every word. We'd all be eavesdropping on each other, measuring our own self-censorship.

The date of the trunk call approached and we began to gear up for it, ready for that phone ringing like it was a starter pistol, or a signal to commence an exam. My head felt thick with unsaid things; declarations and anecdotes, secret grievances and pangs of guilt. The night before the call I lay in bed sorting and assembling, evaluating, editing and discarding, sick for the sound of his voice and the knowledge that he would be listening, the words tumbling and ebbing and churning together in my brain. Not the big, expected words, the easy ones, but the small, precious words you only found at the very end. It all seemed so fragile and breakable. I could hear the rustling of paper from my sister's bed, the sound of a pencil scribbling something out.

'What are you doing?' I said.

'None of your business.'

We were as keyed up and jumpy as racehorses when the call finally came the next evening. I watched my mother speak into the receiver, frowning and stopping and starting, her shoulder curving away from us as she listened.

Nobody to put the pool up without you and I fixed a puncture on my bike by myself your chair looks so empty without you when are you coming home when is it going to be normal again

then my sister taking the receiver and smiling shyly, listening and answering sweetly in monosyllables, using up all that money Mum had told us about, not saying anything, just replying

Little Pete's got a new tooth and I didn't mean to laugh when you left I was really crying, I don't know what happened

then the phone receiver was handed to me and when I listened I heard the whistling empty echo of thousands of miles between us and here it was, my only chance in a year.

'Hello, Dad, I'm missing you!' I called cheerily, boisterously; the one you didn't have to worry about, the one who liked blue.

•

Everything unsaid trickled, repressed, back into silence—an underground tributary, a thread of unacknowledged self, tender as the root of a tooth. This to me defines the sheer haplessness of childhood: the ability to recognise what must be kept hidden to survive. It flows through us while we stand wretched and utterly straitjacketed by a world too complex for us; it is an endless, subdued relinquishing of the will. 'I could control you with a look,' is something my mother says now to my sister and myself, with something like reminiscent pride in her voice, that she could keep us in line while her husband was away, leaving her with three young children. They seem like measures of another age now—to never speak unless spoken to, to never answer back or contradict, to garner praise by staying dull and dutiful and inoffensive—like pointless, hard-won medals in a war everyone would prefer to forget. Except for the inexorable secret life that grows away from this dominion, like tiny weeds that grow sideways in the darkness under an unyielding slab of stone, threadlike and white and spindly but still forming somewhere, enduring the deforming pressure but still in complex circumvention towards the light.

In the year of my father's Vietnam posting, carefully checking our small treasures in our music boxes and waiting for our turn to mark off and obliterate another day on the calendar, my sister and I understood the difference between his quiet presence and the silence of true absence. That silence, so palpable and heavy, renders you mute in return. You are left with small things, your stored treasures, the brief shocking moment of recognition when you glance at your sister's face as you hand back the phone, and see sympathy, raw and unmistakable. Then your eyes drop away. You know you didn't imagine it, but even this—maybe especially this—stays unsaid. Things unsaid fill up every room.

•

Before he died I self-published the memoirs my father had been working on for years as a surprise for him, but the timeframe never reached the period of his time in Vietnam. On a tape I have he tries to begin it, his voice a hoarse painful whisper due to the surgery he'd just undergone for thyroid cancer. He describes how the Australian soldiers stationed in Vung Tau with him helped build and maintain the An Phong orphanage nearby, filled with Vietnamese war orphans.

'The army would bring all these little kids down to the back beach which was near our base, for a swim and a barbecue,' he recalls. 'There was one little bloke who stands out in my mind, who just stood back on his own. I went over to him, and he held my hand, for the whole day. Poor little bugger. Next time they came back, he ran up to me, and again, he was okay, but again he never left my side. That day when he got up on the truck to go back, he handed me a little parcel, a little hand-wrapped parcel. With a clean folded hanky inside.'

On the tape I hear my father's voice crack and break. It wrenches with sobs.

'I'd given him nothing,' he whispers, 'but he'd given me this. And these are the things that used to break my heart.'

The story of that little boy was about the only thing our father ever told my sister and me about Vietnam, and only then because we asked him about the handkerchief, which remained one of his most treasured possessions. In a story in one of my books, I used to think with a savage sense of having been cheated, it would have turned out that we would have adopted that little boy. That was how it should have ended, clicking into place with satisfying story-like inevitability, in a bigger world where bigger hearts ruled. I opened my books after that, and doubted their veracity. They were just pasteboard, really, holding together pages of paper in a certain order; their magic began to seem a little childish. Real life, colourless and hard and demanding to be endured, was the thing that would still be there when you woke up in the morning.

Over thirty-five years later, I listen on the tape to that poor little boy still breaking my father's heart, then the sound of him manfully swallowing, trying to continue to speak. The words scrape faintly and huskily through his ravaged voice box, scarred with tumours, like every sentence hurts. In the background of the recording I hear my baby daughter start crying, demanding to be fed, and it seems like the cruellest irony that of all the things his cancer robbed him of, it took away his voice, ensuring that the rest of those stories would never be told, after all.

•

My golden-haired, cherubic brother was just over a year old when my father returned. Considering he'd missed his son's first year of life in its entirety, my mother was anxious to have something, some 'first' he could be present for, and so she had valiantly fought a losing battle to keep my brother from toddling before Dad was home to witness it. She'd strapped him, squirming, into his stroller at the airport as we saw the plane carrying our father touch down and taxi towards us. As we waited, craning our heads in anticipation for Dad to appear through the doors at the end of the long corridor, she must have let the baby down for a brief respite from the confines of the stroller. My sister and I strained at the barricades we'd been expressly forbidden to step beyond.

When I saw the figure of my father striding towards us in the distance, thin and tanned and lanky in his fawn short-sleeved uniform, I became, for the second time in my life, a momentary stranger to myself. Heedlessly, I ducked under the barricade to run towards him. I think I remember feeling my sister hesitate, wavering between following me and maintaining obedience, and me running out alone, and my father bending down to sweep me up, the expression on his face one of unutterable relief.

He rose and kept walking, towards my mother and sister. A few more seconds and we were all over him . . . well, everyone except for my brother, who took one look at this stranger and burst into howling tears. Putting his newly acquired toddling skills to use, he took off in the opposite direction.

Now that I am a parent myself, I imagine how that must have felt to my father, watching his child run terrified from him, feeling the rest of us cling to him like he was a lifebuoy. I imagine everything he vowed in that moment, to subject none of his family to what he'd been through, to bear it in silence. Pain like this, I can see now, heals in us like an unset broken bone; the fracture knitted together uncertainly under the surface, something you can never quite trust to bear your weight.

As is the way with childhood, I look at that scene now and I doubt the exactness of my recollection. Memories get tumbled together like stones in this life, knocked together until they acquire a sort of polish, and hoarded into our own personal set of irregular gems. Our fingers slip along them, arranging and rearranging, sorting and rejecting.

I wonder whether this particular memory is burnished with retelling and revision, sealed under the cracked, fallible emulsion of old Polaroids. I wonder whether these elements are only here because they feel like they belong to the same strand of treasured, sentimental objects, beads and shells and teeth, strung together and counted through for comfort like a recited litany.

I observe them now, each shining smooth-edged piece, dense and solid and unerringly part of me. Here is the child running recklessly towards her father, the baby son running from him, the older sister hesitating between impulsiveness and the barricade, endlessly torn. Everything pivots on the tall uniformed man walking towards us all, his face stricken with all he would never speak of.

He grows larger as I run towards him, his face gathering more and more aching secrets into itself the closer I get. He's holding in his hand a white folded handkerchief. Any moment, I think, he will shake it open, and raise it in surrender.

LIKE MY FATHER, MY BROTHER

Michael Sala

My brother wants to know what I am writing about. I tell him that I am writing about him and me, when we were young. My brother has a quality that women used to find fascinating. I don't know if they still do. It has something to do with the boyish glint in his eyes, the way it plays against his smile.

It reminds me of my father, who had that same youthful expression even when the wave of hair on his head was dead white and years of smoking had pulled his skin into an ashen mask around the angles of his cheeks.

We are standing together in a pub. My brother holds his drink in front of him like the host of some cocktail party, and his other hand is draped across the shoulders of his girlfriend. His girlfriend is pretty and polished, with glossy brown hair that shivers around her shoulders when she laughs. I have already noticed that she looks a lot more at my brother than he does at her.

My brother cocks his head, flashes his boyish grin at me and says, 'I hope you haven't portrayed me as some sort of monster.'

•

The first clear memory I have of watching him, my brother and I are not alone. He is kicking a ball, juggling it from one foot to the other. He does this effortlessly. I am watching him and my father at the same time. We are in the park. There is a naturalness to my brother's movements that fills me with wonder. The ball looks as if it will never hit the ground. My father smokes a cigarette and stares at my brother as a pillar of ash lengthens on his cigarette. His mahogany eyes burn with an intensity that disappears when they turn my way.

•

In the pub, I am wearing a shirt that my brother gave me, and though I am skinnier than him, it strains across my chest. He stands there with his girlfriend and I sit on a barstool across from him. Another girl with a restless gaze and silky bob of dark hair sits beside me. Her name is Anna.

'I feel like we are being watched,' she tells me.

'We are, but who cares.'

Anna's glance stabs my way, but I don't know how to read it. I have never been good at that sort of thing. I feel as if I am waiting on the starting block and I don't know what to do with my body.

My brother suddenly steps close. 'Mate, you need to loosen up a little.'

He says it loud, with that relaxed, boyish grin on his face. He undoes the top button of my shirt, and then the next one. 'We have to bring out the Greek in you.'

A song comes on and he begins dancing. It's a parody of dance but he doesn't let go of the sexiness entirely. In the last few years, his features have shifted, as if an invisible river is wearing down the angles of his nose and cheeks, but his body is trim and black hair glistens at the opening of his shirt. His broad shoulders roll through the music. His girlfriend is giggling. My brother grins playfully as he dances but something is missing in the pose. I see not so much a boy, as a man pretending to be a boy. That too is something I remember of my father.

I am the last one to have seen my father, and that was more than twenty years ago. At the time, my mother had bargained him into paying for my ticket back to Holland, which we had left some years earlier, and where he still lived. He wanted to see my brother because he was the oldest and this mattered in Greek tradition, but my mother insisted that he should see me first.

My mother won her battle, but it was an uncomfortable victory. My father was the reason we had come to Australia. But in a strange country, married to a man that she didn't love, my mother had grown homesick, and back then, she still had an overwhelming faith in the ability of people to change. 'I can't forget,' she told us once, 'that I used to love him very deeply. And, despite everything, he will always be your father.'

We disembarked at the airport in the middle of winter and my father picked me up while my mother went to stay with my grandmother. My father had changed a great deal since I had left Holland, physically at least. He looked skinnier than I remembered, less substantial. The colour had leached from his olive skin and his hair, black in my memory, now loomed above his forehead like an enormous drift of snow.

Something else had changed. I had always called him Daddy as a boy, not because I thought of him as my father but because I thought that was his name. But now I could only call him by his real name, the name that my mother used when she spoke of him in a tone of both sorrow and caution. I called him Phytos.

On the drive to his house I sat in the front seat, staring out at the flat landscape drenched in grey light, and it occurred to me that I had never been in the front seat of his car before. I was sitting in my brother's place. After a long silence, Phytos told me that I looked like my mother.

Despite the cold, he drove with the car window down. A cigarette dangled from his lips, and smoke trailed from the wide, high arches of his nostrils. Phytos glanced at me again and I thought he was going to tell me something funny.

'I have a surprise for you,' he said.

When we got to his house, it turned out that the surprise was an old friend of mine, someone I had been a cub scout with as a boy. The two of us had made a pile of trouble once by going out of bounds during a camp. We had climbed into the attic of the building where we were staying and I had fallen through the roof. The boy's name was Martin. He was fourteen now, only a year ahead of me, but he seemed much older.

Martin had lank blond hair and a thin, corded neck. He pulled a cigarette from the packet that my father offered, lit it, and showed me a really neat trick. He drew deep and exhaled into a tissue.

Revealing the yellowish brown nicotine stain on the inside of the tissue, he told me with a cynical grin that this was why you shouldn't smoke. He and my father chuckled like war veterans and they both pulled on their cigarettes.

Martin did karate. He was eager to demonstrate his training regime. He jerked his body through an elaborate series of moves and then showed me how to do short, sharp push-ups against a wall. Lots of repetitions, he told me, that was how you got speed in your punches. He did a hundred of those push-ups every day. His arms were milky, lean pillars of muscle. We all sat around a table and arm-wrestled. He could beat Phytos easily, but then so could I.

'You're growing up,' Phytos told me in his oddly pitched English, still saturated with the Greek, 'turning into a real man, an *animal*!'

I remembered that he used to call my brother an animal. I smiled back at him and didn't say how surprised I was at his physical weakness. I had always imagined him as handsome, but there was a sunken quality to his face, particularly around his eye sockets, despite the brightness in his gaze.

Still breathing hard from his karate moves, Martin lit up another cigarette and turned to Phytos. 'You should show Mike your videos.'

Phytos raised his eyebrows. 'I think he's a bit young for that sort of thing, aren't you, Michael?'

'I'm not too young at all,' I said quickly.

'Come on,' Martin urged. 'He can look away if he doesn't like it.'

'What would your mother think?' Phytos stared at me with a gaze as smooth and polished as wood, his mouth hooked at one end as if we were sharing a private joke.

I told him that I didn't care what my mother thought. She was far away, and I was a man now.

'Just remember that a *man* doesn't have to tell his mother everything,' he said as he put on the video.

I sat on the couch beside Martin. The movie was foreign. I guessed that they were speaking German. We watched a woman in a nurse's uniform put her hand inside another woman's vagina.

'Look at that.' Martin leaned into his crossed arms and tensed his fists so that veins rose into the pale skin. 'Yeah, give it to her.'

'Don't get ash on my couch,' Phytos said, touching his head.

He put an ashtray beside Martin and kept on tidying the house, making sure that it was as clean and carefully ordered as the moment I had walked in. All of the walls were white. There were no pictures. The neatness of the place was disrupted only by a plant that had outgrown its pot. Its tendrils, thick as femoral arteries, shot along the window frame and up to the ceiling, and its fleshy leaves dangled along the architraves.

'You have the best dad,' Martin said suddenly.

I watched him briefly, swallowing and drawing at the cigarette between his wet lips, exhaling smoke through his nose the way my father did, then my eyes pulled back towards the television. I had a hard-on. I was grinning and the muscles of my cheeks strained at my jaw. My heart shuddered against the bottom of my throat. Most of all, I felt a shameful relief that my brother couldn't see me.

•

You're too young. This was something my brother said often when we were growing up. He said it once when we were standing beside a place shut off from the world by a tall barbed wire fence. Signs that said *Keep Out* and *Danger* hung along the fence, but my brother had found a slit cut into the wire and he held it open as he stared back at me. I told him what I always did, that I wasn't too young at all, and he let me follow him.

I didn't ask my brother what we were doing. I never did. We passed a shooting range, and long chains that looked like they were used to restrain dogs. Paths ran between oaks and pines and past concrete structures with locked metal doors. We came to a place where a huge old tree spread its branches beside a narrow road.

Nearby stood a building punctured by lights and I could see people moving around inside. I wanted to stay out of sight. A sea of tiny nuts lay around the tree facing us. My brother strolled forward, squatted in plain view and began eating them. He turned and looked at where I cowered in the bushes with a broad smile.

'They taste good, Mike,' he said.

I forgot everything and walked over to him. A man in an army uniform came riding past on a bike. When he saw us, he stumbled off his bike and ran towards us with a tight, focused expression. It was the kind of look that I'd seen on my stepfather's face a hundred times. My brother was off. He yelled at me to run too. The man was surprisingly fast. When I felt his breath right behind me, I turned and tried to warn him off in a shrill tone. He seized me by the back of my shirt and carried me towards the building.

By the time my brother got home, it was dark outside and I sat at the dinner table with my mother and stepfather.

My stepfather shoved back his chair and looked him up and down. 'Where have you been? What have you been up to?'

My stepfather was a large man, overweight, his hands stained with work and tar from the pipes he smoked. He had a way of standing right over us when he asked questions, his arms and shoulders locked as he waited for answers.

My brother glanced across at me. He had straight, dark hair and my father's brown eyes that turned hard and flat in anger, though right now they were full of curiosity. He said that he'd lost me while we were out playing. My stepfather turned and I felt his gaze. We were eating sandwiches for dinner. I chewed on my sandwich and shrugged.

Later, as we lay on the separate levels of our bunk bed, I told my brother how I'd been made to sit in a room with fluorescent lights, a bunch of men in uniforms around me. The men had looked at me until I started crying. They had given me a glass of orange juice and a biscuit and told me never to come back.

'I waited at the fence for hours,' my brother said.

I thought that he'd pile abuse on me then for not having run quick enough, but he fell silent, and the silence grew long. It occurred to me suddenly that he was ashamed.

I knew that I had done the right thing by not telling. These were the important things; never to ask for explanations, never to talk about what we did. My brother and I shared a room. In the months after I was born, my brother had tried to bury me. He would scour the room for objects that he could pile into my cot: toys, clothes, footwear.

Later, he usually ignored me, but there were moments when he didn't. My mother told him off once for carefully laying a packet full of drawing-pins, points upwards, in my bed. She said that it was his responsibility to look after me, that we only had each other.

My brother's violence often came unexpectedly. He would turn with a sudden blankness in his eyes and punch me in the arms and the stomach and chest. Sometimes I would scream so that our stepfather would come in and hit us both, but often I kept quiet and so did he. I had seen my brother fighting at school. He beat people quickly and efficiently, no matter how much bigger or stronger they were, and while they were still nursing bloody noses, he'd be off doing something else, smiling like the whole thing had never happened.

It was the same with me. Not long after his attacks, he would come strolling back into view, preoccupied with something else, a pleasant grin on his face when he glanced in my direction. His whole expression would dazzle me, invite me to forget, and I would find it impossible to maintain my fury. But in the days that I spent alone with my father, I started to see the smile differently.

•

Towards the end of my stay, I bought a record with my father's money. He had been giving me money the whole time as if neither of us really knew what else we should be doing together. I bought Queen's

Greatest Hits and played it full blast in his tidy, strangely empty house. He listened tolerantly the whole way through and watched with a kind of curiosity bordering on affection as I played air guitar.

Martin was there too, doing his endless repetitions of push-ups against the wall. When the last song finished, Phytos told me suddenly that he still cared about my mother, despite everything, despite what he had lost. Showing his perfect teeth, he said that she was a lovely person but just unstable, prone to imagining things that weren't there—or, he added with a confident glance at Martin, things that had never happened.

•

When I returned to Australia, it was the height of summer. My brother didn't ask much about Phytos. He had always seemed slightly bored by our father and his only disappointment appeared to be that he'd missed out on seeing his old friends. At first I couldn't bring myself to talk about the trip at all, but then things began to loosen inside me.

'Phytos says nothing happened,' I told my brother a few weeks after my return.

At first I thought he hadn't heard me. We were sitting on the couch. My brother was watching the cricket. He could sit in front of the television for hours when the cricket was on, and his face would grow empty and still.

'What do you mean?' he asked at last, without looking away from the television.

'Between you and him. He says Mum made it all up.'

My brother laughed but he didn't say anything. I mentioned seeing my friend Martin with Phytos quite a bit although I didn't say what we'd watched together.

'Yeah,' my brother said. 'Some of the guys on my soccer team used to hang at his house too. Even when I wasn't around.'

He turned and gave me a brief smile. He had a way of smiling without showing his teeth that had nothing to do with putting on charm.

By this stage, my father had phoned up a couple of times. The next time he phoned, my brother asked to speak to him.

'Phytos.' My brother spoke softly into the phone. He listened for a moment then said, 'I hate your fucking guts. You're a coward. Don't call here again.'

He put down the phone and went into his room. He came out with his spearfishing gear.

'It's blowing a westerly,' he said. 'Bet you the water's dead flat.'

I had been watching him jump off rocks into the sea for years. I would stand on the shore and glimpse him way out and alone in the turbulence of the sea and my stomach would churn. Dolphins dipped and cut through the water much closer to the shore than he was.

The first time he took me out spearfishing was during that summer. We plunged off the rocks and started paddling; out, it seemed, towards the tankers on the horizon. We paddled for twenty minutes, way past the shark nets. I couldn't see the bottom; only islands of shadow and strange turns of light, and fish, longer than my arms, that slid past as if I didn't exist.

Every now and again, my brother kicked down into the gloom and left me drifting above him in a cloud of bubbles. Alone, at the surface, I shivered and choked at each watery breath in my snorkel until I saw him rising towards me. Often, the carcass of a fish hung from his spear. He nearly always managed to shoot fish in the eye. When he was nearby, I would lift my head and stare back at the thin ribbon of the shoreline and yearn for it, but the thought of paddling back alone filled me with terror.

By the time we returned to shore, I couldn't feel my hands or feet and my teeth chattered so fiercely that I thought they would shatter. I asked him whether he ever got scared out there by himself.

'No,' he told me.

'What do you think of when you're out there?'

He showed his teeth. 'Nothing. Just the fish.'

My brother was by this time sixteen years old, well proportioned, and broad-shouldered. My own limbs were longer and felt strange to me. His short, dark hair was tousled and rough with salt water. There was often a subtle but intent scowl on his face that sat like a wall in front of whatever I imagined that he was thinking. He crouched with one knee on the rocks and opened the belly of each of his fish with a practised motion. He tossed fistfuls of guts to the seagulls that wheeled and descended around us.

Staring back over the blue drape of the ocean, he remarked that he was impressed how I had stayed out with him for nearly two hours. He had come prepared, in a thick rubber wetsuit, while I wore only my swimmers. I had never heard him say that to me before, that he was *impressed* with me. I didn't tell him the truth.

I have this dream sometimes, that I am small and standing at a door. The door is orange and it has a window above it. Through this window, which is slanted open, I can hear my brother and my father. I am outside the door. They are playing a game on the other side. I am calling out, trying to get their attention, but the door remains closed.

My brother often sold me his old clothes. He would dangle them in front of me and offer them at a price. There was never any negotiation. If I refused to pay the price, he threw them out with a mocking, regretful expression. I bought many of his clothes but they never sat on me properly. I was taller than him, but skinnier, and his clothes were already worn by the time they got to me, so that I looked like a lost scarecrow. I rarely saw myself wearing them though. I made a point of not looking at myself. Instead I focused on the way I had seen my brother wear them, the ease with which he moved inside his skin. I was fascinated by his surface.

All of my brother's friends used to call me by his name. They added *junior* at the end as if I were his son, and so I was known, but apart from the history we shared, I was more aware of our difference. My brother had a broad Australian accent that he had acquired within a year or so of our arrival, and he blended in at school in every way. My own accent still carried the thick, stumbling textures of Holland. I was much taller than the people around me and solitary.

My brother could pick up any sort of sporting equipment and act like he had been using it for years and he had an easy contempt for those who didn't have that natural ability.

When he was eighteen he said to me, 'Have you ever actually stopped to *look* at yourself?'

There was such derision in his tone that I flew into a rage. I described in great detail how he had always put me down, how he had oppressed me, made my life hell despite the fact that I had only ever admired him. He turned white, as if all of this was news to him. After that, he'd sometimes find ways of praising me. He'd tell me that I was better with words than he was, that I was the clever one.

I was used to admiring my brother because it was all that I had ever seen other people do. On the last day of my trip to Holland, when my father drove my mother and me back to the airport, Phytos began discussing with a feverish kind of enthusiasm the possibility of seeing my brother the next time.

Suddenly Mum said, 'Mike has all these wonderful qualities that you've just never seen.'

'Oh look,' Phytos said after a moment of silence, 'I guess I just never really noticed them because he's so different to me.'

'Different how?'

'You know, sensitive, fragile. A bit like . . .'

'Me?'

'Maybe, maybe,' he said.

He added, with his peculiar foreign manner of phrase, that my brother was easier to love because he was more in his own image. The unabashed way in which he said this while I sat in the car with him struck me with a kind of awe. I don't remember how this conversation ended, but it was dark and trees shot up from the flat landscape like spears into the smoky grey sky.

My father hugged me at the airport and I kissed his cheek. Despite how I felt about him, the well-kept surface, with its hint of stubble and a sophisticated whiff of aftershave, evoked in me a distilled sort of happiness, and I remembered how seeing my father when I was a kid in Holland had meant the headlong rush into a most wonderful and seductive feeling of potential.

My mother and I got on the plane and sat side by side, in silence. The plane taxied along the runway. There was a low, dull smother of clouds pressing on the landscape, making it vague, and rain sliced across the narrow window beside me. The plane turned and paused. Then it jolted forward and raced along the tarmac with a fierce shudder. Grey filled the window and then tore away to reveal a dazzling, clear sky. It was surprising to see that sky, to remember that it existed.

•

In the toilet at the pub, I stare in the mirror set into the gleaming white tiles, direct a frothy stream of piss into the urinal, and weigh my romantic potential. Chest hair shows at the unbuttoned juncture of my shirt. I follow my brother's advice; I draw on my inner Greek. I have no idea what that means though. I have no memory of the places my father came from, and only a few memories of him. For me it has always been guesswork.

I make my way back into the crowded bar and return to the place where I left my brother and his girlfriend and Anna. My brother has just been on a diving trip to Fiji and talk has turned to sharks.

'I hate swimming in the ocean,' Anna says, 'because I always think of sharks.'

'I'd bet you'd feel safe with me,' I tell her when the bustle of the pub separates us momentarily from the others.

Her eyes dart into mine and she looks away.

I take her hand and move in close. 'I'd love to kiss you right now.'

Anna uses my hands to gently leverage me away.

'You shouldn't,' she says. 'I'm not attracted to you at all. I'm sorry.'

I lean back on my bar stool and the noise of the pub presses around me. Anna and my brother's girlfriend go off to the toilets together. With his girlfriend gone, my brother's gaze moves across the women in the pub with a naked intensity before it comes to rest on me.

'How's it going, Mike?'

'I just tried to kiss Anna.'

'Really? I thought you were just friends.'

'There was more going on than that.' I shrug and feel heat gather in my face. 'For me at least.'

'Ah, I know the feeling,' my brother says. 'I'm still in love with Maddie. When I go to Sweden, I might see if I can give her one last shot.'

'Aren't you in love with your girlfriend?'

His lips press inwards and his face softens into something desolate. 'Almost, but no. It just isn't there.'

For a moment he looks lost and I can imagine him as a boy. I want to ask him all sorts of questions then. His girlfriend and Anna return and that expression vanishes. A new song comes on. My brother undoes another button on his own shirt and resumes dancing, the moves sexier, more absurd than before. I can't stop looking at his face. He invites me to join in with a dazzling, comradely nod. Anna is leaning over her cranberry and vodka, staring away. My brother's girlfriend has eyes only for him. She shakes her head at his display with loving good humour, then gets up and joins in.

'Come on, Mike,' my brother says.

I think of other times that he's said that to me while I stood on the rocks at the edge of the sea, or on the brink of some other adventure. I am sick from too much alcohol and feel as if someone has poured glue into my heart. I jump in. I start dancing. I wonder what is going through my brother's head but I don't know how to ask.

Later, as the two of us walk home from the pub, I glance across at my brother. Although he has drunk much more than me, his face is as contained as ever. I feel an intense, lonely urge to get beyond that expression. I tell him that I watched porn at our father's house.

'Really?' he says. 'Why didn't you tell me earlier?'

'Dunno.' I find myself blushing as if it had all happened this very morning. 'It felt like a betrayal, I guess. But when I was with Phytos, I couldn't help myself. I just wanted him to *like* me, to include me in things.'

My brother laughs softly. 'That's why I used to get so angry at you. You had no idea what that would have meant. No idea at all.'

We walk on in silence.

'Good old Phytos,' my brother says after a moment. 'I wonder what he looks like now.'

I wonder the same thing sometimes.

'Reckon you'll ever see him again?'

'Don't know. It'd be funny though, wouldn't it?'

He aims a playful kick at a bottle lying on the footpath and pushes his hands into the pockets of his jeans. I haven't seen him play soccer in a long time, but he has a habit of kicking at things—pieces of rubbish, plants, the occasional cat. He does it without seeming to notice.

'Yeah, funny, alright,' I say.

I walk beside him and think of how strange it is having such a father in our lives, for the two of us to be bound together in that way.

When he surfaces in our conversation we call him 'Dad' once or twice for comic effect, but we always fall back into Phytos, which in my mind has the dusty resonance of an old curse. We sometimes argue about who looks more like him, and in the stillness of photographs it's me, but then I can't put on his voice the way my brother does. And the smile that obliterates doubt in almost everyone, including the wearer, the dazzling smile that made me want to try anything as a boy, that is my brother's.

I stare across at my brother, the face set, that brilliant glint in his dark eyes. I tell him that we have never talked about what happened between him and Phytos; that I'd like to. The thought actually frightens the shit out of me, but a part of me needs to know just more than the hazy detail. I know that he won't tell Mum anything else. He wants her to sleep at night. He flashes me a grin then stares off down the road. We'll talk about it, he says. We'll have a beer and talk about it someday.

THE CRICKET PALACE

Charlotte Wood

Wendy pressed 'send', knowing that Leonie had almost certainly not expected her to say yes. It was Leonie's second wedding, after all, and had been arranged at short notice. They wanted to marry while they were still on their trip, her email said, but the whole thing would be *very casual*.

And Wendy was seventy-one years old, and Greece was a long way away. She knew it was quite possible Leonie did not really want her to come.

Too bad, she thought. *I am going to Greece.*

Sitting in front of the computer she remembered Athens, with Jim. Staying near the Parthenon, in a small hotel room with a large crack across its dingy porcelain basin, and making love every day because it was holidays, and walking and walking until late into the evenings. A fistful of old lust gripped and turned, briefly, inside her.

She looked across the room at the jar of remaining ashes on the telephone table. She kept what was left in a squat terracotta jar with a warm grey ceramic lid, which they had bought together many years ago in Shanghai, at the insect market. The jar was a home for a fighting cricket. Most of the cricket houses at the market were small, many made of rusted, cut-down food tins. But this—this was a mansion for a cricket. It was satisfyingly smooth and cool to hold, and its girth was covered in columns of fine black calligraphy. Of course they never knew what the characters meant, but they had called it the cricket palace.

For years Wendy used it to keep salt in, next to the stove. But when the crematorium people gave her the ugly plastic urn, her most urgent thought was *Get him out of there*, and she emptied the ashes into various containers about the house: a small inlaid wooden box Jim gave her once, a silver sugar bowl with a hinged lid that had belonged to her mother, and the cricket palace.

A good while later—too long later, most people seemed to think—Wendy and her sister Ruth, Ruth's husband Alan and their children Leonie and Paul, as well as the few friends Wendy still had left, stood awkwardly on a steep, narrow slope just off the walking track in the national park at Bradleys Head, and Wendy's voice went thin as she read a poem, and she tossed Jim in desultory handfuls towards the knuckled ground beneath the angophora trees.

She hated leaving the little flung piles of white gravel there in the scrub, had an urge to kneel and scrabble the bits back up with her fingers, but she knew Jim would have liked it. *Just chuck me here at the end*, he had said often enough as they marched that bush track above the harbour.

But there was still the cricket palace. Sometimes, when she talked on the phone, she lifted the lid and swirled her finger around in the gritty powder.

When Ruth saw the terracotta pot on the telephone desk a few months ago she'd said, 'Why've you got your salt there?'

Wendy told her, and Ruth screeched. 'Ugh! I don't know how you can do that! How horrible!'

Wendy had a great desire to rush across the carpet and smack her sister's face.

•

Wendy assumed she would be the only one of her generation to go to the wedding. In a private part of herself she hoped she was the only one invited, but of course Leonie would have to ask her parents. But they didn't like travel. And Alan's prostate procedure was scheduled only weeks before the wedding.

So it was a surprise when Ruth, who had been to London once at the age of twenty-three, and came back quick smart, declared that she would go to the Greek island too, with Wendy.

Sisters! she cried down the phone. *It will be a sisters trip!*

On the plane they fastened their seatbelts, and Ruth leaned to one side, scoping the aisle. She had filled the empty seat between them with things she had bought at the airport, scurrying around the shops while Wendy read. The seat was filled with magazines, a leopard-print velour U-shaped neck cushion filled with polystyrene beads, a pink shawl that Ruth called a pashmina. It was not really a pashmina, it was synthetic, but Wendy didn't say anything. She had left her own real pashminas at home.

Ruth, leaning sideways, kept glancing up the aisle and then nodding conspiratorially at Wendy. 'Only a few people now,' she whispered, trying to suppress a triumphant smirk. 'It's unlikely.'

Wendy wished Jim were here. He had been dead two years but she wished, so often, that he were here.

Once, in the dark hours, with the plane's dull roar hurtling them through the black skies and everyone else asleep, Wendy looked up to see Ruth swaying down the aisle on her way back from the toilet. She took little steps in her thick pink socks, peering down at the seats as she went, trying to find her home. She looked old, teetering there in the gloom.

•

At the little airport on the island a grizzled young man wearing a shoddy grey suit and a crumpled yellow woollen tie held up a piece of paper with their names handwritten on it in small unsteady biro.

'Oh dear,' muttered Ruth. They were both exhausted. Wendy did not want to admit it, but the plane travel—first to Athens, and then to the island—had been ghastly. Eventually, she had found, it was difficult to distinguish the smell of the food from the smell of the other passengers. Her back ached. But she saw with satisfaction that although Ruth was eight years younger, she walked equally stiffly along the grey linoleum of the airport.

Still. Wendy did not wish to agree with Ruth that this forlorn young man looked disappointing, so she took charge. She strode over to him, smiling. '*Kalimera*,' she called in a clear voice above the airport hubbub.

He looked alarmed. 'I'm Australian,' he said.

Ruth pushed past him towards the carousel. 'Oh yes,' she called over her shoulder to Wendy. 'That's Jeremy's friend.'

Out in the car park Wendy stood by, being gracious, while the young man—Derek—hoisted the women's suitcases into the back of his small four-wheel drive. Derek had lived on the island for some years. Ruth's gaze flicked up and down him, contemptuous of his nerviness and dishevelment. And as soon as she heard the central locking clunk open she clambered surprisingly nimbly into the back seat, pulling the door shut behind her.

Wendy turned to reach for the front passenger door handle and then saw—suddenly, unbelievably—they were *here*. A Greek island.

She took a sharp breath, and stood for a moment in the hot still air, gazing up to the hill above them. The town was white and brittle and frilled like beach coral against the hard blue sky. The sudden beauty of it unbalanced her. She and Jim had never travelled to the islands, only to Athens. She felt her eyes water—she wished Jim were here squeezing her hand, wished they were both thirty and breathless with this shock of splendour and each other.

But Ruth scowled at her through the window, and Derek stood frowning at Wendy across the car roof.

She smiled at him. 'It's so . . . beautiful,' she said lamely.

Derek looked morose and yanked open his door. 'People who don't live here always think it's beautiful.'

As the car lurched through the car park, out into the street, Wendy dragged her gaze back from the Greek town to Derek.

'Have you had much to do with the wedding preparations?'

He shot her an odd look. After an instant he said, '*No-o*,' and looked as if he might laugh. He said, 'I have a few dramas in my life at the moment.' Then he leaned forward, squinting out under the sun visor, and revved the car in a savage burst up around a corner onto a larger ring road.

Wendy looked back at Ruth, who made a face that meant, 'He's crazy,' but also gave a little smirk that meant she was glad to be in the back seat.

'I'm just doing them a favour,' said Derek. 'I work for myself, so they obviously just thought I could up and leave everything and come and get you.'

They climbed the hills. Down below them was white limestone and green water. Derek ground the gears.

'Well,' said Wendy, 'we're very grateful. Aren't we, Ruth?'

'Yes,' came Ruth's bored, unconvincing voice from the back.

'What sort of work do you do, Derek?' said Wendy.

He looked depressed. 'I'm a lawyer.' He reached forward and wrenched a large purple plastic container with a lid from the cup holder and drank from it deeply. Wendy watched him, with his rumpled clothes and his sorrowful face, and wondered if he were a drunk. She gripped her seat and looked out of the window again, about to remark on the Greek mythology she had been reading on the plane, but Derek said, peering through the windscreen as they tore around a steep bend, 'The internet is very useful, isn't it?'

'Oh *yes*,' cried Ruth from the back seat, her little face suddenly appearing by Wendy's shoulder.

And Wendy could leave the two of them talking, as Ruth began detailing the bookings they had made, the pleasures of something called PayPal.

Wendy's fingers wrapped around the little plastic salad dressing container in her pocket. She watched the turquoise water beyond the dark branches of the pines sweeping past below them.

Suddenly Derek braked hard, and the car swerved to the side of the road and lurched to a stop. His door burst open and he leapt from the car. Both the women yelped. The car, driverless, began rolling slowly down the hill.

'Oh my God!' cried Ruth. Wendy gasped. But then Derek's long arm reached in and yanked the handbrake on, and the car stopped. He stood out on the road and flattened himself against the car as a large dusty truck heaved past. Then he removed his jacket and climbed back inside, stuffing the jacket under his seat.

'Bit hot,' he said, revving the engine again.

By the time their bags sat on the paving stones outside the house on the hill, Ruth had abandoned any pretence at manners. She charged off with the house key while Wendy thanked Derek too many times and wondered whether she should offer to pay him.

His car gone, she stood on the terrace of the tall white house they had chosen from a picture on the internet. Grapevines curled along a series of crossed wires above her, and a small iron table and two chairs were set in a convivial arrangement beneath the canopy. A little iron balcony overlooked the terrace from the first floor. The air smelled of pine and ocean. She was in the Greek Isles, the Islands of Magnesia. It sounded mythical and momentous. It was still so hot that the air seemed to vibrate.

Inside the stone house it was all coolness and gloom. The heavy wooden shutters were closed, and the floors were flagstone. She could hear Ruth calling from upstairs, aghast. 'You're not allowed to *flush toilet paper*!'

Wendy climbed the stairs, the dark banister thick in her hand.

Ruth was reading a small sign on the bathroom wall explaining that the ancient plumbing could not cope with toilet paper, and the covered bin was there for your convenience.

'That's dis*gust*ing,' Ruth said.

Wendy stepped away from the bathroom and then saw that Ruth had taken the small single-bed room for herself, leaving Wendy the master bedroom. Ruth's things were already spread around the poky little room, her suitcase opened and sandals lined up beneath the wardrobe.

She stood in the doorway of the main bedroom with Wendy.

'Isn't it *lovely*?' she said, and waited.

Wendy knew she should protest, that they should argue for some minutes until she finally persuaded Ruth that this was *her* big holiday, it was *her* daughter's wedding, and insist that all Wendy's own life she had had the chance to travel the world and stay in beautiful rooms like this, and now it was Ruth's turn.

But they leaned there looking into the room, at the simple double bed with its pale blue sheets and the white curtain at the window where a single shutter slanted open, allowing a sliver of bright light to fall across the Turkish kilim on the wooden floorboards, and suddenly all the hours since they left home came crashing down upon Wendy, and all she craved was to lie down, immediately, upon that square of clean sheets.

'Thank you,' she said to Ruth, and marched into the room.

•

Wendy woke with a start in the darkened afternoon. From outside, beyond the shutters, came the sharp clapping of a child's rubber sandals running along the shallow steps outside the house. A woman's voice shouted in Greek and the child shouted back, all sound carried perfectly, crisp and audible, along the tall stone corridors.

She turned to look at the little yellow Tupperware container on the bedside table. It was from an old, old picnic set. The ageing plastic was crazed with fine dark lines of age. She had snatched it up in the last minutes before the taxi came, and scooped the ashes in with a teaspoon and jammed down the greying lid before popping it into a zippered compartment of her handbag. She had held her breath each time the handbag went through the X-ray machines. She had no idea what she would have said.

She knew it was ridiculous. Or deranged, or something.

She heard Ruth's mobile telephone ring, her shy, hesitant voice, and then its relief. Wendy sat up, throwing off the sheet in a buff of sweet cool air. Leonie and the groom, Jeremy, and their friends were staying all around the island, in various houses.

Wendy sat listening, waiting for Ruth to call out to her that Leonie wanted to say hello. But after a while she realised Ruth had stopped talking, and then she heard the shower running downstairs.

She lay back down in the bed and drew the sheet up beneath her chin.

When Leonie and Paul were little, Wendy and Jim would bring them presents from their travels—a fur-lined hat made of yak leather from Nepal, or wood-and-paper parasols from China. Of course Wendy knew the children would rather a Barbie doll or an Action Jackson, but she knew too that the hats and parasols—and the folklore books, and the French stockings for Leonie as she grew older, and the cufflinks from New York for Paul—all of these were investments in her future with her sister's children. They were learning about the world and all its wild, colourful possibilities, something they would certainly never glean from their own parents, from Wendy and Jim.

She was never pushy. Neither of them were. She and Jim lived their own lives, with their own friends and jobs and travel. And then, drawn by this richness, sometimes one or other of the children would come and stay for a weekend or a week, or visit for an afternoon for photography lessons from Jim, or be taken for a ritual expensive restaurant dinner with a friend of their choosing when each of them finished high school. Wendy felt that, by example, she had taught them to cook and to travel; she gave them Marquez novels in their twenties and Elizabeth David cookbooks for their wedding presents.

Wendy knew Ruth and Alan did not think much of her. She thought they might describe her to their friends as *hoity-toity*.

Once she had walked into Ruth and Alan's living room in Thornleigh when the children were in their early teens to find the whole family sitting on their ugly, squashy vinyl couches massaging each other's bare feet while they watched television. Paul and Leonie and Ruth and Alan, all in a sort of distracted, fleshy chain of idle fondling and stroking. Wendy had not known where to look. It had seemed to her obscene. Alan knew it, and enjoyed her discomfort. He called out to her, *Siddown, Wendy. Want a foot rub?* and had laughed at her prim smile, her stiff, bodily revulsion.

When Ruth's children came to Wendy and Jim's house there was always a dinner table, and serviettes, and sometimes (not always; they were not pretentious) a decanter. She had never been pretentious or prim, but in Ruth's house she was made to feel it, repelled by what was natural to Ruth and Alan, and battered by their hardhearted jokes.

When Ruth and Alan came to Wendy's house the tables were turned, but Wendy took care—Jim did not need to, it came effortlessly to him—to treat them generously. She was careful to instil a sense of warmth and comfortable, well-travelled chaos about the house. Nothing was untouchable. The children were encouraged to pick things up, even the most delicate things: the dried seahorse they had found on a beach in Sri Lanka, the little blue bird's egg from an orchard in Puglia. She and the children would hover over the things, their heads touching, and she would say to them, *One day you must go there. We might even take you.*

Once, long ago, Ruth had said to Wendy in a grave, warning voice: 'They're my children, you know.' And Wendy had not said anything.

She had not said, *Yes but you don't own them, they can make up their own minds.*

She had never said it to Jim, or even acknowledged it fully to herself, but in some hazy depths of her future Wendy had hoped she and Jim, in giving to the children without expectation, in standing back and urging them out into the world, would be rewarded. She saw now she had hoped Ruth's children would, of their own adult volition, choose to become Jim and Wendy's children too. Or even, perhaps, instead.

Wendy was shocked at the raw clarity of this admission, here in the dark room. But the disgrace of it was immediately extinguished by the much larger, cold fact that things had not turned out that way. For the fact was that once they left home, Ruth's children quickly drifted away and hardly ever saw Jim and Wendy at all.

And then, two years ago, Wendy had turned over in the night and reached out, as she often did, to lay her palm flat over Jim's calm, sleeping back. And she had found it stone cold.

She was filled with dread again, here in the room.

She reached out and took hold of the little plastic tub, and clutched it in her fist beneath the pillow.

•

Ruth peered mournfully at the menu, and Leonie leaned back in her chair. They were having lunch in the little beachside taverna where the wedding would be held in two days' time. There were tables and wicker chairs set on a concrete slab, in the shade of a large awning.

All around them were olive trees, and musty yellow grasses, and across the pale gravel track of the road was a grey-pebbled beach, a bank of deep turquoise water, the sky.

Wendy watched her niece across the table.

Ruth and Wendy had met Leonie down on the waterfront, where the boat masts tinkled and sang, and motorbikes buzzed along the dusty road. Seeing her from a distance, Wendy was filled with a rush of love. Despite the adult facts of Leonie's life—her own children growing up, a bad divorce and her job in the upper echelons of a large bank—here, standing in the sun with the sea behind her, one hand shading her eyes and the other arm waving vigorously in the air, Leonie still seemed the lanky, eager teenager Wendy had drawn into her arms so often.

She hurried ahead of Ruth across the street to greet her niece, calling, 'Leonie!', and holding her arms wide.

But Leonie cried, 'Watch out for cars, Wendy!' in an irritated voice, and clasped Wendy in the briefest of dry hugs before turning away, with a broad grin, to her mother. Wendy had closed her mouth and stood by while they embraced.

Now, at the taverna, a breeze shifted the olive branches. Ruth was still grimacing at the menu, fussing over what there was that she possibly could eat.

Leonie was forty, but looked younger. She was of that new generation of middle-class women who employed an army of other women to take care of their bodies; she and all her friends had pedicurists and hair colourists and massage therapists and personal trainers and beauticians giving them facials, all the time. She went away for weekends to spa retreats with groups of women friends. They were shiny-haired and their bodies were youthful, trim and tanned. Now Leonie wore a sarong and a thin-strapped singlet, and her limbs and her elegant bare feet were smooth and brown, her neat toenails polished bronze.

'What about Greek salad?' Wendy said to Ruth, her patience draining away rapidly.

'But that's got that *cheese* in it!' said Ruth, with a grimace of disgust. Then she gasped. 'Goat. Oh my God.' She closed the menu and slapped it down on the table, and craned around at the other tables, staring at their plates with open-mouthed fear.

Leonie seemed unembarrassed but Wendy was ashamed, to be sitting here on a Greek island with her sister, a grown woman—an *old* woman—who refused feta, spat out olives, wanted butter instead of olive oil. Ruth caught her sister's expression, and cried—it seemed with pride—'I've *always* been a picky eater, Wendy! You know that!'

Wendy looked out at the sea, and at the great walls of limestone shearing up on either side of the little bay. There would be a private small space out there, between the rocks, for a person's ashes. If she was even going to do anything with them. She didn't yet know. The force that had thrust the little tub into her bag was not reason but some quick flare of fear. She had never travelled abroad without Jim. She could not leave him behind.

Eventually, the waiter standing by, Ruth stabbed a finger at a picture. '*That*.'

Wendy and Leonie each ordered a salad of feta and tomatoes and oil-soaked toasted bread and chopped olives, and glasses of beer.

As she looked out at the gritty beach, an image formed in Wendy's mind, of herself crouched by a rock pool after dark, after the wedding, when others were dancing. But Jim had never even been to the Greek islands, let alone with her. It would be strange, and wrong, surely, to leave even a tiny bit of him mixed here in the sand.

'*Efkharisto*,' Wendy murmured to the waiter as he set down their glasses, while the others said *thanks*.

As he walked away, Ruth, her plump arms folded, looked at Wendy with open dislike. 'What did you say to that fella?'

'I said thank you.'

Ruth raised her eyebrows and drew her mouth into a long pout to show that Wendy was being pretentious. Leonie sat back with a half-smile, watching them both. Ruth shook her head and said to Wendy, 'You're a mystery to me, you really are.'

Leonie spoke at last. 'So, how's the house, Aunty Wendy? Your room sounds gorgeous.'

Wendy felt her cheeks grow hot at the accusation.

Ruth's chef's salad came; a small plateful of waxy yellow cheese cubes, chopped green lettuce with no dressing and half a dozen squares of cubed ham from a tin. Ruth tucked in cheerfully.

It was too late now to insist about the room, Wendy supposed. Should she insist? Change the sheets and just move Ruth's things in there? But this would be accepting Ruth's way of never saying what she wanted, of always stepping back with lips pressed together, arms folded, and then complaining about being made to wait. It angered Wendy to think of bowing to it.

'Derek is nice,' she said, to change the subject.

Leonie groaned. 'Bloody Derek.'

Ruth said, through a mouthful of ham, 'He nearly killed us!'

Leonie groaned again, leaning forward to lay her head melodramatically on her outstretched forearms on the table, then sat up. 'He's Jeremy's old friend from uni. He's lived here for years. He's a pain in the arse—sorry, Wendy—but he's sort of useful.' She sipped her beer.

She gazed thoughtfully out across the water, with her chin in her hand, and then said, 'Derek's alright. He's just sort of . . . depressing.'

Wendy felt a surprised stab of pity, and solidarity, for Derek.

•

The day before the wedding, while they slept after lunch, there was a knock at the door. Wendy groped her way down the dark stairs and padded across the flagstones. When she opened the door, Leonie strode in with another woman, and called up the stairs to her mother as she went to the fridge and pulled out a jug of iced water.

The other woman's name was Lucy. She had thick bushy hair and a loud sharp voice, and wore bangles that clacked up and down her arms when she moved. Lucy was her make-up artist friend from London, Leonie told Wendy, and she had offered to *do them* all for the wedding.

Ruth, clambering down the stairs, was already calling, 'Oooh, lovely.'

Wendy had never really worn make-up, except the occasional smudge of lipstick and some rouge, as they used to call it. When she was younger she scorned make-up; it was a thing suburban women like her sister were interested in. But also, more secretly, Wendy had found that any make-up other than lipstick—the other things: foundation, and mascara, and eye shadow—made her look strangely like a dressed-up man. So now while the other women discussed make-up Wendy laughed lightly and waved her hand *no thank you*, as she refilled the water jug and returned it to the fridge.

The woman Lucy met her eye across the room, and shrugged and said, 'Well, if you change your mind.'

Then Ruth's son Paul came striding in, carrying a heavy-looking cardboard box. Wendy had not seen him for eighteen months, and he looked even taller, and now tanned and more masculine. He was forty-three now, and married with two children, but Wendy still thought of him as a wastrel university student, full of potential and wit and unbloomed talent.

She hurried around the table towards him, calling his name. He grinned and said, 'G'day, Wendy,' and leaned his head down sideways for a kiss, before kneeling at the fridge to put the box down. When he set it down, he didn't then get up to greet Wendy properly, but began tearing open the cardboard box and stacking bottles into their fridge, carrying on a conversation with his sister and mother that seemed to have been started without Wendy.

It had been decided that tomorrow Wendy and Ruth's house would be 'the girls' house'; that there would be a champagne breakfast, with Lucy and her cosmetics set up on the terrace, where any of the women guests could come and have their make-up done in the hours before the wedding.

The house was to be overrun. Nobody had asked Wendy's opinion about this, although her money was paying half of the rent. As she stood in the room and listened to them all talking, it galled her to think that since Jim died she was no longer a person to be consulted.

She didn't say anything. She knew it would be ridiculous to complain. It was a wedding. *Ruth's* daughter's wedding. She was lucky to be here at all.

She left Leonie and Paul and the friend and Ruth, and went out walking.

The steep streets of the town were populated by hundreds of slender, pretty cats. They crept along balconies and strolled the shadeless stone stairs. They swarmed around the orange plastic bags of garbage that appeared on odd days at selected laneway corners.

Wendy had been told by one of Leonie's friends that a man with a donkey came clopping down the stairs to collect the rubbish, but in three days she had not seen or heard any donkey, though the rubbish disappeared every day or so somehow. She heard the little motorbikes, bumping noisily up and down, their sound coiling off into the distance. And yesterday she heard the sonorous, yearning prayer-song of a priest in the church far above them. There was a clock somewhere that struck bells on every hour. But no donkey.

In a small shop of antiquities and folk art, looking for a wedding present for Leonie and Jeremy, Wendy bought a small beaded handbag. She had not thought before, but she would need something to take to the wedding that was not her workaday leather handbag. This one was small enough to be elegant, but large enough for tissues, lip balm, keys and money. And for the little container, she thought. In case. Why had she brought the ashes, otherwise?

She had begun to feel a secretive, low-level anxiety about the container, as if she were carrying some prohibited substance with her through the holiday. Above all she did not want Ruth to see the ashes when she came bustling into Wendy's room, as she would, to rummage through her suitcase to borrow a scarf or a pair of earrings. For since Wendy had accepted the best room it was clear, though unspoken, that Ruth must have anything she pleased for the remainder of the holiday, including choosing for herself the earrings Wendy had planned to wear to the wedding. To keep the little Tupperware tub from Ruth's appalled discovery Wendy hid it at the back of her bedside table, slipping it inside a shopping bag beneath some holiday brochures.

As she wandered around the shop, Wendy came across a display case of small beaten-metal votives. The proprietor told her in his beautiful English that these were called *tamata* in plural, *tama* in the singular. They mostly depicted a part of the body that was ailing, he explained, and a person would make the *tama* and take it to the church as an offering, a symbol of what the prayers were needed to mend.

There was an ear, two separate hands, a heart, a baby, a foot, and a shoulder. Wendy chose the heart. It was made of fine, pretty silver. Leonie would put it on a shelf and think it exotically decorative and romantic. Origins did not matter to people like Leonie and Ruth, who had mass-produced cement Buddhas and 'Moroccan' lanterns from Ikea around their swimming pools.

Ruth liked things that were *cute*: a dish-scrubber that looked like a giraffe, a knife-block in the shape of a man being stabbed. Wendy knew her private derision of Ruth's taste was snobbery. But she couldn't help it. Whenever Ruth showed her some decorated household object—washing-up gloves with fur cuffs and a diamond ring, or a leopard-print doormat, or a chicken-shaped egg-timer—and said gleefully, 'Isn't it fun!', Wendy wanted to shout at her that they were not children. Why must everything be entertainment?

Standing in the shop with the little beaten heart in her hand Wendy tried to remember if she had always been this ill-tempered with Ruth, or if it was only since Jim died that she had said goodbye to the possibility of trivial, empty pleasures.

She paid for the little heart, and the man wrapped it in soft green tissue paper. It was a good present; pretty and romantic and Greek. And Leonie would never know that the *tama* had been made because someone once thought their heart might be broken.

•

On the morning of the wedding Ruth's mobile rang time and time again. In the late morning, women began to appear at their house with their hair held in outlandish shapes by large rollers, giggling and hooting, disappeared again, then reappeared holding an electrical extension cord or a pair of hair tongs, or a paper bag full of pastries.

Still others came and went with armfuls of olive branches and red bougainvillea, to be dumped for a time in Ruth and Wendy's bath, and then taken away again. Jeremy showed up briefly, cleanshaven and smelling lovely, and kissed Ruth and Wendy before he left, calling, *See you when I'm a married man!*

There was an air of holiday excitement. The house and the terrace echoed with high voices and light laughter, and the smell of coffee and the popping of champagne corks. Wendy stood on her bedroom balcony and looked down at the throng of women seated around the terrace.

Lucy, her long hair loose and her bangles shoved high on her forearms, sat on a stool in jeans with her legs wide to accommodate the knees of another woman perched on another stool before her. The woman chatted and laughed as Lucy smoothed her fingers upwards over her cheeks, or told her to look up while she painted her lashes.

Other women were arranged about the terrace, some standing, some lounging in chairs. They held champagne flutes aloft, and munched on pastries held away from their bodies so as not to catch any sticky flakes. Some were half-dressed in slips and jeans, while others wore glamorous frocks that sparkled, and shiny jewelled sandals.

They were beautiful. They shone. They had an ease with sensual pleasure—an unquestioning, guiltless talent for it—that women of Wendy's generation lacked. Women of her age had either spurned this preening as vanity, or else borne the effort of grooming as something dutiful, hard-edged. But these women were different. Physical delight came to them as naturally as breathing.

Wendy stepped back into her room and saw her face in the mirror: dried-out, colourless, pinched.

She sat on the bed for a minute. Then she went down the stairs and out onto the terrace. Some of the women called happy greetings to her as she sidled across the paving stones to Lucy.

'Of course, Wendy,' Lucy said. She looked at her watch. 'Get dressed; I'll do you after Ali, and then I'll have to get out and get the bride done.'

Someone handed Wendy a glass of sparkling wine, and she sipped it, and took it up to her room. She felt some flush of freshness tingling over her. She was beginning to enjoy the girlishness of this occasion without, for once, feeling foolish and fraudulent.

•

She was sitting in the shade on the little stool with her eyes closed, with Lucy's cool, moist fingers feathering over her face, when another young woman arrived. She had a blonde ponytail and a pierced nostril, and stood uncertainly, holding a bucket and a broom. The cleaner.

'Oh, I forgot!' said Ruth. But they waved the girl inside, and she disappeared up the stairs. Soon they heard a vacuum cleaner's thrum.

An hour later, when everyone but Ruth had gone, Wendy saw herself in her bathroom mirror.

The bathroom smelled fresh and her bedroom was orderly, the bed made with fresh pale green sheets and her things stacked and folded tidily on the chair and the bedside table.

Wendy leaned into the mirror, trying to focus on her earrings as she slipped them through the holes in her lobes, but she could not help sneaking glances at her face. Eventually she straightened, and stared.

She didn't look like a man.

She didn't appear to be wearing make-up at all. Her eyes were clear and blue, and the planes of her nose and her cheekbones had strength and dignity. She seemed taller. What had Lucy done? Apart from the gloss at her lips Wendy found the make-up impossible to see. Perhaps it was her eyesight. But her face, in the mirror, seemed to radiate some force of life, some charge of beauty that came from being alive, that she had not ever seen in herself before. It was *this* all the young women had; this blaze of life. And now Wendy had it too. She stared and stared.

Ruth was calling from the bottom of the stairs, and Wendy trotted about her room, calm and regal, gathering things into the beaded handbag. And then her heart seized.

The little tub, the ashes of Jim, had gone.

The bedside table was clean. But the plastic bag with the magazines and brochures was gone.

The bins were empty. The one in the bedroom, and the bathroom one with its carefully folded wads of toilet paper, all empty and clean. She remembered now the girl leaving, hauling behind her one of the large heavy-duty orange plastic garbage bags Wendy had seen in the streets.

She sat on the bed, her breath coming fast and cold. She put her hands out flat on the cool bed sheets on either side.

Ruth shouted up the stairs now, 'Wendy, they're waiting.'

A shivering began to fill her chest. She breathed. She knew the ashes had gone, but still she began to bolt around the room, tearing at things and lifting scarves and bags and hats.

'Wendy! For heaven's sake!'

At last she made her way down the stairs and pushed past Ruth, out across the terrace and into the lane.

'Wait for me!' Ruth called, as she locked the heavy door.

Wendy climbed into the back seat of the car, sunglasses jammed on her face. She clutched her handbag and the straw hat and a tissue, staring out of the window, trying to swallow the lump of pain in her throat, forcing back her rising tears.

Next to her, Ruth was plump and garrulous. Their arms pressed together, and Wendy could feel her sister's warm, happy skin against her own.

She had done something terrible, something she had believed she could never, ever do. She had separated herself from Jim. Distracted by trivial, selfish pleasure, she had *forsaken* him.

She wanted to be sick.

As the car moved Ruth said, 'What a marvellous day!' and through the window Wendy saw a pile of the orange garbage bags slumped against a wall in the heat. Three hungry cats licked at a torn corner of a bag, where filth and decay spilled onto the old stone stair.

•

At the wedding reception it was Ruth who looked as if she had lived in Greece for half her life, and Wendy was the tight-smiling outsider, sitting at the end of the table with some old people, friends of the groom's parents who had travelled from England.

A man next to Wendy was from Oxford. He leaned across and said, 'I hate Greek food. I don't know why they can't serve it hot, do you?' And then sneered, showing his yellow teeth.

Sitting across from Wendy was Derek.

She watched her sister down the table. Ruth wore a white silk blouse and chocolate satin trousers, and her brown hair was swept up glamorously. Wendy had never seen Ruth with her hair up. She looked twenty years younger. And she wore Wendy's earrings, citrine and peridot drops, which glinted and shimmered as Ruth turned her head, chatting merrily with a young man in a beautiful green shirt. A woman on the other side of Ruth put her fingers up behind the earring, remarking on it, and Wendy watched Ruth absently finger it and say, *Citrine, from Greece actually*. She didn't even look up the table to Wendy when she said it.

The man from Oxford saw Wendy watching Ruth and the man with the beautiful shirt, and he said in his loud English voice, 'I didn't know so many of Jeremy's friends were homos, did you?'

Across the table Derek sniggered into his glass. He was wearing the suit again, but without the woollen tie. He drank a lot.

A little boy dashed between the tables, dumping plates of food in the centre. *Mit mit!* cried the boy, when he set down the meatballs, and *Feesh feesh!* when the plate of little fried fish came.

The man from Oxford had turned away to talk to someone friendlier. Derek looked at Wendy, and asked, 'What are you doing up this end?'

He was tugging at his left nostril with his thumb and forefinger. It was quite disgusting, but she liked him.

'Oh, I don't know,' she said gallantly. 'They have to put people somewhere, don't they? I suppose they think old people have things in common. Why are you here?'

He snorted unattractively. 'Ah. They put all the misfits up here.'

She didn't like him so much now. She watched him drain his glass of the pale red wine they were serving. He reached across his neighbour for the jug and filled his glass to the brim.

Wendy drew the jug towards her then, and filled her own.

She understood, as she sat back in her chair, that it wasn't just Derek's drinking that had seen him relegated to this end of the table; everybody was drinking a lot.

It was that sad people were not really wanted at weddings. That was why she had been put up here with Derek.

The man from Oxford turned to her again. She smelled his sour breath.

•

Long after the speeches Wendy sat, not listening to the man from Oxford's voice drilling into her about his shares, the plummeting price of something or other.

The sun had set, and in the dusk the awning of the little taverna swung with coloured lights.

Down the long table, Ruth was surrounded by Leonie's friends, attentive and sweet, their heads bent towards her and eyebrows raised, smiling expectantly if she began to speak. Now and then Wendy could tell from the friends' expressions that Ruth had said something ignorant, or mean, but Leonie's friends did not remark on it; they quickly regained their smiles and changed the subject. Everybody knew their roles here, at a wedding. And the bride's friends knew Ruth was the bride's mother, must be cared for and cosseted. So they reached for glasses for her, poured her wine, beckoned a dish back from the other end of the table if she liked it.

A great tide of savage, bitter envy swept through Wendy.

She got up from the table and wandered away from the balloon of light, leaving the man from Oxford to turn his droning voice to Derek, who sat stone-faced and drunk in his chair.

She picked her way across the gravel and the pebbles in her bare feet, and then she reached the water's edge, her feet sinking to the ankles in the clean grey grit. She stepped back and sat down on the pebbles.

She did not want to be this maudlin old woman, tearful in the dark at weddings. This afternoon she had seen another woman, very briefly, in the mirror. But that was the terrible thing she had done. She had wanted to *be* that other woman. Renewed. And because of that she had let poor, beloved Jim—for it was actually *him* she had disregarded—be left behind. *Thrown away.*

She burrowed her two hands up to the wrists into the sand beside her, put her head to her knees, and cried.

Then someone was staggering up from the far end of the beach, calling, 'Wendy! What are ya doing?!'

She didn't answer.

'Are you being sick?' called Ruth, who was drunk.

Wendy stood up. 'Of course not!'

But she did feel a little drunk now, having rushed to stand upright, and the sea slurping back and forth.

'Oh,' said Ruth. 'I did.' She giggled sheepishly, and wiped her mouth. 'Think I drank too much of that wine.' She burped. 'Sorry,' she said solemnly. They stood looking at the sea.

Then Ruth, her voice full of emotion, cried, 'I miss Alan!'

The swell of bitterness inside Wendy crested, and crashed down. She turned on Ruth. '*Alan!* He could have come but he couldn't be bothered. You'll see him next week! You have your *children*. What could you possibly have to *miss*!'

Ruth said nothing, but looked out at the dark water. She sniffed. In a little while she said, in a simple, peaceable voice, 'I'm allowed.'

She sat down, dumpily, in the sand.

Wendy stayed where she was. The sea heaved and moved. Jim was dead and gone, and she had no children. She had made her life; now she was lying in it.

This is all that's left, she thought. *And it's Ruth.*

She stood over her sister and they both looked at the water. Music from the wedding came in drifts from behind them.

One day soon, watching the water on the swimming pool in Ruth and Alan's backyard, thinking back to the wedding in Greece, Wendy would be suddenly tired of being secretive and complicated and alone. She would be tired of her disdain for Ruth. She would be tired to the bone of Jim being dead, but even more tired of missing him, of the watchfulness and diligence it demanded, the effort and duty of it. She would go home and tip the last of the ashes from the cricket palace into a small dip in the garden bed, and press the earth down with her fingers.

But now, here on the beach with Ruth, she simply stood.

Eventually Ruth got up from where she sat, letting out one of her long, old-people groans as she rose, and Wendy put out her arm to help her sister steady herself while she brushed the damp sand from the back of her trousers, and they turned and walked back towards the party lights.

FAMILY RADIO

Roger McDonald

A dust storm blew until it reached the riverbank, where it stalled in the sky, a cliff, purple-bruised, highlighting one side of the Louth road as red, the other as green. A steam pump made from an old boat's boiler drew water from the clay-smelling river, irrigating lucerne in leaky sweeps and flooding lanes of an orchard, where oranges hung in the trees.

At the Watsons' 'Blindale' on the river road, Tony Watson lay around on the shady verandah boards like a bog-eye lizard waiting for a fly, turning the pages of a Marvel Family comic and feeling sick with a malaise without name. Happiness was a sensation so rare that it was unrecognisable when it came. Now he had a name for it: Blindale.

After a shower under the tank stand Tony wiped a sweaty mirror, stared into his grey eyes between the cracked splats of silvering, and made his voice into Churchill's, fighting 'em on the beaches, the British Bulldog's vowels and growls rolling from the voice box of a pale-skinned chicken-chested boy; shifting then to a nasal Nazi interrogator promising, 'We haff ways off making you talk.'

Tony came into the house and heard the cat snoring. Everything gave him pleasure: the cat snoring, the blanket the cat slept under, design and nap thereof, the ring of damp soil at the tank stand where zebra finches came for water, the sight of the yellow sponge cake with passionfruit icing under the mauve gauze fly cover on the kitchen table. It was a cake to celebrate his hitting his teens. He hummed along to the sound of the wind under the roofing iron. This was home and it wasn't a dream: knitted tea cosy, butter board, carved emu egg on the living room shelf, Gundabooka Mountain waddy-donger tied to the hallway wall with fuse wire, and Pop's Velocette motorbike propped at the garden gate when Pop came in for a cuppa. Tony thought himself into the photos the family had, of the son who died (diphtheria, buried in a sky-blue coffin). They'd taken on Tony to fill the gap.

'My brother, Chicka,' Tony whispered, awestruck by this idea of himself, the way it built and built and might never be covered over, if he lived long enough to see what could happen. 'Tony Watson,' he mouthed, looking down at his arms with their light gingery hairs. He reached for a tambourine and gave it a hissing shake at the level of his jug ears. Before this move his name was O'Malley, a little strop of a weedy biffed and bruised boy in a dormitory scrummage. Father: unknown. Mother: deceased.

Tony followed Mum Watson through the hallway to the front door, a screen door snapping open to a wide verandah and a view of red dirt, diesel drums and a shearing shed half a dust-churning mile away. More dust, from an arriving car, drifted across the front of the house. Mum stood with her fat white legs apart and reached over and took Tony's hand. There was the sound of topknot pigeons flying low overhead—small tinkling bells of hope, they were.

Major Marks, wearing his Army jacket in the gritty blow, brought Judy in. The Salvos were always the ones. Judy Compton-Bell had frizzy hair, freckles, a snub nose like Orphan Annie. At eleven years of age she was ready for play. Tony grinned, and they ran inside together.

Tony drew her in pencil, tiny circles all over her cheeks, on a sheet of butcher's paper. The wind blew the paper all over the room. They dressed up and played weddings at her command. He pulled her along in a billycart, the bridal car, and read stories at night, doing all the voices. Mum and Pop Watson stood in the hallway, listening. They'd lost one. Now there were two.

As far as Tony could ever remember (and his way of remembering wasn't always this straight), Judy Compton-Bell was the last person he allowed to make rules relating to his domestic life. When he peeled a Blindale orange (the pith like kapok and the juice running down his arm) and hurled the peel over his shoulder, it landed on the dirt making a perfect J.

'When I was married . . .' he liked to say. Or: 'At my wedding . . .' It gave people something to think about—Tony Watson with a woman in his life who wasn't a former prime minister's grass widow or a similarly positioned needful one with whom (note the grammar) he attended the charity balls of the Eastern Suburbs set. The gist of it was: 'I was putty in her hands . . . Not a grown woman—great heavens—Judy Compton-Bell was my kid sister.'

'This was back in my Army days,' Tony likes to say, watching for a reaction. See him in his first long trousers, stovepipes worn when shaking the donation box outside Fitz's pub in Bourke. 'My Life As a Salvo' will be chapter two of his bio when he puts pen to paper. A story of interest, surely, but with an in-built quandary in the telling, the problem being that by the time Tony was taken under the Salvos' wing (that is to say, taken in by the Blindale Watsons and their honest ilk) he was twelve years old, and of his first twelve years Tony has nothing to say. Never will have, either. So there you have it: there can never be a chapter one and so no book when all other celebrity know-alls of a certain age have one. Something sticks in the craw: the leached, bleached, despairing information that has made him who he is. A fretwork of hints, lies and hopeless inventions. A feeling of stupidity and failure, of having been born as a mistake, half alive, half dead—a worm—the strongest sense of where he came from given by a scarecrow woman from the ladies' lounge of Fitz's pub who came out onto the street and knocked the collection box from his hands, and told him, with whale breath, that his mother had been that fuck-house, O'Malley.

Relating to whom, however, there might have been something to embellish—if Judy Compton-Bell hadn't taken charge of a sequence of early-life events in a book of her own, blabbing tales of their Blindale paradise. Tony would like to wring her adventurous little neck for telling the world that he'd come to Blindale from institutional foster care, when he'd long stated in press releases that he was a born Watson, 'rolled onto the linen' on the Louth road. It made him look stupid, and he was called a con-job in the *Tele* and *Mirror*—only just possibly gaining appeal from never being able to be pinned down to any sort of wholesome truth at all. And the truth about Judy at the Blindale Watsons was that she was a paid boarder from a station in the outside country, a child parked with good folk for the convenience of a mother wrapped up in herself and a father at a loss to know what to do.

Where was Judy now, you might ask, after a lifetime of chasing around the world? Sailing aboard a seventy-foot Greenpeace steel yacht in the approximate vicinity of sixty degrees south, a venerated crew member taking seawater samples on behalf of fish; her bulk emails (satellite sent) throbbing on Tony's desktop computer screen twice weekly. Her cruncher in *Bluebell's Voyage* (her lone-sailor-around-the-world topseller) was: *I grew up with Tony Watson, a ward of the state.*

Now she writes: *I am down among the icebergs.*

He wishes she'd stay there (not really). His broadcast opinion of environmental activism is that it says more about the people protesting than about what they are trying to save: so get up a tree and stay there, he barks into the mike, you bunch a' monkeys. It's all to keep his listeners revved, blowtorched, attentive. Works like that with Jude. Keeps her close on his heels. Lose 'em, lose your life. How does this work? What's the recipe for eternal listening life, you mean? Don't ask him. The words are lightning on the branches of dead trees. The words are fistfuls of dust thrown in the wind.

'A bunch a' galahs,' he'll say—though if one bird brings him up short (in memory) it is galahs in the Bourke park, near the band rotunda, crowding along telephone wires when the Salvos played.

All the old derros they'd pulled from the gutter would be sitting on park benches nodding their appreciation. Tony was on the trombone, a tricky instrument to master. Judy would be there, wearing a black straw bonnet with a scarlet ribbon tucked into the pleats of the bonnet trimming, rattling the tambourine and giggling sidelong at Tony's cissified wrist action on the trombone slide. By the following day or the day after, the rescued would have the screaming blue heebie-jeebies again.

A compulsion dictates with Tony: he's always tried fitting in with the lowest common opinion, from a conviction of belonging where he comes from, but never being able to say where that is. For this reason he thinks his opinions never count (though never lets on), and this stops him from working them responsibly. To be real he must grate, irritate, exasperate and peeve. He knows that Judy defends him in her corner as never meaning what he says. But nor does she listen to him. As befitting a former ward of the state, Tony is always reaching past the mike to some sort of paradise the government doesn't want him to have, while Judy's always saying that paradise is what you're standing on, but it's under threat.

A Kodachrome shows them standing on a kerosene crate grinning at the camera, Judy wearing a muslin curtain, Tony with a pair of baggy trousers held up by a too-large belt and one of Pop Watson's felt hats flopped down to the level of his eyebrows. Other not-quite-so-old photos show Tony with his hair parted in the middle in a style worn until the Beatles put an end to the lairising look and Brylcreem and hair combs altogether.

At Bourke school there'd come a day of remembered importance when a young man named Warwick Mickless was seated next to Tony after a fair bit of whispering between teachers at the door of the room. Tony was fourteen, Warwick Mickless fifteen, a drover's son who couldn't read or write (or hardly), and Tony was asked to help bring him up to scratch before his next drove. Promoted from the class below, Judy was placed on the other side of Warwick from Tony. She was the cleverest girl in the school, winner of spelling bees and general knowledge quizzes—beating older kids (though there wasn't much competition)—and at Sunday School reciting the Bible backwards, winning cardboard boomerangs and a trip to Bible Camp at Bathurst, from where she returned with some sort of bacterial bug so was sent to the Far West Children's Health Scheme, at Manly, to recover. That was where she saw the ocean for the first time and went to the Aquarium to look at the fish.

Warwick was another sort of wonder, his long doggy face bearing burn scars from being rolled into the ashes of a campfire as a baby. They did 'Clancy of the Overflow' as a hush fell over the classroom, and Warwick, in a deep (halting) voice, read what seemed to be his very own part, thumbnail dipped in tar and all that. He'd never lived in a house, hardly knew what it was like to sleep with a roof over his head.

At the Brewarrina rodeo Warwick was a sensation; he picked up the ropes after the buckjumpers had thrown their riders, leaning down from a galloping pony and snatching them from the dirt. Then, with the reins looped over his arm, he leaned back and rolled a cigga.

Tony was handed the mike to read the adverts between events. You should have heard him carry on. There was a trick he had, where the pony's galloping gait and swivel turns gave tempo to a line of patter. It was rock-and-roll, and made Tony known around the rodeos and district shows before he was seventeen.

Tony, Warwick and Judy formed a trio in those in-between years. Being seen with Warwick was to be seen with a star. Tony, his little mate, was acclaimed for verbal skills, but sometimes scorned, on the side, as befitting one with the power of words. Judy's favourite term of approval was 'hot dog'. 'Hot diggety dog,' said Tony when the three got together. On Friday nights when they went to Randall's flicks for the double bill, Tony laughed at the clever bits and looked at Warwick to see if he got the subtler jokes. Sometimes he did; he was a fast learner. When he worked his hand down Judy's blouse he winked at Tony to count him in on his luck.

After the flicks they went over the dialogue and Tony remembered slabs of it which they acted out, sitting on the verandah till all hours and hearing Mum's stifled giggles from the sleepout.

Following the Intermediate year Judy went to Meriden at Strathfield. A sportsmistress took her sailing in a Gwen-class dinghy, and that was when a lifetime of simpatico communicado started each way by lettergram, news of the day, Tony and Judy in touch weekly at the very least, their two worlds, their two bubbles of life, leaning on each other till the colours ran like rainbows to the very end.

2DU Dubbo was where Tony made his start. His golden tonsilation was more in the style of an ABC bloke's as a result of the ABC being the only network with a transmitter strong enough Out West to give him something to imitate. He'd come there via counter-jumping at Permewan Wright's and part-time cattle and sheep auctioneering for Pitt, Son and Bender in Bourke, Bre, Warren, Coonamble and Narromine.

Sydney had Joe the Gadget Man selling people what they didn't need; the West had Tones Watson. You ached with laughter hearing Tones do his hundred and one voices. 'Just Orf the Train', 'Milkun the Goat', 'Who Brung You?' and 'Lennie the Plague Locust' were just a few of the skits that brightened our dry toast in the mornings.

Dubbo was a party town. There was nowhere else to go. Tony arrived at the door with a bundle of 45s hot from the record companies and gave some away. 'Eines harten Tages Nacht' ('A Hard Day's Night') was already a collector's item the year of its release, and he kept that one for himself (still has it). Onwards then towards the year of 'Sergeant Pepper'. Tony wrote his own jingles and testimonials, achieving status in the eyes of Macquarie network executives through a broadcasting belt more or less contiguous with the growth range of native cypress, from the Queensland border down to approximately Peak Hill. Later—in Sydney, making his name—he liked to rib ABC types on the occasions when they met, as being a bit too Sir Robert Menzies with it, and not being of the people. Any young fellow seeking his advice about a career in national radio he warned to wear lead underpants. Was he ever tempted to go over to Aunty himself? You must be out of your mind (though he never lost his 'plum').

Tony had a studio visit from Warwick, who'd been to some outfit that made tapes of hopefuls playing guitars and yodelling cowboy songs, and transferred them to 45 rpm extended plays for a whopping fee. A ludicrous amalgam of doggerel and strummed chords was Warwick's offering. 'There's no easy way to be any good,' said Tony, as he walked Warwick to the door. They did not see each other for years after that, not for decades, it's true, though birthdays and Christmases weren't forgotten. There was a feeling, always strong, that their connection was close to a blood relation. But there was a feeling of offence, as well, and as they didn't have blood relations to judge this by, they didn't know that a feeling of offence equally defined what they so definitely felt they lacked.

On 17 April 1967, live telephone conversations were made legal broadcasts and Tony Watson was born—let me calculate: for the fourth time? There were to be no further incarnations. Answering back to the nation (eventually) on ninety-eight syndicated stations, Tones would keep on doing it till the wind blew itself out, by which time the clock of the years would hook around the dial into the spiderwebs of disbelief, and if you doubt me, recall when you peered through the soundproof glass and saw liver-spotted Tony with a slack turkey-gobbler jawline doing the countdown still.

Tony was known Out West as a terrific snob—but home-town-hatched, familiar in his scorn, loved to death for loving them along the shrivelled Darling. He never forgot those cards and letters, birthday and Christmas presents, nor telephone calls where he never announced himself by name but was the unmistakable owner of that tremulous *helloo*—as the promos used to say, 'smooth as a triple malted'. Of late, the promos merely call him the King Of, a tired appellation for a tired old ratings' ruler, while pundits headline in the industry press: WHEN WILL TONES PULL THE PLUG ON IT? Judy asks the same question.

Tony had a curious experience recently, on a Qantas flight to London. The bloke he was sitting next to said, 'Your voice reminds me of someone.' Tony preened and said, 'My voice reminds you of me, my friend.' He was Tony 'Give Me Your Ears' Watson: the bloke who'd invented talkback or near enough. But no, said the bloke, it was someone else. Had Tony ever lived in the Territory? 'Nooh,' said Tony. They advanced through degrees of separation until they came to the name Warwick Mickless. 'That name rings a bell,' said Tony with self-protective affability. He didn't want to give too much away. There was the dead son, Chicka Watson, whose ghost he'd brought to life, just by living, and there was Warwick Mickless. Then there was Judy. The four of them—dead and alive and alive and alive—occupied an indefinable space, elbows linked, feet scuffing through the dust of Bourke backstreets as through some sort of foreverland, dipped in Technicolor. Tony somehow, without realising it until of late, had lived his life in a mood of indefinite postponement, becoming one whose entire being was based on launching his voice into the world of the microphone at nineteen past nine every morning (after a barrel of adverts), and holding together that world, by an act of word-spinning, till noon. The feeling was of a sentence starting at the bell and not finishing till the gong. It was all one blast of breath rushing along. As early as the evening of the same day Tony would have the blue heebie-jeebies over microphone deprivation. At cocktail parties and openings he'd find himself either ranting or sulking. One day, for one so made, there would be a reckoning.

Warwick Mickless, said the man seated next to Tony on the plane, had a radio spot on a Darwin ABC rural program, 'The Stock Route', reporting on tropical breeds of cattle. The bloke said, 'Wocka's a cracker, he keeps the Top End in stitches.'

'Does he now?' said Tony with a low chuckle. '"The Stock Route"'s a listening must, even for people who wouldn't know what a cow was?'

'It sure is.'

'Ho, ho,' said Tony.

It was a little too much for the wordman of note to swallow. After checking with Neilsen's he found he was losing listeners in Darwin faster than anywhere else. Something would have to be done (as it always was). His childhood playmate, surrogate sister, Judy, beats him to the draw on getting her story in print, and now his illiterate pupil (that Brewarrina Centaur) challenges his lifelong playpen by having a radio spot, struth, doing some public good, so claimed, while getting a laugh, a point upon which Tony dwells in the post-midnight hours.

What is the good he's done? Red Shield Day jams the switchboard annually. The Westmead Children's Hospital has a wing named after him. Many a soup kitchen gets his cheque, and he's to be found down there, in the stinking washcloth light of East Sydney, ladling out scrambled eggs through cold winter mornings.

But all Tony can think is that banishing bad to the shadows sums it up. His bad. His shadows. The best Tony has ever been able to do is sell things. Selling people what they don't need by virtue of having it wrapped in words: corkscrews, flame weeders, luggage wrappers, eggtimers. His garage is full of gratis junk. (Eggtimers make him weep.) There's also real estate and luxury cars: he owns a good deal of the former, drives three of the latter, knows he doesn't need as much as he has, far from it, but wants to get rid of it less than he wants to keep it for the reason of holding on to himself. Words made these solid objects out of thin air.

Interesting the letter that reached Warwick Mickless (signed *Tones*). It included a neat transcript of a bunch of Warwick's pieces, collected by the clipping service Tony used. The grammar, sentence construction and vocabulary were corrected in red ink. It looked like an attack of mad spiders on the page. *For your benefit*, Tony signed off, *old friend*.

This brings us almost up to the present—to a day last year when Tony rang Alan Corker at Whistling Flats, and closed on a parcel of land in the Southern Tablelands he'd been looking at, after selling his place at Bowral, where he'd lived, on and off, for years—always with the thought that somewhere less tamed and manicured by visiting gardeners would be a requirement before the end, if reality was to meet truth in the image of who he was, as being sprung from a patch of raw dirt in a raging windstorm.

The deal was five thousand acres of which about one-fifth was usable for stock, the rest comprising dry forest running up into steep ridges and gullies, rocky outcrops, messmate, brown barrel and alpine ash, formerly milled. Then upwards and on to a spine of granite tors, from where, as Corker told it, you could see out over an entire province of the Great Dividing Range. 'Halfway to Bourke,' said Corker, dramatising the view, at which point Tony felt his heart lurch with the possibilities of possession. 'Sold,' he said, experiencing a rush, a gush, of feeling. The two men shook on it. They were to be neighbours. Corker's chunk of land, the Bullock Run, was on the western boundary.

Corker uncapped a whisky bottle and set up a couple of Pyrex glasses on a tree stump. From a reedy gully he extracted a billycan of clear water and asked Tony to say when. After they toasted the purchase Tony wrote a cheque for the deposit, and by the time Corker poured two more snifters of the Famous Grouse they were well away on a friendship riff.

There was more to this, an oddity of congruence. Among auctioneering legends, Careful Bob Corker, Alan Corker's father, had been the veritable Don Bradman of his profession. Tony remembered Careful Bob ranging north to Haddon Rigg during the 1960s, where Tony, in blue Oxford shirt and Wool Board tie, shaggy hairdo and tight white moleskin trousers, had a season of selling rams. Corker liked the portrait of Careful Bob that Tony presented, a man the rest of the world had pretty much forgotten. Tony recalled gruff humour rising to the melody of a bush singer as the bids came flying in. 'You've got him!' said Corker. Even the sheep paid attention, said Tony; the crowds on the railings stayed hushed. Careful Bob was a small overweight man the double of Harry Secombe; his upper forehead white as parchment, his face raspberry-red when he lifted his narrow-brimmed hat to a lady.

'There's justice in that description,' said Corker. 'You have a way with words.'

'I'm running out of them,' said Tony.

After their drinks Tony wandered along a bush track, keeping to himself, wondering what he'd done. Corker followed at a discreet distance at the wheel of the Toyota. When Tony climbed back into the car Corker had the radio tuned to Classic FM.

'So you're a friend of the ABC,' said Tony.

'You could say that,' said Corker. 'I do a lot of long drives—five, six, seven-hour stints. Radio keeps me company. It's been my education, sort of. Then there's the music. It's always the music with me.'

This was what people said, digging a hole for themselves, when they weren't able to come out and say they loathed listening to Tony 'Give Me Your Ears' Watson. Tony knew that Corker's buying group (underpinned by West Australian money) spent big on his show: it was why the Corkers of this world, honest brokers who needed him, couldn't say they hated him. They didn't know it was best to let fly, giving Tony the benefit of feeling cornered by desperation and dismal neglect. Didn't know that his success was forged in silence.

Not that Tony sensed anything like hate from Alan Corker, an unusually warm and confiding sort of bloke. But just for a moment there, in the front seat of the car, Tony turned and projected from his upper chest and larynx into a space only a few inches in front of Corker's nose something that sounded like 'Arrgh!'

'Are you alright?' said Corker, hitting the brakes.

Tony recovered himself.

'I'm on the ABC next month,' he said. '"The Media Report"'s doing a tombstone number on my forty years of being me.'

'I'll be listening.'

'You and about three others, that's the stats.'

'Come on, the mountain comes to Mohammed, you ought to be pleased.'

'My sister, Judy Compton-Bell,' said Tony, 'must have given them a push. She's deputy chair of Friends of the ABC, quote unquote. I put up with a tremendous amount of bull-o from her. I'm putty in her hands.'

'Judy Compton-Bell—she's your sister?' said Corker.

'To wish it were otherwise,' said Tony, 'would be very heaven.'

'Her book's in our library. There's always a waiting list. I remember that night in '98, the Sydney to Hobart . . . It was wild enough up here—wind and weird fog—couldn't imagine what it was like out there on the water, till I read what she wrote.'

'Garn, she's unsinkable,' said Tony.

•

'It was the oddest thing,' said Tony, when he took Judy out for dinner after she returned from Antarctica a week or so later. 'I had the feeling all the birds were talking to me, calling out my name.'

'As the centre of the universe, is this any surprise to you, dear?'

'A bunch of white cockatoos flew over. They screeched my name from out of the blue. There were these grey little parrot things.'

'Gang-gangs?'

'Watch your tongue. It used to be like that when I was a kid. There was even a topknot pigeon, just ahead of me, looking at me from the ground—God, how I loved them—and a pigeon with a zigzag on its chest, like the mark of Zorro.'

'A wonga.'

'Speak English,' said Tony. 'Hissa, huzza, hissa hissa hissa. Huzz-ah!'

'What's that?'

'A lyrebird, stupid.'

As he spoke, Tony cupped a hand and shook it beside his ear.

When they rose from the table they made a time to drive down south to inspect Tony's bush block. Judy gave him the name of her doctor—she was always looking out for him. Worried sick about him, was how she expressed it.

'But there's nothing wrong with me,' said Tony.

'There's a good reason to keep it that way,' said Judy, kissing his cheek. He looked rather drained and exhausted. It was towards the end of his contract, his farewell few weeks behind the mike: years had been spent anticipating the end and worrying about Tony's reaction. Judy and her pals went on about it.

'I'll be sticking to you like glue,' said Judy. She felt that if things went well she'd be getting the old Tony back—the boy who played with her, games without end, with dedicated fondness of spirit. If not? Such desolation.

Complaining, upbraiding her, Tony went to see her 'complimentary' practitioner in Randwick. That was the way it was spelled in the handout.

'It would help,' said the doctor, a nutritional bloke, 'if you could fill out this questionnaire.'

'Jesus,' said Tony, 'must I?'

All very well to be asked intimate questions about history of diseases, operations, sexual infections and number of sexual partners (Tony wrote in that square: *Information available on request, if deemed relevant*). What knocked him sideways was the genetic slant on things, page after page, where your cousin's uncle twice removed's propensity for strokes or palsy pointed a finger down into the seat of one's pants.

The doctor, who rather fancied himself on the psychological scale, wanted to know a lot more than Tony was willing or able to tell.

'You can have no idea how this makes me feel,' said Tony, hovering with his pencil and hitting on a rhythm of two ticks, three crosses, three ticks, two crosses, and so on through several pages addressing the nothingness of being.

When he phoned Judy to say what a load of crapola it was, she said, 'Tony, come on around.'

'Where?'

'To my place.'

'When?'

'Now.'

A dusty tan stetson hung on the hallstand of Judy's Rushcutters Bay flat. There was a knobbly cane of mulga wood leaning against the wall. A pair of dark glasses with side shades, 'burglar glasses' for the elderly, lay where they'd been placed by the owner of them, whose identity Tony guessed.

'This is a set-up,' he said, as he came into the room.

Warwick Mickless rose from a chair.

'Tones,' he said, completely without sarcasm (sarcasm Tony deserved).

This craggy giant of a man—he looked eighty—had pouches under his eyes, yellow horsy teeth, a cattleman's blebs and blemishes of crusty skin cancers on the backs of his hands. Standing beside him was a small Indonesian woman, Betty, his wife.

Tony had the feeling that he was looking into the mirror, an impression gained by the way he hated what he saw, it was so much the best of all his own possibilities ripened and dried like wood. Then he looked away, turned back, and realised that he wasn't having some sort of optical fit the way the room fractured into cubes and rainbows. Judy fetched a box of tissues into which he plunged a fist.

•

Now to the present—well, to yesterday, to be exact; the previous afternoon shading through to a crisp, starry night, and then from that purple deepness into a morning where throughout the state at breakfast, on ninety-eight syndicated stations, there came no smash-bang of kettledrums to usher in the daily dose of you-know-who.

'Aren't you going to listen to your successor?' said Judy.

'No, I'm not,' said Tony.

Anyway, the reception was appalling, so how could he listen to who-was-not-there-to-be-heard?

He twisted the dial, recalling the whistles and whoops of the old valve set at Blindale, with its green silken speaker cover into which Tony and Judy had long stared, seeing in the dim glow of the valves their entire futures being lived in imagination. And, as it turned out, much as they'd longed those futures to be.

On Aunty reception was better. In these back ranges there was a good reason why the ABC ruled the airwaves and even people who couldn't be less interested listened to whatever was on, because stuffing one's ears with words was a human must.

'Immediately following the news we have "The Media Report",' said the announcer.

'Oh, Jesus,' said Tony. 'Here she comes. Now she is on for young and old.'

He stood at the back door of his Owner's Cottage, listening to a bowerbird squabbling with a lyrebird, and the radio playing the interview from the kitchen bench. He mouthed what he himself said, almost by heart. A rhythm of short and long sentences, abrupt declarations, deliberate silences running to tantalising suspensions of speech (a Tony Watson touch)—during which he pictured listeners, paused in what they were doing, wondering what the next word would be.

The crumbs of forty years, this felt more truthful to him than any of his thousand-dozen jaunty attacks on all and sundry. If he'd been a carpenter talking about the craft of planes and saws, drills and sanding techniques, he could not have been more on to himself. Judy, watching his face throughout, gave him a hug.

'Why, I was alright,' he said, when it was all over. There was nobody in the room to hear him say this. Nobody in that larger room, either, going on and on through boundless space. Outside, sitting on a stump, Judy was crying.

Alan Corker rang: 'I heard you, Tony. You made a lot of sense. I didn't know you were an orphan. Never heard anyone talk better about coming from nowhere, having nothing.'

'I'm depressed by my own intelligence,' said Tony. 'It goes to show how easy it is to talk intelligent crap.'

•

Judy met Alan Corker when she came down to supervise arrangements for getting Warwick Mickless and Betty installed in the Manager's Cottage. Betty said she would die in the mountain winters, but Warwick wasn't so sure, even after a lifetime of his thermostat being adjusted to the Top End. He might even like it here. On the way in, as they'd come through a paddock of mares and foals, Warwick had climbed from the car to open a gate and, when they were through, he started walking out among the animals, bringing them up to his hand.

When they were all in the cottage with mugs of tea, Judy brought out their presents, wrapped in white tissue paper and tied with blue-striped string. For Warwick it was the tooled leather change purse, with a motif of desert pea and quandong fruits, that he'd made in boyhood days of saddlery repairs and stock camp evenings, and slipped to Judy after a night of heavy petting at Randall's flicks. She was returning it to him now with the thought that Betty should have it.

For Tony the gift was a battered Salvationist tambourine, bought in an op shop on Bondi Road.

Tony held the instrument to his ear, giving it a hissing shake.

'This is the wind,' he said, 'wrapping itself around the bluebush on the old Louth Road.'

Tony turned to Warwick: 'Come on, say something funny.'

'You never knew it,' said Warwick, 'but when you started on the air, all round the country, I'd listen to you on this old trannie I had in my saddlebags. This was when I was at Katherine, not far from town.'

'Cut to the chase, cowboy.'

'There was a way you had, it was like a horse, you walked, trotted and galloped. I used to think . . .' Warwick paused.

Tony looked at him: all teeth and hairless hackles.

'You used to think what?' he challenged.

'Well, that you mightn't a' done what you did, said what you did the way you said it, without seeing it done by a pony.'

'Might or mightn't,' said Tony, pulling his jaw shut. 'I always thought it was the wind that drove me, that wind that never shut up on the river road, and I wanted to get inside out of it.'

'When I got stuck with *Bluebell's Voyage*,' said Judy, 'and I didn't know what to write next, I remembered what you once said, darling, when we were kids.'

'What did I say?' said Tony, swivelling in Judy's direction. 'What's all this getting at me about?'

'You said all the words were there waiting, everything we'd ever say in our lives. You said the words were in the wind.'

'Well, even without us the wind keeps blowing,' said Tony, and without knowing why, felt radio drop from his life, needs, and necessity.

TROUBLE

Tegan Bennett Daylight

Emma and I were walking home from school together. It was September, spring, with a cheerful breeze running along with us, new leaves lit and flickering, the houses hung with wisteria and jasmine. We were walking with Peter, who had been troublesomely in love with Emma for several years. If she'd been alone he might not have dared to follow her, but her younger, noisier sister made it easy. I was, without knowing it, combative; sparring with me had relieved the nerves of more than one of Emma's boyfriends. Emma walked silently beside us, a spray of jasmine dangling from one hand.

A truck, uncommon in our money-quiet suburb, screamed past us. When it had gone, Peter said, 'A truck drove into my house once.'

'No, really?' I was balancing on the low stone wall that ran beside the road. 'Tell us about it,' I said, hopping off the wall to land next to him.

He glanced at Emma, who continued to watch the pavement in front of her, which was lumpy with tree roots.

'We lived on a corner,' said Peter. 'It came too fast on the way round, and its brakes failed. It went straight through the fence and into the side of the house.'

'Amazing,' I said.

'It was a big deal!' said Peter. 'If I'd been playing in the yard it would have killed me!'

Suddenly inspired, I said sweetly, 'Do you often play in the yard, little boy?'

Emma snorted with laughter and Peter blushed angrily. He was quite a handsome boy, with thick blond hair and long eyelashes. 'It was years ago. I was much younger.'

A magpie whose nest we were passing swooped suddenly, clicking its beak in Peter's hair. He swung at it in fright. It flew up into the branches ahead of us and perched there, glaring.

'Come on,' I said, prodding Peter in the small of his back.

'You're much bigger than it is,' said Emma.

We went forward, turning to face the bird as we passed, then continuing to walk backwards. The magpie snapped its beak again and hopped along the branch speculatively, but did not swoop.

•

When I was eighteen Emma and I moved to London, using money that our grandmother had left us. We had a place to stay: a flat, belonging to wealthy friends of our parents, who lived for the most part in their farmhouse in Surrey. They were in their sixties, and had no children. The flat was furnished with cream carpet and cream brocade sofas. The windows had double glazing, so that the traffic outside could hardly be heard, although it made the ground bounce under your feet when you went outside. The kitchen shone. We took our boots off at the door when we came in, and the carpet would always be warm underfoot.

In our second week Emma started applying for work. I went with her to her first interview and sat outside on the street, in a quickly shifting rectangle of sunlight. First the sunlight was on the steps of the office, which was in a silent lane of low sandstone buildings with pretty window boxes. No cars. Then it moved to the pavement, so I sat there, my back against the cold stone. When the light moved onto the road itself I stayed where I was, growing colder, watching it cross the narrow space.

The door next to me opened and Emma was handed out by a man in a white shirt and linen pants. My legs had gone to sleep. I tried to get up to say hello but the door closed before I was upright.

'Did you get it?' I said. I put one hand on the stone wall for balance while I flexed my stiff feet.

'Pretty much,' said Emma.

•

They were a civilised group of people—all men except Emma—working in a white, light-filled space with its tilted desks set up at a sociable angle. They rarely designed actual buildings—everything they did was a renovation, a conversion, of one of the many difficultly small houses, apartments and offices owned and rented by the well-to-do of London.

Emma's office was only a few tube stops from our flat, and I met her for lunch sometimes, but mostly I sat at home, too weary to struggle along in the fine bubbles of her wake. I couldn't get warm. It was only September, and the flat was centrally heated, but I was doing nothing except sitting at the table in our white kitchen, whose window overlooked Vauxhall Bridge Road. Sometimes I ate porridge oats, dry, from a bowl. There was something solid and sustaining about them. You could make porridge in your own mouth, mashing the oats into a warm paste with teeth and saliva. I could eat two or three bowls at once. I looked in the newspaper for work. Sometimes I had baths to try to ease the cold ache in my sides and legs.

One evening Emma brought a friend home from work. When they came into the kitchen I slipped down from my stool, shoving the book I was reading to one side. I wished they'd found me doing something, being busy. I saw myself in the face of the microwave, stomach held in, eyes ringed with black, mouth thick with red lipstick.

'Your voice sounds English already,' I said to Emma, unable to speak to Jerome. He was black, and the most beautiful man I had ever seen. He grinned at me, knowing he'd caught me off balance. He wore a grey t-shirt, close-fitting, and dark jeans. His smile made the skin on the back of my neck feel hot and tight.

'Not to me,' he said. His voice sounded flat London. He was looking around at the kitchen, at its broad white counters, deep drawers, its double-glazed view of the traffic and the city beyond that. 'Nice place,' he added.

'It's not ours,' said Emma quickly.

I looked at her curiously.

'We're paying rent,' she went on.

Mates' rates, I almost said, but it would not have been fair to her.

They wanted to know if I would like to come out to dinner with them. I knew Emma would have talked Jerome into this. He kept his body turned towards hers.

I didn't. I said so. I didn't have an English accent; I was not in England enough to acquire one. At home in the flat with the porridge and the paper, my voice was not needed at all. A friend had once said to me that I was like a shark that had to keep swimming—if I stopped talking I would die. It did feel as though I was sinking.

I stood up when the door had closed behind them and went into the bedroom. There was only one bedroom, with twin beds. There was a long mirror fixed to the wall between them. I looked at myself, lifted my Clash t-shirt and clawed a bit at my soft, white stomach. Then I lay down on my bed. Soon I was too cold, so I pulled off my jeans and got under the covers. After a while, I fell asleep, and didn't wake when Emma came in.

•

My cousin Karen and her best friend were also living in London, somewhere real, that they had found for themselves. They were nursing in one of the hospitals in the centre of the city. They did a lot of night shifts, and had plenty of time to visit me during the day. Karen wore a leather jacket covered with studs and told me how she'd stamped on the toes of a man who'd shoved her at a Smiths gig. Her docs had extra-thick soles. Her face was set in a defensive snarl, which faded after an hour or so in the creamy quiet of our flat.

'I'm fat,' I said to my cousin—something I could never say to Emma.

'I'm fat too,' said Karen, who was looking in our fridge. Her spiked blonde hair brushed the shelves as she bent down to take out a block of cheese.

'I've got a new way of losing weight,' said Ruth from the living room. She was lying full length on the cream sofa, her boots splayed on the cushions.

'Yeah?' said Karen. We came to stand in the doorway, Karen holding the cheese.

'The twist,' said Ruth, staring down at her boots.

'What do you mean?' said Karen.

'You know those fifties movies? You never see a fat girl, do you?'

We watched as she swung her boots to the floor and stood up. She began to twist on the white pile of the carpet, her dyed hair flopping into her face. It was like the traffic that you could see through the window—odd, jerky, no soundtrack, except the hushing of her boots on the carpet.

Karen laughed scornfully, and began to tear open the plastic wrapping of the cheese. 'It wasn't the twist. It was the Ford pills. They were all taking laxatives.'

'I wonder if that works,' I said. Ruth kept twisting. Karen and I met each other's eyes.

•

Oh, Jerome. I heard Emma say this one night. I had been asleep but woke at the sound of the key in the lock. I was suddenly rigid in my bed. The bedroom door was open. What should I do?

But they were only saying goodnight. I turned quickly on my side before Emma came in, and didn't answer when she said softly, 'You awake?'

The next day was Saturday. Emma made me come with her to the National Portrait Gallery. We were early, and sat on the steps in the pale sunlight, watching the pigeons milling and crashing in the square.

'You should stay at Jerome's house if you want to,' I said. I was clacking the toes of my doc martens together. I had recently noticed that I could not sit without some part of my body moving.

There was a pause. People were beginning to line up around us; we kept having to lean sideways to let them pass.

'I wouldn't want to leave you alone,' said Emma.

'I'll be alright,' I said. Then added, 'You're not my mother, you know.'

'What if someone broke in?'

I looked straight at her now, as witheringly as I could. I kept my feet still. There were three separate security doors between us and London, and anyone who did manage to breach them would not bother coming down the lengths of carpeted corridor, turning the corners, passing the stairwells, all the way to our flat. I couldn't imagine commanding that much attention from anyone, not even a murderer.

•

Jerome had a friend who managed a chain of bookshops. There was a job available in their smallest branch, which was on the fifth floor of a department store in Knightsbridge. In my letter of application I invented a bookshop back in Sydney, and named it after one of my university friends. I rang her up—long distance, still an event in those days—and asked her to make up some letterhead and write me a reference.

At the interview, the manager of the tiny book section said, 'You seem very nervous. Why are you so nervous?'

I was nervous because I had written the letter too quickly, I didn't have a copy, and I couldn't remember what I'd said about my time working at Woods Books in Enmore. He was holding my friend's letter and I kept trying to peer at it. I could see that she must have used one of the computers at university to type it up. I could see that she had changed her signature to make her seem more like the proprietor of Woods Books. I couldn't tell if it was obvious that she, like me, was only eighteen.

I think I was probably clacking the toes of my boots together again, too. I said, 'I just really want the job.'

'Well,' said the manager, looking down at the letter, 'I suppose I'll have to give it to you then.'

I watched him as he sorted through his desk drawers for the right forms. His name was Rory. He had white skin that looked as though it would be cold to the touch, a tightly knotted woollen tie and a patterned waistcoat. He would have been only three or four years older than I was but his *I suppose I'll have to give it to you then* was elaborately patronising. I tried to imagine being friends with him—perhaps eating lunch with him—and felt my mouth make an involuntary grimace.

•

But I was glad of the job. I was grateful to be on the move again. I loved catching the tube in the mornings. I loved feeling as though I was the same as everyone around me. I enjoyed feeling exasperated with the tourists who stood in front of the turnstiles, holding their tickets, trying to work out how to get through. I wore headphones and listened to the Smiths or the Triffids. I learned to make my face impassive as I stood in the swinging aisles of the train, hanging onto a strap. I learned not to look at anyone. My friend from uni who'd lived in London had not learned this lesson fast enough—a woman in her office used to shout at her, if she caught her, 'What the fuck are *you* looking at?'

Do Australians gaze openly around them? I am trying to imagine myself doing this. I can see myself exchanging smiles with people on the bus, but maybe this is not true.

•

Every few weeks Emma got a letter from Peter, who was finishing his commerce degree in Sydney. I got letters almost every post, having channelled my lost voice into aerogrammes. My friends drew pictures and sent me bits of their lives—some hair, a leaf folded into the blue paper. Emma showed me one of her letters before putting it in the bin. Peter said that he hated his degree, and hated the other students. *I always wanted to be a pilot*, he wrote, *but my mother wouldn't let me. I shall never forgive her for that.*

'Why doesn't he do it now?' I said, handing the letter back to her. 'He's twenty-two. He doesn't have to do what his mother says anymore.'

Emma just looked at me, then did what she always did, ripped the letter, once, twice, and stamped on the bin pedal to flip the lid up. I didn't know if she was writing back to him.

In my aerogrammes I told my friends how wonderful, how amazing London was, and with Emma, Karen and Ruth I dutifully went to see bands, new movies, exhibitions. I was so often bored when I went to see bands, but found it hard to admit this to myself. This was London. I had read about these bands in the *NME*. If I could get drunk enough I would not be bored, but often my capacity for the large, plastic cups of brown, watery beer fell short of drunkenness. I got sleepy standing there next to Emma, holding my cup, watching the other two dancing, yawning till my ears ached.

I made a friend at work, out of necessity. Her name was Sarah, and we were united in our hatred of Rory. Poor Rory. His face seemed always to be sweating—pearls of it on his upper lip and forehead—while I was still cold and getting colder, clutching my coat around me as I stood in the lift going up to our floor. Sometimes I wore my coat all morning. Rory was not bad-looking; he had a classic English look: dark hair and plenty of it, regular features. But the sweat, and the froglike skin, and the whining drawl he spoke in. I nicknamed him Rory the Reptile and taught Sarah to play *How much would you charge?* We always ended up at the same place—*How much would you charge to sleep with Rory?* Sarah was one of those conscientious players who tried to put a realistic price on things. Fifty pounds?

One hundred pounds? I was always unreachable—a million pounds. A *billion* pounds.

I hadn't, of course, slept with anybody, but Sarah had. She had a boyfriend called Michael, who often used to stay at her house. Her parents wouldn't let him sleep in her bedroom, though, so they had to sneak into each other's rooms at night. She told me everything they did. All day she talked about Michael and I suppose I encouraged her, for we were the only people who worked in our dwindling section, and I had no other friends. It was her or Rory.

'We couldn't make love this morning because Dad was up early. But we had a shower together after he left.'

I would be on my knees in the storeroom, slitting open a box of books with a Stanley knife. Sarah would be sitting at the desk with the invoice. It was my job to unpack and count the books while she marked them off.

'Michael told me he wants me to buy some sexy underwear. So he can tear it off!'

'Can you two hurry it up! I want to get those on the shelves before lunchtime!'

We glanced at each other and rolled our eyes as Rory walked away. Rory was not fat, but he had a broad bottom like a woman's. I despised him for this, the way I despised myself. Sarah thought he was gay, but that was too obvious. He wasn't anything. I knew people like that at home. Perhaps others thought that was what I was like. I never had any boyfriends. But I had desires, powerful desires, and needs, and I was young enough to think that Rory did not.

•

In London no one touched you, except on the tube, and that was either by accident or horrible design, the hand that wormed its way past other bodies to slip between your sweaty legs. People would shove you backwards if you tried to pass them on the escalator, but no one ever looked at you. Once I wore a dress that had a swirly skirt, and as I fought my way onto the escalator a blast of hot wind came and flipped the dress up right over my head, so I was snatching and scrabbling to get it back down again. It was so stupid it made me laugh, but when I'd finally got the dress back in place not a single person was looking at me. They all stared, steadfastly, straight ahead.

Emma and I certainly did not touch, unless it was by mistake, Fatty and Skinny bumping around the inside of our luxurious flat like balls in a broken pinball machine. I might not have had sex with anyone, but at home people had at least touched me. My girl flatmates and I hugged each other, called each other 'mate', gave each other massages when we had been smoking dope. Most of my male friends were teetering on the brink of being gay, but this didn't make them any the less physically affectionate. Maybe it made them more so. I often held hands with a male friend when we went to the movies or a party.

•

Once I was standing by the fiction shelves, re-alphabetising, when I heard Rory, beside me, gasp; a sharp little intake of breath that made me look up. What he'd seen was Emma, coming towards us from the lifts. She was pretty, I thought, watching her. Her pale hair had grown and she wore it in two plaits. She had on a woollen coat, deep red, with buttons, a sort of Mary Quant thing that she wore with her long boots.

Rory was working on his smile when Emma said to me, 'I came to see if you wanted to have lunch.'

Her office was quite near, in Covent Garden, but she'd never come over before. She was looking around, sizing the place up. We were too high in the building to ever be busy; our section covered only a corner of a floor that was mostly taken up with fashion for large people. The bridal registry cowered in another corner, but you could see it wouldn't last.

'This is my sister,' I said to Rory. 'Can I have my break now?'

I could feel him looking more closely at me. Emma and I were not unalike. We had the same eyes and skin and big straight noses. It was more as though, using the same materials, an adult had built Emma and a child had built me, fumbling over the bottom and the arms and legs, forcing the clothes on, adding red raffia for hair.

'Half an hour,' said Rory, finding his voice.

'Is that all?' said Emma. 'What about an hour?'

'She'll have to work late,' said Rory, straightening himself.

I grimaced at Emma, and she raised her eyebrows back at me. 'We'll have sushi,' she said. 'Get your bag.'

•

After a month or so I gave up eating in the cafeteria at work, no longer exercised by horrible fascination over the other staff's eating habits.

At first I had just sat and watched as slender, clear-faced girls collected trays of lasagne and chips, bowls of chocolate pudding, and Diet Cokes. Everything came with chips. London was the only place I had been where you were offered chips with Chinese food. Not even Parkes, not even Dubbo had food like that.

It was partly the food, but partly also that I didn't like people to see me eating. Later on I would wonder why I'd thought myself so fat—I was merely *plump*, a word that I hated nearly as much as I hated *chubby*—but back then there seemed to be no doubt about it. Whenever I could, now, I went over the road to Harrods to buy my lunch. In the food hall you could get a mango, or a bag of dates or figs. I always tried to get outside if it was sunny, but often enough I spent my whole lunch break in the food hall, sneaking figs from a paper bag while I stood in front of the bread display, or the butchery. Everything was beautiful in the food hall—the tiled floors, the columned rooms, the elaborate plaster ceilings. There were no windows, but the lighting was generous and warm. There was nowhere to sit, but I sat all day at work anyway, and there were always enough people to prevent me from feeling conspicuous as I wandered around.

One lunchtime I was waiting at the fruit counter when someone beside me said, 'Hey.' I looked up. The voice belonged to Tony, our floor manager. I had never spoken to him before. He was a tall, skinny man who always wore the same loose-fitting suit. He had a walkie-talkie clipped to his trousers and thick, slicked-back hair. Sometimes I saw him conferring with the white-shirted security men. I don't think he liked Rory; he rarely came into our section. But I saw him in the distance sometimes, talking to an outraged customer. Women in particular became angry very easily, and it was his job to soothe them and make them want to come back.

He had a gentle Cockney voice and quite a large mouth. He grinned at me. 'Hungry?' he said.

I blushed and blushed.

'Seen you in here before. This lady was first,' he said to the woman behind the counter.

'No, you go,' I said, stepping back so fast I trod on someone's toes. 'I was just looking.'

•

It was not that I *wanted* to be a virgin. It just seemed to have happened. I had missed a chance once, with a nice boarder from the nearby boys' school. I wished now that I had taken advantage of him. But all I'd had to do was look at him to drench him in blushes. He would turn up at our house to see if I wanted to go for a walk and be unable to talk to my mother while I thumped upstairs for my sneakers. And then we would walk down the green lanes of our suburb, leaves whispering, me talking too fast, him not talking at all, our shoulders occasionally, unhappily bumping. I was too embarrassed about my own lack of experience to take his on as well.

In London I couldn't see how anyone, even a nice, shy, terrified boy who *couldn't get anyone else*, would be attracted to me. All the young women I saw were softly beautiful, smooth as doves, or if not beautiful, finished somehow. Like Emma, with her Mary Quant coat and knee-high boots. And she was warm, while I was shivering in my bomber jacket and short skirt. Even the few punks still left in 1986 were perfectly made-up, their red or blue hair slickly smoothed into mohawks, their clothes shiny and black and convincingly studded. Nobody that I saw looked messy, the way I did, unless it was Karen and Ruth, with their creaking leather jackets and their weary, mascaraed eyes. I knew that somewhere there were men who appreciated girls like me; girls with clear white skin and round cheeks and big white boobs and slutty, grubby hair. But men; not boys. I was not ready for that yet.

•

We'd been told that it would rain often in London, but I hadn't thought about the kind of rain it would be. I was used to rain or no rain: a tropical torrent that swept up out of nowhere, or days of incessant sunshine that crisped the parks and made the pavements burn your bare feet. In London it just rained, greyly, endlessly, like a weepy friend, always sorry for herself. I bought umbrellas but I was always forgetting them on the tube and having to walk home with my head down, my dyed hair leaking red down my neck.

One Thursday evening I got home, dripping, and Emma wasn't there. Usually on Thursdays she finished half an hour before I did and would be cooking, the lights of the flat turned on to make a yellow box of warmth. As I switched the hall light on, the phone rang. I walked down to the kitchen and picked it up, looking out at the river of headlights on Vauxhall Bridge Road. It was Rory, who I had seen only twenty minutes before, buttoning himself into his long raincoat as we stood waiting for the lift. He wanted to know if I would go out to dinner with him.

How to describe the cold despair I felt on hearing those words? It was enough to endure that I had not made a success of living in London. This was the worst—this was not just lack of success, it was anti-success, the most wretched of failures. Rory must have recognised something in me, something that echoed inside his own miserable heart. He must have thought I was so desperate that I would say yes.

When I'd said no, unhappily fabricating a jealous Australian boyfriend, knowing that Rory didn't believe me, I put the phone down, and almost immediately it rang again. It was Emma. She was having dinner with Jerome, and if I was *sure* it was okay, she would stay at his house. I nearly laughed. I said it was fine and put the phone down again. I switched the kitchen light on, and then, walking out into the sitting room, the lamps and the television. All this luxury. At home I'd been living in a terrace house with nearly a dozen tiny bedrooms. Mine had been small and damp, but there was always the sound of someone on the stairs or in the kitchen. I looked out at the traffic and the bright lights of the off-licence, and the people coming up from the tube entrance, and pulled the curtains shut.

I will always love you. That was what the last page of Peter's last letter said. I'd taken it out of the envelope, which had already been ripped open, and read it. It was a letter like a suicide note, only he wasn't committing suicide but quitting commerce to join the defence forces. Finally he would realise his dream of becoming a pilot.

I left it on the kitchen counter. It wasn't deliberate; the microwave beeped. My tinned soup was ready, and I forgot to put the letter back in the envelope. *Top of the Pops* was on, which I always had to watch through splayed fingers. Then I rang a friend at home and we talked until I could tell her about Rory, tears leaking out of the corners of my eyes as I laughed. I went to bed and slept heavily, without needing to be aware of Emma beside me.

Next morning I was in the storeroom, kneeling on the floor beside the overstock shelves, with a book open on my lap. I'd just unpacked a box of children's classics and I was reading *The Magic Faraway Tree*.

I didn't hear him approaching, just felt, suddenly, a warm hand cradling the back of my head, the way a mother does a baby's. I looked up, startled. It was the floor manager, Tony. He smiled at me, and said in his soft London voice, 'Alright, trouble?'

Behind him I saw Rory, hands on his fat hips, glaring at me. I flushed, and smiled up at Tony and nodded. He nodded back, took his hand away, and left.

I could see that Emma was home as I crossed the road from the tube that evening. Our kitchen light was on. There was someone with her; Jerome, no doubt. I took my time scraping my feet on the metal doormat at the entrance to our building. It had been a long day; Rory was not talking to me, which was more tiring than I could have thought possible.

They hadn't been there long. As I shut the door I heard the squeal of a wooden stool on the tiled floor, the sound of the fridge opening.

'Hello,' I called. I stopped to look at myself in the bathroom mirror, seizing a towel to rub over my hair. Some of the red came off on the towel. The back of my head still felt warm where Tony had touched it.

When I came into the kitchen Jerome was reading Peter's letter, one long arm outstretched to hold Emma off.

'It's *private*!' she was saying.

I put my bag on the floor. They didn't notice me.

'Give it back!' said Emma. She was making surprising headway, given her size; Jerome had to brace himself against the bench with one foot to stop himself falling off the stool. Then he simply took his hand away, and Emma cannoned into him. She snatched the letter and stood back, panting.

'I thought you'd finished with him,' said Jerome, crossing his arms.

'I couldn't *finish with him*,' said Emma. 'I never started.' She put one hand to her chest, as if feeling her trotting heartbeat.

'It's true,' I said. 'It was unrequited love.'

They both turned to look at me.

'Whose love?' said Jerome. 'Whose love was unrequited?'

He was so beautiful. He was wearing a green scarf, high around his face. You could see the green in his dark eyes. His skin would be smooth to the touch.

'*Peter's* love,' I said. 'He's had a crush on Emma for years.'

'So why hasn't she put a stop to it? Why hasn't he given up?'

I glanced at Emma. She had become very still, though tears gleamed in her eyes. I shrugged.

'Were you sleeping with him?' said Jerome to Emma.

I felt my body glittering with embarrassment.

'Of course not,' said Emma.

'You're lying,' said Jerome.

'Oh, don't be a fucking idiot,' I said, suddenly impatient with him. *This is why I don't have a boyfriend*, I thought. Jerome was not beautiful at all. His face was rigid with anger, his lips pinched righteously together. What a waste of time, all this to and fro, this fighting over nothing. I picked my bag up again. 'I'm going out.'

I had already planned to meet Karen; we were going to see another band. I forgot my umbrella again; I ran across the road in the rain, through a clot of cars, and went into the off-licence. I called her on the payphone and asked her to come straight away. I put more lipstick on, looking at myself in the door of the fridge, and bought a four-pack of tall, strong beers. I waited for Karen in the doorway and drank one of the beers. A double-decker bus trundled around the corner, Karen leaned out of a top window and shrieked at me, and I made a run for it, half-blinded by rain.

I climbed to the top floor, my beers banging against my leg. You were allowed to smoke upstairs. Karen lit a cigarette as I sat down beside her. She was smoking Silk Cut.

'If it rains again tomorrow,' said Karen, 'I'm going to kill everyone in London with an axe.'

'You'll be tired,' I said, staring through the rain-streaked window at the crowds forcing their way along the pavement.

'It's a big job,' she agreed, exhaling smoke.

We started to laugh at the idea of her wearily hacking her way through the populace. It was so hopeless. We were having such a terrible time. We hated London, and ourselves. I leaned my forehead against the seat in front of me, and laughed until I was weeping with it.

'Forget the band,' said Karen, when we had wiped our eyes. 'Let's just go and get drunk.'

When I got home the flat was quiet. The kitchen light had been left on. I padded down the hall carpet to our bedroom. I swayed a little. Jerome and Emma were asleep in her single bed. He lay behind her with his knees bent up behind hers, as though they were one shape. I pulled the covers off my bed and dragged them down the hall to sleep on the couch.

•

We didn't get any more letters from Peter, and Emma didn't mention him, or the fight with Jerome. She had successfully sealed that rupture in the smooth surface of her existence; sealed it so that nothing about Peter and his unhappiness could leak into the rest of her life. We were sisters, Emma and I, which meant we were the same, even though so different. I knew what she was doing, and even wished for some of her strength, her separateness. I understood how important it was for her to keep herself apart from people like Peter, who made a mess of things, who spoiled love with their silliness. I understood, too, that I would always have something to do with the Peters, that awkwardness and trouble would always follow me, because awkwardness and trouble are a part of being alive.

Still, I didn't want Peter, and I didn't want Rory, but I didn't want Jerome either, for all his beauty. I wanted Tony, who'd put his hand on me gently, lovingly. Who'd smiled at me in the food hall. Who'd spoken to me with his body, without needing to be grandiose, without desperation, without the kind of anger that so often mars a man's attraction to a woman. But I still wasn't ready for him. I smiled and blushed whenever I passed him, and once he winked at me over the shoulder of Annabelle, who managed the bridal registry, but we didn't speak. I wasn't even sure that he knew my name. What he'd done probably meant nothing to him—it was an unconscious gesture, a small comfort, a way of avoiding conversation. But none of that mattered: he had touched me, kindly, and the relaxing it had brought about in my body would go on for a long while.

THE SINGULAR ANIMAL: ON BEING AND HAVING

Ashley Hay

This little life, lying across my lap. Big eyes open, looking at the wind playing in the curtains, the light catching their fabric, looking up at me now and then, trying to smile and swallow at the same time. This little life, still so new: working out where he is in the world. Working out what his world is, what any world is, who he is.

Our son. Our only child.

•

I was evangelical about it, always leaping against the assumption that this child was bound to be the first of several.

'Of course,' said the lady in the baby-stuffs shop, 'the advantage of this pram is that when you have your next child, you can clip on one of those skateboard attachments and your toddler can ride there while your newborn's safe in here.' She executed a smooth sort of reverse-park glide designed to show off the stroller's handling, its manoeuvrability.

And although I should have just smiled, kicked the wheels, looked under the bonnet—or the equivalent for stroller appraisal—I felt the words take shape in my mouth, heard them push into the air to disrupt the shop's bustle of other bumpy women like me, other neat and tidy assistants: 'We're not having any other children. Just this one.'

'No, you'll have another,' said the sales lady, patting the pram's handle as if to reassure it that it wouldn't be a one-use purchase.

'Of course,' said the lady at my childhood beach, tickling our baby under his chin, 'what you have to do is have another one as soon as you can.'

'We're not having any other children. Just this one.'

'You need to have the next one as quickly as possible,' she replied, unflappable in her flapping towel.

'But it's so much nicer to have siblings,' said a variety of people, perhaps thinking this was a less proscriptive way to make us see the error of our ways. 'So much nicer, and so much easier.'

And, 'Once you've got the first one, you'll end up wanting more, no matter what you think now.'

And because of the evangelism, I jumped each time, trying to explain, to justify. For the most part, I stuck to the numbers. How old I was; how old my husband was. That we were no spring chickens was, I thought, pretty unarguable. People demurred.

I tried a more mathematical approach and came up with a model of hands—our child could hold my hand and my husband's, and still leave us both with a hand free for each other. This represented a kind of perfection in my head, a kind of complete and safely enclosing circle. People shook their heads again.

Then I tried pointing out that I was an only child, that a family of three had served me perfectly well, that I'd had a ball.

Which only made me more suspect again.

'Don't you find it remarkable,' another only child whispered to me at a dinner party, 'the things that people feel able to say when they find out you've got no brothers or sisters? About what you must be like, and must feel like, and must wish for? And just how rude they can be?'

You must have been spoiled. You must have been so lonely, bossy, selfish, precocious, self-important. You must be antisocial—you must be a loner; you must find it hard to make friends. You must wish you had a sister, a brother.

You must feel like you've missed out on so much.

Such a set against singular creatures: I read somewhere that the decision to have one child is even less acceptable to most people than the decision to have none at all. I read somewhere about a woman who was tempted to divorce her pro-single-child husband because she was so 'terribly worried' about her son growing up with no siblings. I read somewhere about a mother who felt that with just one child her family was still, somehow, a childless family of single people. But with three children, well: 'Now I feel like I am a mother,' she said.

•

It's a funny word, 'only'. It can ring with drum rolls and acclamation—'the one, the only'; it can echo with the isolation, the emptiness of lonely, alone. The English-speaking world is rare, having separate words for only's 'one-off' connotation and for its 'alone' one. The

English-speaking world is rare, too, for the deep suspicion the majority of its speakers have about only children. There's no distinction in semantics: for most people, most of the time, 'only' in terms of 'only children' means alone, solitary, lonely. Those other nuances—individual, exclusive, unique—hardly ever get a look in.

•

In this photograph, Granville Stanley Hall is all beard and authority, the epitome of an eminent late-nineteenth-century American.

Born in 1844 in a small Massachusetts village where sheep outnumbered people by a ratio of eight to one, he could trace his family back to the *Mayflower* on both sides, and he had a particular passion for climbing hills. His father was a broom-maker by trade, and Granville took obvious pride in being perhaps one of the few people able to say in the early years of the twentieth century that he himself had made, 'and can still make, a broom'. He is also credited with founding the discipline of educational psychology.

At first glance, Granville Stanley Hall seems like precisely my kind of man—class poet on graduation, pursuer of a polymathic career that bounced around divinity, literature and philosophy and let him settle, briefly, in a Chair of English before he travelled to Germany in 1875 to study the new science of experimental psychology. He was the man who invited Sigmund Freud and Carl Jung to visit America in 1909. He was the man who undertook a formal and academic study of tickling, during which he coined two seductive and lamentably under-utilised words: *knismesis*, for a light, feathery kind of a tickle;

and *gargalesis*, for the 'harder, laughter-inducing' kind. Who wouldn't warm to someone whose scientific surveys asked about the way laughter spread across a child's face, about which features were 'first and what last involved'? Who could help but be drawn to someone whose published work declared that 'in 107 cases laughter or tickling results from merely seeing a finger pointed with movements suggesting tickling; slow circular movements of the index finger, then stopping these and thrusting it toward some ticklish point, especially if with a buzzing sound, make many young children half-hysterical with laughter'? Or that 'adult men more often laugh in o and a, while children and women laugh in e and i'? Surely anyone whose contributions to human knowledge include a taxonomy of tickling, an anatomy of laughter, must be a force for good.

Which is why it's such a shame that Granville Stanley Hall is the villain in this story, given that it was just one statement of his that did all the damage to the Anglophone world's perception of only children.

According to Hall—a man with two siblings of his own, a man who'd spent all his childhood summers in the company of a large and exuberant country family—'being an only child is a disease in itself'. He wrote that as part of a study undertaken in the late 1890s, and given that it stood as the sole study of only children for several decades, it simply kept being cited, giving it the patina of currency, accuracy, inviolability. In a 1928 paper that drew on Hall's work, the writer declared that 'it would be best for the individual and the race if there were no only children'.

Even now, more than a century after Granville Stanley Hall wrote those nine fateful words, most stories about only children—and even the positive ones—at least nod to it. It's a singular sentence that allows us to see what someone described as an event as rare as the birth of a star: the birth of a prejudice.

•

I am five years old and dressed as a frog. My outfit comprises a kind of romper suit made of yellow (for tummy) and green (back) taffeta lining with hand-sewn sequins (the water droplets of a frog recently emerged from a pond); green tights; green felt flippers tied onto my hands and my feet (more sequins; more water drops); and the headdress. This is a green taffeta skullcap with two modified ping-pong balls decorated and sewn on for eyes. There are possibly also more sequins.

It is bespoke, it is a miracle of amphibianity, and it is the last word in under-six elegance. In 1976, I wear it to the Austinmer Public School Frolic; I believe myself to be the belle (or at least the batrachian) of the ball. We follow it up with a gorgeous mushroom-coloured mouse suit the following year which employs a slightly heavier weight of taffeta lining, a reprise of the skullcap design with a new set of ping-pong-ball eyes, and a tubular stuffed tail of such pleasing weight and length that I can still feel the satisfaction of spinning fast on the spot to make it swish around.

The pièce de résistance, however, is achieved for the 1982 Austinmer Public School Book Week Character Parade, which I attend as the web from *Charlotte's Web*: a navy-blue bodysuit onto which is attached a miraculous web French-knitted out of silver twine (the glorious extent of which isn't apparent until I hold my arms out like a T-square) with the words *Charlotte's Web* French-knitted in the centre and a glamorous spider hanging to one side, as if she's just finished spinning. She's made of two grey pompoms, with pipe-cleaner legs and dazzling beaded eyes. I can't remember if she had eyelashes or not, but in my memory she does.

This is how my family does costumes, thanks to two parents of vast imagination—a mother who's an artist with a history of creating fabulous outfits, and a father who's an engineer with hidden talents in ping-pong-ball adaptation, French-knitting and pompom fabrication.

I watch the other kids arrive in their shop-bought superhero outfits, their shop-bought cowboy hats and holsters. My flippers sparkle. My tail swings round. My silver web shimmers in the sunlight. Unique.

•

In this photograph, Bi Kaiwei looks thin to the point of gauntness, his eyes closed and his mouth tight. He lives in Wufu, works in a chemical plant there, had a little girl, Bi Yuexing, who was thirteen years old. His daughter, his only child; she was killed in the Sichuan earthquake in 2008.

If it's impossible to write about only children without invoking the single-person ghost of Granville Stanley Hall, it's also impossible to write about only children without invoking the billion-person population of China and its famous—or infamous—one-child policy. 'Have fewer children; live better lives,' the government slogan declares. And in 2008, the world was paying particular attention to some real lives behind that phrase. On the one hand, the stories were about those only children killed in Sichuan's rubble—more than seven thousand, some said. On the other, with the Beijing Olympics imminent, they were about the pianistic prodigy Lang Lang. As the young Chinese superstar who would be centre stage when the Games began, he embodied not only the happy-endings of international opportunity and success but also the worst kind of pressures and expectations that Chinese parents—and often, people suspected, any parents—were suspected of harbouring for their lone offspring. Here were Lang's parents paying half a year's salary to buy their two-year-old son a piano. Here was Lang's father moving thousands of miles with the young boy to pursue his musical education while Lang's mother stayed behind and kept up her job. Here was Lang's father, furious that his son had missed two hours' piano practice, thrusting pills into his son's hand and insisting he take them or throw himself from their tiny balcony. Because missing practice meant certain failure. Because failure meant death—there was no going home and admitting that your little boy was not going to be an international megastar.

A father advocating his son's suicide: the suspected story of China's suspect little emperors and empresses—as their millions of only children were tagged—writ large.

The problem seemed to be one of many eggs and just one basket. In the wake of the Sichuan earthquake, some bereaved parents expressed their grief in terms of having had to pin their every hope on just one child. 'And this is the return we get,' said one mother.

Children mourned in the language of profit and loss, of capital and investment. *This is the return*.

In the photograph of Bi Kaiwei, he is holding a photograph of Yuexing; you can see how tightly his fingers clutch its glossy edges. His body looks rigid with grief, as if his entire being was focused on the little girl in the picture, the mess behind him where she died. When the Chinese government announced it would lift its one-child policy for parents whose children had died in the quake—provided they weren't too old to try again, or hadn't already been sterilised—I wondered whether he and his wife could or would try to have another child. Because in in the first stories that reported the children's deaths, and the later policy reversal, the implication was that the parents' grief would have been less, or could be lessened, if they were no longer restricted to having just one son or daughter.

The implication rubbed and jarred: if I died, these stories suggested, my parents would feel better if they had someone else to fall back on. If something happened to my child, I would feel it less if I had another one. They were strange ideas for an only child to think about—strange ideas, too, for the mother of one. As Bi Kaiwei's wife would know: pregnant with another child by early 2009, 'I feel this is the return of our daughter,' she said. Yet, she continued, 'even though I'm comforting myself, telling myself this is her, I still don't feel very cheerful. I'm very depressed.' She and her husband visited Bi Yuexing's grave every day.

•

I am four years old and standing in a cupboard in the laundry. This cupboard can be, variously, a shop, a lift, a bank, a travel agency, depending on my mood, but today it is what it is, a broom cupboard, and I am pretending to be Alice.

Alice-in-the-Broom-Cupboard is the imaginary friend of a character in Russell Hoban's book *A Birthday for Frances*. Frances, in the book, is a badger.

Outside the cupboard, my mother is doing the ironing. If the cupboard was a lift, she'd say, 'fourth floor' or 'haberdashery' from time to time. If the cupboard was a bank, she'd say, 'Five dollars in change, please.' But when the cupboard was home to Alice, she simply let it be home to Alice.

She does not, fortunately, subscribe to Dr Spock's theory that children invent imaginary friends to make up for some deficit in their lives. Perhaps it was a shortfall of 'hugging and piggyback rides', he suggested, recommending that any child still nattering to an imaginary being by the age of four should be shipped off to a 'child psychiatrist, child psychologist, or other mental health counsellor [who would] be able to find out what they're lacking'. At the age of four, I am not and never have been deprived of either hugs or piggybacks. At the age of four, my own gallery of imaginary friends is not only intact, I also like to pretend that I am the imaginary friend of a badger out of a book. And no one tells me I shouldn't.

If imaginary friends were symptomatic of a problem, then the problem was thought to be more pronounced and more common among only children. Of course it was the lack of siblings, the lack of conversation between peers, the lack of interaction in long days.

We were lonely little souls, deprived of real conversation with real playmates and desperately trying to make some up for ourselves. Best not to talk about it; best to hope we grew out of it as quickly as we could—with or without the assistance of Dr Spock's retinue of experts.

I can't remember what being Alice-in-the-Broom-Cupboard required me to do, other than stand in the broom cupboard. I can remember the sound of my mother's voice as we chatted through the door, the sound of steam as her iron went on gliding and surging, gliding and surging. And Alice-in-the-Broom-Cupboard is still part of our family, referred to and remembered in the way of Percy the Parrot (whose adventures my father channelled for me), the Six Fairies (channelled by my mother), and Mrs SeeWee, my imaginary neighbour in the garden who lived beyond a doormat that sat—inexplicably—in the middle of a bed of sasanquas for years.

One of the first things I did when we thought about becoming parents ourselves, more than thirty years later, was track down a copy of *A Birthday for Frances*, so that Alice could come into being for that next, then-theoretical generation.

•

Here is a selection from the world's gallery of only children—proffered for their various levels of inspiration, consolation or remonstration. Here is Lance Armstrong, Lauren Bacall, Leonardo da Vinci, Albert Einstein, Indira Gandhi, Isaac Newton and Frank Sinatra—plus one US president (FDR), two US first ladies (Nancy Reagan and Laura

Bush) and one almost-one (Tipper Gore). Take solace, too, one-off progeny, from the fact that you are more likely to appear on the cover of *Time* magazine than your siblinged friends.

And here is an alternative phrase that could ameliorate the downsides of that English 'only'. Step into French, and an only child becomes *une enfant unique* instead—redolent with drum rolls and acclamation.

•

I am eighteen years old, a few days out of home, starting university, starting the next part of my life. On this late summer morning, my mother's phone rings, and it's someone suggesting that my parents might like to host an exchange student now that I've gone. The silence in the house without its one available young person—they must want someone else around to fill that gap.

My mother declines: they're not really looking to replace me. They're not really wishing they had someone else around. They're happy I'm off doing what I want to do; they'll look forward to the holidays when I come home. They stand firm in the face of more than one of these suggestions. My mother, as the years pass, gets busier and busier—there's no way she'd have had time for an exchange student.

Later, when I move overseas, it happens that they sell my bed, change the locks on their front door, buy a car that only seats two. We make jokes about this—not only did they not need to replace me with an exchange student, now they're excising me from their space completely. Some people, when I tell this story, take it seriously, which makes me wonder if this is the sort of sneaky behaviour parents-of-several do get up to when their houses finally empty.

And later again, when I'm pregnant, I ask my mother for the first time about being an only child, about whether they ever thought I might not be—or should not be. It's never occurred to me to ask before.

'I always wondered,' she says, playful, 'what I'd do if I had another small person and didn't like the second one as much as I liked the first . . .'

•

Here are some statistics; here are some correlations. The work finally done on only children that offered alternatives to G. Stanley Hall showed that they tended to speak earlier and gain their vocabulary faster, gain higher marks in aptitude tests and in school, and not only progress to tertiary education but follow through and graduate. They tended to have better self-esteem, to be more patient, to be more sharing. In terms of happiness, politics and career choices, they were indistinguishable from any member of a larger family.

As countries prosper, families tend towards fewer children. Similarly as women's education levels rise. And as levels of personal faith decline, people tend towards fewer children too. By late 2008, single-child families outnumbered two-child families in America for the first time—although the number of Americans who thought one child was the ideal number was still a miniscule three per cent.

Here are some theories about the benefits of being or having a single child. Fewer children in a family mean the resources that family has available have to be divided fewer ways—whether that's time for reading together, money for tertiary education, or the availability of frog and mouse suits. There's no way even a master French-knitter could whip up Charlotte's webs for five offspring on short notice.

Imaginary friends are now seen not as a dangerous tendency that should be curbed as quickly as possible, but as a hallmark of creativity—if your child doesn't have a Mrs SeeWee, some say, you'd do well to invent one to impress their teachers. And fewer children mean women are freer sooner to do other things, whether that's returning to work or heading in a whole new direction. Only children as emancipation.

But research can show you whatever you'd like to see: of the first sixteen studies of China's burgeoning population of only children, two found they displayed more 'socially desirable' behaviour, one found they were more spoiled and selfish, and less independent and emotionally healthy, and the vast majority—the remaining thirteen—found there was no appreciable difference between the onlies and the severals at all. A connection was drawn between an increase in the Chinese crime rate and an increase in single children. The preponderance of males compared to females that was the perhaps unintended result of the policy could be responsible, it was suggested, for almost two-fifths of the surge in crime the country was experiencing. But then another connection was drawn between the one-child policy and any positive contribution China was making to address climate change: 300 million fewer births meant 300 million fewer people making their demands on the world's resources.

More than a decade ago, American environmental writer Bill McKibben approached parenthood from an ecological angle. The world and its resources had played a large part in the decision he and his wife made to have Sophie, a single child, and he wanted that world, those resources, to at least figure in the thinking some other people gave to the important question of their family's size. 'I'm not saying that my friends, or anyone else, are wrong to have several children,' he wrote, 'or that they should feel guilty or defensive . . . all I'm saying is that we live at a watershed moment in our ecological history when we need at least to *consider* this question, a question we almost never talk about.'

But alongside his concerns about the world's food, the world's energy, the world's space, the world's future, he grappled with the authority he had—and as someone with his own sibling—to decide that his daughter would be siblingless. Beside all the familiar concerns—would she be shy, selfish, spoiled, unpopular?—he asked whether she would have to endure an especial loneliness after he and his wife had died.

I understood how much he worried about Sophie and the state of the world and its future. But the idea of especial loneliness, especial orphan-ness, had never occurred to me. Everyone is orphaned when their parents die, irrespective of how many brothers or sisters they have, just as every first-born child gets to be an only one . . . for a while.

And only children—at least in my experience—tend to be good at accumulating people, at creating their own quasi-families, at bulking up their numbers with a profusion of friends with whom they often have closer relationships than the ones they see over in sibling-world.

I asked my one-of-five husband if it would matter to him that this one-of-one child of ours had no siblings.

'No,' he said, 'not at all.' As simple and definitive as that.

•

I am thirty-seven years old and lying on an operating table at Brisbane's Mater Hospital, unexpectedly caesareaned, unexpectedly delivered. My head is turned to my left, and my nose is centimetres away from the nose of our tiny baby, looking to his right, looking at me while my husband leans in from the other side. This person we've spent nine months wondering about, imagining. For most of that time, chatting away to him, telling him stories, it felt like he was the latest in my long line of imaginary friends.

'The look on your faces,' says the anaesthetist, clicking our camera, 'the look on your faces: *look what we made*.' The three of us, framed in our hospital blues, together in the world for the first time.

Later, in one dead-of-night feed, I look at this little being lying in my lap, his father lying next to me. In the half-funk of darkness, I wonder about the genetics of this, and whether I see my son not as the amalgam of two people, two families, two clear and distinct lines of descent, but as some kind of sibling—a sibling through vertical generations, rather than the more usual horizontal ones.

He shifts a little, grabs at my finger without looking at it, and I cannot describe the size or shape of the warmth and the excitement and the anxiety and the responsibility that settle around me. This can't be how you feel about a sibling; this is how you feel about a child. This is, as a friend had said it would be, a whole other way of loving.

When I glimpse myself now in a mirror or a window, I see somebody's mother—just one somebody. And I see myself more clearly, more distinctly than I ever have before, as if I'm recognising myself properly for the first time.

This little life, lying across my lap, his head as soft as velvet, his skin as smooth as silk. It's four in the morning and while my son lies here with his cheek resting on one hand, his father is next to me, asleep, his own cheek resting on his own hand. Outside, the light is coming up through silver, through mauve, and the first kookaburras are beginning to sing. Inside, the three of us are breathing together, safe and warm.

There's no correct maths for families—they're the embodiment of infinite variety, irreducible to models or theories, right or wrong sizes or shapes or numbers. This is my family: these are the numbers and the people that feel right, from the generation above to the generation below.

That's all.

THE YARRA

Nam Le

Hours before sunrise my body's already soaked with sweat, as though in anticipation of the real heat. Melbourne's in drought. The city a plain of dust and fire. I wake amidst dreams of Saturday sports as a schoolboy, shin guards and box chafing where the sheets have twisted; noise, collision down the pitch as faraway as a deeper dream. There are tupperware containers at half-time, frozen wedges of orange. Then a sudden switch and charge, players all around me, the rising breathing in my ears—I am sprinting, dread-filled, from here to there, and here the ball is kicked to there, and there it's booted—at the very moment I've chased it down—somewhere else. The sun is on my face and then it is dark. My brother, my blood and bones, confessor and protector, came in last night, he must be sleeping downstairs, and—as always when he comes—I find my hand on my heart and my mind wide open and wheeling.

I get up and wash my face. The water from the cold faucet is warm, and smells of dirt. Downstairs, a reflexive propriety forestalls me looking at the sleeping form on the couch, and then I look. My brother, Thuan, comes bringing no clues where he's been. As always, he lies on his back. His mouth is open, his eyelids violent with their shuddered thoughts, and under the thin sheet I can see the heavy limbs, flat and parallel as though lying in state. He has a powerful body.

I make some coffee in a plunger—not bothering to keep the noise down—and take it outside to the back deck. Surrounded by cicada song I sit down, stare out. Something is wrong. Why else would he have come? I wonder where he's been but then why does it matter? Away's where he's been. I think of his last visit three years ago, then Baby's visit a few months later—how quiet and uncertain she was, how unlike his girlfriend from those rowdier times. Before leaving she hesitated, then asked for thirty dollars; I gave it to her and never saw her again.

Against the darkness, other faces from that shared past occur to my mind with stunning vividness. Even closer, thicker, than the dark is the heat. Another scorcher on the way. Somewhere out there a forest is burning, and a family crouching under wet towels in a bathtub, waiting as their green lungs fill with steam and soot muck. I test the coffee's temperature. As often happens at this time of morning I find myself in a strange sleep-bleared funk that's not quite sadness. It's not quite anything. Through the trees below, the river sucks in the lambency of city, creeps it back up the bank, and slowly, in this way, as I have seen and cherished it for years, the darkness reacquaints itself into new morning.

He's there now, I sense him, but I say nothing. Minutes pass. A line of second lightness rises into view beside the river: the bike trail.

'You still got my old t-shirt,' Thuan says. Even his voice sounds humid. He comes out, barefoot and bare-chested, stepping around my punching bag without even feinting assault.

'Sleep okay?'

'If you mean did I drown in my own sweat.'

He's feeling talkative. 'You came in late,' I say. 'There's a fan.'

He pads around the deck, inspecting it. Since he was last here I've jerry-rigged a small workout area, a tarpaulin overhang. I painted the concrete underfoot in bright, now faded, colours. He lowers himself onto the flat bench. Then under his breath he says, 'Alright,' as though sceptically conceding a point. He shakes his head. 'This bloody drought,' he says.

'I know, I've been going down there,' I say, nodding at the river. 'Bringing water up—for the garden and whatnot.'

'Why?'

'You know.' He's making me self-conscious. 'The herbs and stuff.'

'I mean why not just use the hose?'

I glance at him. Where has he been that there aren't water restrictions? Then I catch his meaning: who cared about the water restrictions? What could they do to you?

A shyness takes hold of me, then I say, 'I dreamt about Saturday sports.'

To my surprise he starts laughing. He lifts up his face, already sweat-glossed, and bares his mouth widely. Yes, he's changed since I saw him last. 'Remember when you broke that guy's leg? And they wanted us to forfeit?'

I tell him I remember, though in my memory it was he, and not I, who had done the leg breaking. We'd played on the same team some years. For a confusing moment I'm shuttled back into my morning's dream: the brittle sky, the sun a pale yolk broken across it. Then the specific memory finds me—the specific faces—the injured kid with what seemed an expression of short-breathed delight, as if someone had just told a hugely off-colour joke; the odd, elsewhere smirk playing on our father's lips as he came onto the field to collect us, batting off the coach's earnest officialese, the rising rancour of the opposing parents.

'The look on his face,' I scoff.

I wait for Thuan to go on with the story but apparently he's done. He's chuckling still, but the sound has no teeth in it and that makes me wary. I feel oddly tested by him.

'Coffee?'

He thinks about it. Then, as though shoved, he falls backwards along the bench, twisting his upper body at the last second beneath the barbell. Hurriedly I count up the weight—one-twenty kilos on a fifteen-kilo bar—not shameful, but nor is it my PB.

'Wanna spot?' I ask, making it clear from my tone that I'm joking.

He jerks the bar off the stand and correctly, easily, completes three presses. When he's done he remains on his back, arms gone loose on either side of the narrow bench as though parodying one of the weekend kayakers on the river below. I follow his long breaths. For some time he doesn't move or speak, and in the half-dark I wonder if it's possible he's fallen back asleep. All around us the cicadas beat on, their timbre unsteady, deranged by the interminable heat of the night. I settle back too. A strong whiff of sage from the garden. Trees and bushes sliding into their outlines. Buying this place when I came into my inheritance was the smartest thing I ever did—despite its rundown state, subsiding foundations, the light-industrial mills and factories on every side. I couldn't have known then that ten years on, at thirty-three, I'd be living here alone, jobless. I couldn't have reasoned that I'd end up folding each of my days into this early-morning mood, trained on the dark river below, sensing that the mood, though ineffable, was one less of sorrow than of loss—and that what I called my life would be answerable to it. I know this: my brother, when he comes, muddies this mood in me. For this I am glad, as for the fact that we are bound to each other in all the ways that matter.

As though invoked, he speaks up. 'I'll be out of your hair in a couple of days,' he says. Then he gets up and goes into the dark bushes, presumably to take a piss.

•

Physical excellence has always been important between us. As a boy, I remember pushing myself in sports because my brother did—following him blindly into school and street games of every type. Unlike me, he didn't read, or even listen to music; for him the pursuit of physical betterment was its own reason and reward. I remember witnessing—when I was eleven and he thirteen—a push-up contest between my brother and the four Ngo boys. Later, of course, the four of them would be media-tarred as members of that night's notorious 'Asian gang' but in truth they were no gang—they were barely even friends—and famously never on speaking terms. What they were,

were brothers. And even back then, in the kids' room at some family friends' party in St Albans, squatting around the prone figure of my brother who was younger than all but one of them, they'd already learned to stick together. The contest carried on. With no clear winner emerging, they progressed to push-ups on their knuckles, then push-ups on five fingertips, then one-armed push-ups incorporating these variants—the Ngos dropping out until only Hai, the eldest, remained alongside my brother. Then Hai collapsed. All of us watched in incredulity as Thuan went on to demonstrate a one-armed push-up, left hand tightly clutching his right wrist, where his body's weight was borne entirely by the thumb and forefinger of his right hand. I was stricken—as much by my brother's single-mindedness as his strength, the fact he must have practised, in secret, for months. (I say this with confidence because it was only after three months, when I'd buffed two coin-sized spots into the bathroom floorboard, that I managed it myself.)

My brother believed that nothing could make you ridiculous if you were strong. His way was to go at things directly; entering a new school, for example, he would do what movie lore says to do upon entering jail: pick a fight—and win. I wondered what he did in jail. Our father, in his own way, failed to beat this into us, and so my brother beat it into me. I thought then I hated him for it but I was wrong. I wanted to know him—I always have. Now I realise it was only when he asserted himself in physical motion—then, ineluctably, in violence—that I came closest to doing so.

I am on the street of my childhood. I am running late, without any time to scavenge through the disused paddock, veer in and out from under lawn sprinklers—even to catch a breather at the bottom of our steep hill. He's by himself, waiting for me. Both our parents at work. I'm late, and when I come in the front door he'll punish me—those are his rules, and they're clear enough. I come in and there he is, right in front of me, his face almost unbearably inscrutable. He allows me time to put down my schoolbag and deadlock the door. I fumble off my shoes. The hot cord bunches up from my gut into my throat, clogging my breathing. I lift my arms to my face and he slubs me with a big backhander.

'Where've you been. You're late.'

I nod, lick my cracked lips, crabwalk quickly into the living room. He follows me to the couch where I hunch my back and bury my face in the dark red cushion. Over and over he hits me, his knuckles pounding the hard part of my head where I won't bruise. The cushion smells of old blood, and spit, and sweat from both our bodies. If I reach behind to feel for the arm, the punishing fist—try to glove it with my own smaller, sweaty palms—he'll twist and sprain my fingers. If I turn to plead, I'll meet his face absent of heavy intent, as if his attention is somewhere else, as if he's bashing my skull to reach something just beyond it. He's utterly without pity and in my stronger moments I envy that. I'm sorry, I tell him. I'm sorry I'm sorry I'm sorry. He drives his knee into my lower back. At the height of panic and pain something comes free in me. Afterwards, I wipe my face on the cushion and try not to track blood, if there is blood, all over the carpet. I search my reflection in the bathroom mirror. If there's visible damage, he'll barter with me, he'll let me off next time, he'll do my chores, buy me jam doughnuts at the tuckshop—so long as I don't dob him in. But only rarely are there visible signs.

'What happened?' Mum asks. She's had a long day and her face is closed and loose.

'Nothing.'

She pauses. 'I'll tell your dad.'

I look at her scornfully. Even she knows that doesn't deserve an answer.

One of the common tacks in media accounts of my brother, I noticed—beyond the routine designation of 'monster'—was to call attention to his inscrutability. None of the other culprits merited such consideration. The Ngo boys, for instance, always looked thuggishly guilty. But courtroom reporters and sketch artists described, artfully and self-consciously, their failure of scrutiny in the face of Thuan Xuan Nguyen; a face typically depicted as 'smooth', or 'mask-like', on someone whose very name rebuffed pronunciation in each of its three syllables. I could understand their frustration. My brother was a person in whom deep faults ran, yet always he seemed to conduct them into something like charisma. All my life I never judged him; to me he represented the fulfilment of my own genomic seed and tatter. I never suspected, after all that happened, at the trial and beyond, that complete strangers might also be capable of my reservation. This is not to defend what he did. This is to say I understood, completely, the media's macabre, manic insistence on the details of that night. The facts of the matter. The altercation and eviction from the nightclub. The first victim chased down and hacked to death by a gang wielding machetes, meat cleavers and samurai swords. The sickening count of wounds on his body. Victims two and three fleeing into the Yarra, carried by the water approximately two hundred metres to the west—shadowed alongshore by the gang. One with gashes on his wrists and forearms, three fingers missing below the knuckle, from a presumed attempt to return to shore. Chances are you may recall these details. The sober-faced riverside TV reports, the strongly worded declarations by members of the mayor's office, the Homicide Squad, the Asian Squad—while in the wintry background, day on day, the grieving families held vigil, wailing in Vietnamese as they proffered incense sticks, lit and let go of tissue paper. You may have even heard me speak, in one of my presentations, about this incident. Most people recognise my brother only through one of his tabloid nicknames: the Meat Cleaver Murderer. He was there on the bank that night. Here's what most people won't know—what I've never spoken about: I was there with him.

•

When it gets light my brother showers and heads out. I laze on the couch in the living room, windows open but curtains drawn, shirtless in front of the rickety fan, rolling a chilled glass bottle of water back and forth across my chest. Otherwise, I try not to move. When the phone rings, it's Mum—one of her friends has just spotted Thuan on Victoria Street. Is it true? Has he come back?

I'm waiting for him when he returns. We have to go visit Mum, I tell him. He stops, then nods, puts his sunnies back on. Outside, the air is so hot it immediately dries out my lungs; I can feel the bitumen boiling through my sandals. This is a killing sun. We walk south, through the Abbotsford chop shops and factories, the streets made slow, strange with heat vapour, the sudden assaultive glare of metal surfaces. People move, then pause in scant shadows. On the main street the tramlines look as though they're liquefying. Too hot to think, let alone speak, we make our way towards the high-rise flats.

'Child?' our mother asks when she opens the door. She's wearing brown silk pyjamas and there's absolutely no sweat on her face.

'Hello, Ma.' My brother touches her shoulder for a second. She reaches up and cups his ear, then turns to smile at me.

When our father died I advised her to sell the house and car and move here—the flat was government-subsidised, located in the heart of a Vietnamese neighbourhood. During that period she was used to doing whatever I said. I see, looking back, it must have been hard going for her—moving from a family home with yard, driveway and garden to living alone in an inner-city warren sentried by closed-circuit cameras. Up urine-doused lifts and down fumigated corridors. Since then, though, she's grown to like it. She likes the proximity to her new circle of friends, to Victoria Street a block away, and—a few blocks behind that—to me. After all that happened, I sometimes wondered how her friendships suffered—I loathed the thought of her being judged by that array of flat faces and slit eyes, besieged by their silent, hostile curiosities—but of course she'd never have discussed any of that with me.

The dining table, predictably and yet astonishingly, is covered with food. Mum comes out of the kitchen with a jug full of mint leaves and cut lemon halves. She pours our drinks, enquires after my herb garden, brings out a colander brimming over with fresh basil and purple mint and coriander. She'll send some cuttings home with me, she says; the residents picked the community garden clean due to the drought. Every now and then, as she speaks, she'll stop to look at my brother.

'You've been in the sun,' she says. She wets a cloth under the kitchen tap and lays it across the back of his neck.

We eat with courteous gusto. These are all our favourite dishes: spring rolls, shredded chicken coleslaw, a plain winter melon soup offset by caramelised salty pork. My brother doesn't talk, so neither do I. The silence becomes the outside wind: up here on the eighteenth floor it's a constant commotion, driving dust and sound through the metal window jambs, shaking the very light. Every so often I see smallish cockroaches stopping, as though disoriented, in the middle of their skitterings. Oblivious, we eat, and before we're done with any given dish Mum carts it off, brings forth a new one. For a moment it's as though we've ducked out from our nearer past; we're back in our St Albans kitchen, nothing to say, waiting for Mum to finish up. Not knowing it would chase us all down—this past still in front of us. Then, she cooked, and we ate. Later, she sat down and couldn't stand up again in a Victorian Supreme Court public toilet, her eldest son counted push-ups in his cell, body wet with heft and speed, I stood in front of strangers and spoke them both down into small dots of sense. Later, she sat with her back straight and head bent, I stood in front of people and delivered up her dead husband.

In cold weather you find the dead roaches behind the radiators, under the electric kettle, microwave, fridge, where they group for warmth. When it's this hot where do they go?

'Child is well?' Finally she's seated, facing Thuan. The dishes are cleared and there's a platter of fruit on the table.

'I'm fine,' he says.

She starts to respond, then stops. Her fingers reach out to test the lacquer of a cut lemon face, left open to the air.

'Really,' he says. He sounds like he means it.

'It's so sad what happened to Baby,' she says. She, too, is thinking about death. 'I didn't even know she was sick like that.'

'Baby? What happened?'

'Thank you for coming to see me. I know you're very busy.'

'You don't know about Baby?' I ask despite myself.

Thuan, frowns, then reaches over and squeezes our mother's shoulder. 'Ma. Guess what.'

'Where you've been, or what you've been doing, is your own business,' she continues. She says this shyly and forthrightly, a settlement of fact. 'I don't need you to look after me.'

'I know, Ma.'

'And Lan, he is very good. He can look after himself.'

'He is very good,' repeats Thuan, completely deadpan.

'I hear about Lan speaking at universities, at the community centre, and it makes me very happy.' My brother throws me an offhand smile, and in a ritual manner she follows up his smile, almost too sweetly. Turning her attention to me: 'He has become a brave and caring man.'

I get up, go to the window. There has always been a touch of formal drama about my mother, and a situation like this—her prodigal son's return after three long years—is bound to draw it out. Through the wind-rattled window I watch some seagulls, hovering in the air the way seagulls do. The air is runny with heat and bleaches the blue sky.

Mum's speaking again. 'I know I can't tell you what to do. But I'm your mother and I don't want my sons to be angry with each other.'

I turn around. My brother's mouth is slightly open, sly at one corner.

'I don't know how much longer I'll be here. I want my sons to look after each other.' She speaks with care, a prepared grace. 'Your father would want that too. Remember when you were children, you looked after each other.'

In grade three, when my parents found out I was being bullied, they left it to my brother to beat up the malefactor. Recess the next day, Thuan climbed out of the concrete playground tunnel from one end, then, a long minute later, Matty Fletcher from the other, smiling with his mouth full and one hand low on his gut. My family used to bring this up at every chance. Now, Mum stops, following the thought to its logical implication. Another track cut off next to a night river. Nothing, during the trial, was so cruel as watching the jury coaxed and coerced by weeks of 'similar fact evidence' alleging Thuan's propensity for violence—until it was all anyone could see of him. She must have been confounded, afterwards, by the new plot of her life—how, whether forward or back, it inescapably led her, as it did both her sons, to that one night—as though it were exactly where we were all meant to be.

'I've been saving some money,' she says.

'Ma.' His insouciance has settled now.

'I need you to come to the bank with me later. To sign some papers. If you have time.'

'Listen, Ma, I don't need money.'

'You're the oldest, so I want you to look after it.'

For a moment no one speaks. In the yellow emptiness behind the window I hear voices, shrill strains of Asian opera riding the hot red wind from a different floor, maybe a different building. The glass-warmed sun on my face. I'm brought back to mornings waking up when my pillow is so suffused with sun, the air through the open window so full of a sense of lost summer, that I close my eyes again, coach those voices at the bottom of my hearing to sing louder, bear higher their meaning.

'Child,' says Mum, her tone finally relaxing. 'You're too good for money now?'

Thuan leans back at the table, slightly embarrassed.

Mum stands up, brushing smooth her silk pyjama top. 'Heavens,' she says, 'it's been so long since I saw you. I'm going to tell you the truth—I didn't know if I would see you again.' Then, with her usual restraint, she checks herself. Smiling privately, as though she's decided she has all the time she needs, she picks up the jug and heads into the kitchen to make more iced tea.

•

'So Baby.'

The lift drops with the sound of metal squealing against itself.

'Two or three years ago,' I say. 'It was an accident, they think.'

He looks straight ahead. 'OD?'

I nod.

'She was still in Footscray?'

'Yeah, probably. I think so. I saw her—she was all straightened out.'

He frowns, maybe sensing my lie. 'Not if she was still hanging out in Footscray she wasn't.' It's the first time I've heard an edge of the old hard tone. 'Jesus,' he mutters. The lift opens, and I follow him through the two security doors back out into the heat.

In the presentations I've been asked to give, I generally concentrate on sociological factors until the inevitable moment I find myself nudged towards the incident. The cops at our door two days later, their duteous, scornful faces, all the scorn sucked into their eyes and the edges of their mouths as if to curb them from asking, What kind of animals are you? That you could do this to your own? These are not, I think, unfair questions. But the people who turn to me for answers aren't looking to my master's in political science, they're looking at my one-of-them face, they're looking at my pedigree of proximity: the fact I'm my brother's brother. Not that I'm one of them, of course. I'm articulate and deferential, I'm charming to just the right degree. It's that they trust me to tell them the inside story. They want to know—beneath the affidavits and agreed facts—*how it happened*. And so when I talk about socioeconomic disadvantage, about ghettoisation and tribal acting-out, about inexorable cycles of escalation, I say these things and I mean them, but even to me they start to sound insincere. What I mean to say but don't—can't—is that everything always starts with a girl, and in this case the girl was Baby.

My brother was nineteen and one night came home drunk, flushed, probably high, and with a girl. This last had never happened before. There was a shadow on his jaw which I assumed was a bruise. After some time the girl said to me, 'I'm Baby,' then turned to him and exclaimed, 'I can't believe you weren't gonna introduce me!' then kissed him, all the while still talking into his mouth. He made some joke and she laughed and I was relieved, hearing her laugh, that it wasn't the cutesy, infant squeaking so many Asian girls liked to perform in front of guys.

'He talks about you *all* the time,' she said, and laughed again.

I decided I liked her.

How long they'd been together wasn't clear. It seemed, from Baby's comfort with him, that it might have been a while. She was my brother's first girlfriend, I think, and I'm not sure why that didn't surprise me at the time. They'd just come home from a fight. I mentally staged it during their telling: Baby's ex had been at the club, an Asian night, stewing deeper and hotter in Hennessee the longer he watched them until, at the final, emptying hour—the lights switched on and music off, bartenders wiping down bars, tallying the take—he'd called up his mates and followed them outside.

Something flew out of the night towards Thuan's head. He ducked, the bottle smashing against a car, setting off the alarm. I knew that club: its main entrance fed onto a cul-de-sac backed in by warehouses, roller-iron doors, a multi-storey car park giving out the only light. Under that spotty, gas-like glow, my brother turned around and saw them—maybe a dozen of them. Their movements loose and stiff with alcohol. He had Baby with him, and the four Ngo brothers—that was it. Breath shortening, the great engine of his glands working till he felt again the thick familiar twists of hormones through his body, he fended Baby back against the blaring car, made quick eye contact with the Ngos, for whom he felt himself flooding with a feeling of deep loyalty, and waited. You can always tell the seriousness of a fight by the speed of first approach. Baby's ex feinted forward, then his crew herky-jerked at them, and instantly my brother knew in his body the entire shape of what would follow. The only surprise was the set of strangers who jumped in to help them; it was only later, in the nervy racing-away euphoria, that they were introduced as Baby's friends from Footscray; only later still, well past the point of ready return, that he learned the guy in the red baseball cap—as affable afterwards as he was vicious during the fight—was another of Baby's exes.

'You should've been there,' Thuan said magnanimously, rubbing the sore spot on his jaw. 'We could have used you out there tonight.'

'You did okay,' said Baby.

I studied her closely—this girl they'd all fought over. She had a face struck together by contrasts: the Asian hair—so black it looked wet—offset by almost European features: chalky skin, sunken cheeks, lips in a burnished shade of red that belonged to some earlier, jazz-smoked era. Her body was slight and wonderfully slouched. She had, all in all, the look of a good girl gone a bit grungy. Thinking of their story, I saw her arms lined by light in the alley, locked crossed amid the scudding bodies, the car alarm caterwauling through her skull. Then I saw my brother watching her. He looked the happiest I'd ever seen him.

'I wish I had been there,' I said, and meant it.

That summer, I spent more time with Thuan than ever before or since; Baby liked my company, insisted on it, and my brother was surprisingly acquiescent—especially given we'd never really had any mutual friends. She called him Little T and so, with even less reason, I became Big T. I came to need her, and probably what I needed most about her was him: the emergent, intricate person he became around her. He developed a way of talking to me through her, in third-person—*Look at him—and he reckons he's not on steroids!* She kept him kind to me like that. At Brighton Beach she stripped to a grey bikini. When he caught me staring, he gave me a look that was warning and mockery, shy and full of braggadocio, knowing and forgiving all at once. Do you see what I mean? We lived then in slow-time; the light more viscous, the breath drawn deeper into our bodies. I had a new brother and a new name—how would I not rally to both?

•

When we get back, Thuan breaks the silence and tells me to head inside—he's going to keep wandering. There's no invitation in his announcement so I go in—glad to escape the punishing heat—strip to my boxers, splash water over my face and chest. I think for a droll moment of working out. Then I resume my place on the couch, following the creak of the fan, the odd foolhardy cyclist whizzing by on the track below.

The wind sears my face awake. I'm sodden and sticky. I find myself incredibly aroused. The wind feels as though it's passed through fire. I press my face into the cushion and reach for myself, drowsing into the familiar memory of Baby that one time. The habitual quickening. She came over to our house wheeling a large suitcase full of clothes to launder. Yes. These trips were timed so both our parents would be out working the night shift. My brother steered and shut her up in his room, not knowing I could hear their every other sound. At the end of the night she unloaded the dryer and folded her clothes into the suitcase.

'Need any help with that?'

'I'll be right.'

'You can carry it down the stairs?'

A flirtatious pause.

'Sure, you can help me bring it down.'

I glided to the window and lifted the hem of the blinds. I was nearly seventeen. They left, as usual, by the small unlit walkway between the fence and my side of the house. And as usual, they tarried in the dark, swaying in and away from each other, whispering, and I cracked open the window to listen in from above.

'So what's the going tip for a bellboy here?' she asked.

Outside, the night was cool and a wind blew full and quiet along the empty street, carrying with it the scent of new flowers, jasmine and hibiscus and bougainvillea. A wood chime sounded from a neighbour's porch.

'Just a quick blow job,' he said.

She spluttered out a low laugh, pushed and punched him. Then they kissed. She kissed him soft and then she kissed him hard, and after some abortive fumblings she spun around and folded herself over the standing suitcase. She wriggled her pants down to her knees.

'Make it quick,' her voice hissed.

He shoved down his own pants and grabbed her pale hips. He leaned and rocked over her. The wheels scrabbled wildly across the concrete but the suitcase stayed upright. From where I was watching all I could see of Baby was the side of her head, curtained off by her jogging black hair. She nodded and nodded and nodded and I watched. Finally they stopped, remaining locked together, almost statue-like. Then she unbent herself, bobbed her knees in a little curtsey, and reached between her legs with two fingers.

'You,' she said, grinning delightedly, jabbing her fingers at his chest, 'are going to get me pregnant.'

He shushed her and automatically she looked around, scoping the street. Then she looked up—and saw me. I jerked back but didn't dare release the blinds. After an appalling hesitation, she lowered her gaze, then straightened her clothes. She took possession of her suitcase handle. My brother stood there half-slouched and stupid. I ignored him. I watched instead the new self-consciousness in Baby's body as she walked away—or did I imagine it?—leaning her weight forward, scraping and sledding her suitcase across the street.

'I never want to see you again,' my brother abruptly shouted into the night. 'Take your stuff and get out of here!'

With a wicked smile she turned in our direction. 'I'm never coming back!' she called out. She heaved the suitcase into the boot and slammed it shut.

Something occurs to me from my childhood I haven't thought about for years. After a particularly nasty beating, if I swore to tell our parents—and his bribes and proofs of contrition weren't enough to dissuade me—my brother would threaten to run away. How strange that I now remember this with something like nostalgia. He would stalk to the closet and take out a suitcase and then he'd start packing it, leaving me mute-stricken as I tagged helplessly and furiously behind him, horrified by the thought of being responsible for his loss—and, far more deeply, of losing him. I'd break, of course, and agree to anything if only he agreed to stay. Was this what it was to love somebody? I guessed it had to be.

A few weeks after my brother's open-air tryst with Baby, we received word that the Ngo brothers had been ambushed at the casino. The crew from that nightclub fight was responsible; they'd driven all the way in, we later learned, from Sunshine. The youngest Ngo, Peter, had had two of his ribs broken with a cricket bat. They'd been out with the Footscray crew from the same fight—the one with Baby's red-capped ex—with whom they'd since become mates. Straight away there was talk of revenge, and soon enough there was another fight, at another Asian night, when Red Cap recognised one of the Sunshine boys. This time, knives were produced, and two people cut.

To Thuan and me, none of this, in itself, seemed critical. These fights happened all the time without ever reaching the hospitals, let alone the courts or headlines. The Ngos were known hot-heads.

And everyone accepted that the club scene was booby-trapped with grudges and grievances, blood ties and vendettas and bonds of blind loyalty. Asian nights had been banned in Sydney for exactly this reason. The shock of what followed in this case lay mostly in the speed and savagery of its escalation. Afterwards, there was a fair bit of carry-on about who could have done what, when, to whom, to excite such action—but I'll confess that, as irrational and unfair as it may sound, and though it can't really be said to have presaged anything, as soon as Baby looked up that cool night, and commanded my eye, and showed me how dangerous her desire was, how matter-of-fact her recklessness, I knew right then I could no longer be shocked by anything that touched her.

For Thuan it was already too late. First, it emerged that she'd been in contact with Red Cap, her ex, all along—that in fact he was her on-again off-again dealer. I saw my brother's face when he found out, felt the shock and deep retreat as though it were my own. He broke it off with her. She contacted me and pleaded her innocence. She was crying, and had never looked more beautiful. It was over, she said; she'd been clean the whole time, she said, and, still believing her, I passed it on. They reconciled. I was wracked with strong ambivalence seeing, even momentarily, my brother so vulnerable. A week later, a friend of mine spotted Baby in Sunshine with her other ex—the one who'd picked the first fight with my brother. I confronted her. At first she denied it, then she stopped short. It was impossible to go anywhere within a Vietnamese enclave without being marked—she understood that.

'Okay,' she sighed. 'I went there.'

I didn't say anything.

'I heard—' She paused, reconsidered. 'Him and his mates are planning an attack. A big one.'

'On who?'

'Johnny. My ex. And all the rest of his friends. Your friends too—the brothers.'

We were in her car, on our way to pick Thuan up from somewhere, and she spoke straight ahead, into the busy windscreen.

'You know this? You gotta tell them.'

'I *don't* know.' She frowned, chewed at her lower lip. 'I know him. He just wants to be the big man. That's all it was, I just went there to ask him to stop all this.'

'What'd he say?'

She glanced over at me, and there was a small, strange crease around her eyes I hadn't seen before.

'He said he'd think about it.'

'Okay.'

She drove on a while, then, as though resolving some internal question, she swung her head from side to side. 'Big T, he wanted me to beg.'

All my life I've been told I'm not very good at reading people. There is, I think, some truth to this. Baby, in particular, was so changeable that any attempt would usually be offside and out of step. But in that moment, I was inspired by an intense insight to say nothing, to sit still and let her ravelled thinking tease itself out. In my concentration my face must have lapsed into a frown.

She looked over, cringed slightly. 'I guess you already know,' she murmured. 'I don't know what to do.'

'Do you wanna pull over? Talk about this?'

'I would *love* that.'

She pulled into a petrol station and parked by the air pump. Again, I waited for her to speak.

'You're sweet,' she said nervously. She tilted the rear-view mirror down and checked her face. Then she told me how, when she'd gone back to plead with her ex, one thing had led to another. Not like that. But she still wasn't sure how it had happened.

'What happened?'

She paused. 'I don't want your brother to think I'm a slut.' Her voice was small but quickly hardening. 'That's what he called me last time.'

We sat in silence as the car ticked. Slut. The word led me to the image of her bent over a wobbling suitcase, pants scrunched down to her knees. Sand and salt on her wet skin. The lie of the bikini on her body.

'Yeah, but you did fuck him, didn't you?' I could feel my heart throttling my ribs as I thought this, and then, unbelievably—as I said it. Now the new word—the new image it called up—landed heavy and wet between us.

Baby jutted out her jaw. She jerked her head in my direction but didn't look at me. 'You can't . . . Look, it's not like I'm going out with *you*.'

'Right.'

'You can't talk to me like that.'

'Right. It's not like he's my brother. Like the last time you fucked around, who was it that patched everything up for you?'

She inhaled sharply. She said, 'I screwed up.' Then she turned to me, her face gone cunning. 'But what's the deal with you two anyway. What sort of fucked-up thing is that?' Her skin was clenched tight around the eyes, her jaw muscles working her thoughts. 'I don't even know why he lets you follow him around. Almost like he's scared of you or something. Like you've got something on him—the way you've got something on me—'cos that's what you do, right, Big T? Spy on everyone? Get all the dirt?'

As she spoke, the space inside the hatchback seemed to shrink. It was as though everything real, dimensional, was happening here, inside, while the windows were actually screens broadcasting a program of outside movement and colour. In this enclosure I became acutely aware of her smell—sweat from where her body had kneaded the seat, the chemical tang of her shampoo.

Without thinking I reached for her.

She flinched. 'I'm sorry,' she coughed, then, somewhat unsteadily, she undid her seatbelt, leaned forward, and peeled her cardigan off. I realised her cheeks were wet. I didn't know what I wanted. 'Sorry,' she repeated, and offered both her bare arms to me. She was sobbing now, quietly. And then I saw what it was she was trying to show me. The two dark mottled bands around her wrist, and two more around her biceps. The bruises yellow and orange and green, and myself enraptured and repulsed by them. The rot and ripe of them. Most strangely, I felt myself powerfully flushed with a sense that I only much later recognised—and ultimately accepted—as betrayal.

I told my brother a friend had seen her go into the ex's house. I told him to ask her himself. I told him—thinking he'd be happy to hear it—that this ex was gearing up for a major attack against the Footscray crew. I told him my source was unimpeachable.

•

The day, finally, is cooling down when Thuan returns. He catches me half-naked in the kitchen. 'I've washed up in plenty of kitchen sinks,' he assures me. He's carrying a slab of Carlton Bitter under one arm and holding a supermarket bag in the other. 'Meat,' he explains, 'for the barbie.'

'Where'd you go?'

He ignores me, sets the bag down, rips a couple of cans out of their tight plastic trap. When he throws me a beer I realise it's exactly what I feel like. The rest of the cans he tips into an esky. By silent consensus we head outside and sit on the deck. Through the gums and melaleucas, the thick pelt of scrub and sedge along its banks, the river is light brown, slow, milky. This river that famously flows upside down. The day's heat hangs in the air but is no longer suffocating. The brightness no longer angry. We finish the beers, and then the next ones, and the next. I hadn't realised how thirsty I was. He tells me he walked along the river, up to the falls. He saw kayakers there, rehearsing their moves, and uni students doing water tests. I picture the concrete-capped, rubbish-choked weir, the graffitied basalt boulders, all dominated by the Eastern Freeway roaring overhead. I wonder whether it brought to his mind another river—the same river—running beside and below a different freeway. I wonder whether, when he stares out at this river now, he connects it to that other river a few kays dead south of here; if he follows it, in his mind's eye, through its windings and loops, through Collingwood, and Abbotsford, and Richmond, and Burnley—to South Yarra.

He throws me another beer. The barbeque is all but forgotten. I'm getting a bit dreamy with alcohol, my mind draggling in the heat.

'So what's going on with you anyway?'

'What?' I say, even though I heard him. I have no idea why I said this. I start to audition sentences to make my answer over but this only affirms the silence. My brother snorts, then hoists his drink in a wry toast. I skol my can, stand up and torpedo it into the bush. I'll pick it up later. A pair of rowers glance at us from the river and wave.

'Jesus,' my brother says, 'I really screwed her up.'

'Nothing you could have done. She was on edge the whole time.' After my last chance, I'm now eager to speak. 'Probably junk too. And those friends of hers—in Footscray.'

'What?' His brow creases. 'Nah, I meant Mum.' He looks at me curiously for a second, then scoffs at himself. 'Though her too, I guess.'

I recall a story Baby told me during her last visit, how a friend of hers in detention had collapsed from withdrawal; the male guards had grabbed her, double-cuffed her, stuck a motorbike helmet on her head for two days so she couldn't 'hurt herself'.

'Mum still going up to that temple?'

He'd come back from jail and I'd fantasised about receiving his confidences. He'd copped the time for both of us—knowing, surely, that I would've done the same. But he hadn't grown more open at all. Nor the couple of other times he'd visited. Only this time seemed different. This was the most communicative I'd ever seen him.

'In Sunshine? I think so.' He doesn't react, so I go on, 'I think once she ran into one of the families there. I heard one of them spat in her face.'

He nods absently. 'And you? You okay?'

The directness of his question stuns me. I saunter my arm out along the view. 'What's not to be okay about?'

'Listen,' he says. 'Can I ask you something?'

'What?'

'That stuff Mum said about you doing talks.'

'It's nothing. Just uni stuff.' I feel myself smirking. 'They just need someone with slanty eyes who can speak in their language.'

'What sort of stuff do you say?'

'You know—just whatever they wanna hear.'

'Like what?'

'Like poverty, or language issues. Cultural marginalisation . . .'

'They don't ask about what happened that night?'

'You mean do I talk about you.'

He shakes his head impatiently. He's working himself up to something and it puts me on edge. 'I mean, don't they ask why? Why I did it? I mean, isn't all the rest of it bullshit?'

'Why *we* did it. I was there too.'

'Yeah,' he says, visibly annoyed at having been interrupted. 'You're right. I forget. I'm sorry.' I wait for him to go on but now I've mucked up his thinking. 'It's all bullshit,' he says again, struggling to recall his argument, and out of some old fraternal deference I find myself looking away. I listen to the frogs gulping for air down by the rushes. The black ducks and reed warblers. My heart is beating harder and harder. I know, of course, what he's referring to—it's the same thing that brings him here each time, then each time strikes him silent: the mind-boggling bullshit of *me*, years on, still with nothing but time, still cashing in, ever more deeply, on *his* time. Those twelve bullshit years piled on the back of a single night's spur of the moment. That night, too, I'd felt the same sick, heady exhilaration talking to him like this—like we were friends.

'You're shaking,' he had pointed out. We'd made it home and both showered; he'd scrubbed his face, I noticed, until it was bright pink. The corners of his temple lined with delicate blue veins.

'I can't piss. My bladder feels heavy as, but nothing comes out.'

He frowned, then reached out and clutched my neck with one of his strong pink hands. I knew the strength of those hands. My stomach hitched. He didn't say anything, and at the physical contact I was shuddered back to our surreal, silent trip in the car; the fog descending upon the freeway canyons, the red blinking lights of radio towers blooming like blood corollas in the mist. The streets had sucked us through the city and shot us home.

'If they come for us,' my brother had said to me.

'No one saw us.'

'You weren't there. If they come for us, you weren't there.'

'Hai and Long and Quang saw me.'

'No they didn't. I'll talk to them.'

'What about you?'

'No matter what they say—so-and-so saw you, so-and-so ratted you out. Don't listen to them. You weren't there.'

'What about you?'

He patted my neck, then removed his hand. The absence was a freezing burn. He was my rough flesh, he was rooted in the same soil, his heart and brain fed by the same blood, and never before had I felt so needful of him. He stood up and abruptly grimaced, clutching his right knee. Then his face smoothed over again. 'I don't think anyone who saw me will talk,' he said. 'But it shouldn't take them long. To find out about the Ngos. And then me.'

'You mean Baby?'

He nodded, then let out a short burst of air.

'What?'

'I'm not saying she'll talk,' he said.

'She's the one who called me.'

To this day I still remember how, when I told him this, he'd shaken his head and smiled. 'I know,' he'd said, as though unexpectedly amused. 'I know,' he said. 'Everything always goes back to Baby.' Now it is summer, my brother sits with me on the deck of my own house and his face, sweaty and cooked well past pink, confirms itself in that same expression—bemused, sardonic, slightly otherwise occupied.

'Listen to me,' he says. 'I'm glad you didn't have to go down with me.' His tone is flat with finality. 'That was the best thing that happened this whole mess.'

'Okay.'

'That was the opposite of bullshit.'

'I'm sorry.'

He waves it off. The light is dimming now and he turns away, but not before I catch a brief tensile movement in his expression. There's a discipline holding his face together. I'm horrified by the sudden realisation that maybe he's lying to me. 'But see,' he goes on, 'what I mean is this. I was there, you were there. I don't remember hardly anything. I was off my head but still.' He pauses, perhaps suspicious of his own earnestness. Neither of us looks at the other. 'Haven't you tried to think about it, why we did it, and you can't tell what's what?'

I decide, in the brief silence that follows, that he's not actully asking me this question.

'What happened,' he goes on, 'and what everyone else says that happened?'

My face has reverted to its little-brother mask—imploring his censure and contempt, his instruction.

'You'd think you'd remember everything.'

I nod. I approximate a wry sound. Then I venture, 'I do. I do remember.'

He stops to absorb this. Then slowly, and to my great relief, his face slides back into its ironic smile. 'Well, you have to. Otherwise, who's gonna give those bloody speeches?'

•

That night. I'd been at a different club. They'd all gone to Jade—an Asian night—and I hated Asian nights. Too many try-hards, too much attitude. I was in the toilets when I got the call. There was a guy next to me pissing with both hands in his pockets. It was one of the most intimidating things I'd ever seen. I was pretty buzzed by that time, and when I answered the phone, Baby's tinny laughing was of a piece with the cackling going on and off in one of the stalls, and then—out in the club—the DJ's chop to a bass-heavy loop, the dewy, overripe smell of teenage girls. I found a quieter corner so I could hear her.

'Swords!' she was saying. Then I realised she wasn't laughing. 'They've got fucking swords!'

Outside, it was drizzling. I ran down the road, past the shawled girls with clopping heels, the corners and culverts reeking of piss, the darkened power poles specked with staples. Overhead, wet telephone wires gleamed completely gold in the streetlight, like charged filaments, even though my mind insisted on them as black, sheathed in black plastic. I reached the car, which I'd parked at a defunct petrol station—now just a low, flat broken roof spewing water onto the oil-stained concrete. As soon as I stopped running, I vomited. I got in the car and caught my breath. I called Baby. She didn't answer. I called my brother.

'Fuck,' he panted. 'Fucking fuck.'

'What happened? Where are you?'

He was running, his breath loud and jagged. The wind took his voice. There was no time to explain. He told me where to pick him up, down near the river. It was only a few minutes away. I arrived at the corner of Church and Alexandra. Across the road from the brightly lit car dealership, human shapes were scampering in every direction. They were all guys, all Asians—some carrying glinting weapons and cudgels. I thought I saw one pull down the beak of his baseball cap over his eyes. Not daring to stop, I slowed the car as I passed, made out what looked like a small pile of dirty clothes on the nature strip. Then I saw, pale and inverted, the telltale hand. There was no blood. The head must have been concealed by a piece of flapping fabric, or maybe the ground fell away. There was nothing to indicate a body that had been smashed and stabbed to bits, but even then I knew that was what I was looking at, and the knowledge rocked in my skull, riled up my blood.

I drove on a bit further and parked on the grassy shoulder, making sure to turn off the engine and lights. I took out my phone, my hands trembling, saw three missed calls from Baby. I tried her again but again no one answered. Then the phone rang. My brother. Where was I? I told him what I'd seen, we had to get the fuck out of there. Not yet. Where was I? Okay, I should meet him on the other side of the bridge. When? Now. Right now.

I got out of the car. The wind had picked up, gusting sideways on my face. I spat and could see my slag sail forever. Behind me the faux-gothic columns of Melbourne High School were upwardly lit. I crossed the road to the riverbank and ran along the bike path, under bare tree boughs creaking and contending in the wind. Some distance ahead of me, windows in condominium buildings glowed in what seemed secret patterns. I ran into the wind. A car bore down on me, its headlights tunnelling through the thickening fog, changing the shape of the road. It passed in a vicious swipe of noise. By the time

I reached the body, which had been strangely left unattended, a veneer had been ripped away within me, an innate excuse brought full-blooded to life. I crossed the bridge.

My brother was three-quarters across. He wore an open-necked shirt as though it wasn't the heart of winter, and leaned against a lamp-lit column as though bored, as though waiting for a late tram. As soon as I reached him he spun around without a word and sprinted down some white-glowing stairs that led to the north bank of the river. There was another track down there, squeezed between the Monash Freeway on one side and the river on the other.

I can't tell you what it felt like, racing through the cold night with my brother. On our right the concrete-and-plastic freeway barricade flickering our progress, on our left the river, and beneath us the paved path springing our feet forward and fast. The wind kicking at our backs. At no point did I second guess what we were doing. I spent my life waiting for him to talk me into something and now the wash of adrenaline through my veins urged me on, faster and faster, as though to chase down, catch my own breath. A voice floated across the river. My brother slowed down, then stopped. His face haggard with exertion but steely, the set of his jaw exuberant.

I turned, breathing heavily, towards the voice. Under the high moon, the river was a trough of light and it was difficult to see behind it. Then I saw. There were two black shapes in the shine. In the darkness opposite there were three more shapes. I soon recognised their voices—the three elder Ngos. They spat and swore into the river.

'Who are they?' I asked, pointing to the two black heads bobbing next to each other. 'Is that Baby's ex?'

Thuan nodded. 'And his brother.'

The two of them seemed to roll and ride over each other on the same spot of river. Every now and then an arm would flail up. Their occasional cries made no sense.

'They're pissed as,' I said.

'Swim over here,' Hai sang out. 'I dare you, come on.'

'Jesus,' I said. 'He's got a fucking samurai sword.'

Instinctively I turned to Thuan and saw, for the first time, his fist gripping a meat cleaver. Looking more closely, I noticed his pants gashed above one knee. His sock beneath that knee was discoloured by blood; on his other foot the sock was white. My lungs filled with air.

'Please,' one of the swimmers beseeched. His voice was low and shaky.

Then, as though they'd just made us out, the two of them began to splash their way towards our bank. My brother looked on impassively. A mist was beginning to settle over the water and the faster swimmer sidestroked awkwardly beneath it.

'That's him,' my brother murmured.

The swimmer came closer. His mouth was wild above and below the water, his eyes blinking non-stop. Vapour sputtering from between his teeth.

'Please,' he croaked.

I watched my brother for weakness.

'He can't swim. My brother can't swim.'

'Don't come any closer,' Thuan said. 'You had your chance.'

'Fuck him up,' Hai shouted from the other bank.

'What chance? Oh God. Oh God, oh God, oh fuck.'

The icy water weighted his clothes, forcing him to kick hard to stay afloat. Behind him, his brother moved more erratically. I could hear him hyperventilating loudly.

'Please,' Baby's ex said. 'Please, he can't swim. He's got asthma. Please, it's enough.'

My brother shook his head.

'She's not worth it, man. Oh God.'

My brother looked at him again, paying new attention. He murmured, 'You don't talk about Baby.'

Baby's ex started moaning. He swallowed some water, thrashed around for a moment. Then, lifting his face and staring directly at us, he kicked in our direction, desperately dragging his body to one of the beams supporting the walking path. He clutched the edge, then tried to lift himself up, his eyes wild and goggly. As soon as I saw him close up—the thick, straight hair, the snub face and buck teeth—I knew him, and I knew that I hated him. Jeers and catcalls wafted over through the mist. Thuan kicked at him but Baby's ex grabbed his ankle. My brother tried to stomp him with his other leg but it was the injured one, and Baby's ex clung on fiercely, fixedly. Hopping in a weird dance, my brother took a handful of his wet hair in one hand, raised the meat cleaver in the other. He looked at it. Then he looked at me and there was an odd new uncertainty in his expression. I drank in that look. It fed my heart roar, my blood rapids. I was filled with strange rage and I wanted to be as big as my feeling. I accepted the meat cleaver from my brother's outstretched hand, fell down in a swift crouch, the ground rearing up at my shins, and felt my arm go back and then forward, the blade biting into the wet jacket, and when Baby's ex released my brother's foot and hung on to the path's edge, I worked the blade at his fingers until they too let go.

They drifted, in a weakening, wordless flurry, back out to the middle of the river. At one point the river raised the legs of the brother, and he lay on his back, head bent forward, looking at the evidence of his body as though in disbelief. To this day people wonder why they didn't swim a few more metres to the west, where they might easily have held onto a leg or abutment of the railway bridge. Or back eastward, to the Church Street bridge. Further east yet, they could have struck out for Herring Island, accessible only by water, and made sanctuary there. As it happened, they stayed in the deep middle of the Yarra. They were drunk, injured, freezing, one asthmatic and unable to swim, and after some desperate horseplay and muffled splashing their eyes went loose and their bodies calm, as though their feet had finally found a shelf in the water, and then they sank, their bodies spinning in slow dark minutes of motion, and they did not re-emerge until two days later when the police divers dragged them out.

My brother bent down at the path's edge. The new silence rendered the brothers' moments-ago breathing clotted and monstrous in its memory. Thuan took off his shoes, dipped them into the slow-moving river, then took them out and wrung the blood and water out of them. He dipped them in, took them out, and wrung them again. Our shoulders touched and pushed off each other as we ran back to the car.

•

'What else do you say?'

'I talk about revenge. Honour. Loyalty and betrayal.'

'That's all bullshit too.'

'Not to me it isn't.'

'Wouldn't you rather just forget everything?'

'I wouldn't change a thing.'

'More bullshit. This is what you want? This life?'

'I'd do it again.'

'Why?'

'For you. Because you couldn't. Because you wanted to.'

'I didn't know what I wanted. It was stupid. Jesus, it's easy for you to say.'

'No it's not.'

'You didn't cop the twelve years.'

'That's why you came back?'

'No.'

'To rub that in my face?'

'No.'

'Sorry.'

'Actually.'

'I would've done that, I would've copped it.'

'Actually, I came back to ask for your forgiveness.'

'What?'

'You heard me.'

'You don't have to. I told you I'd do it again.'

'That's what I mean. I'm sorry I made you that way.'

•

The next morning he was gone. In hot February my brother came back to me, and stayed for only two nights and one day. I haven't seen him since. My life, such as it is, I owe to him. If guilt is for what you've done and shame for who you are, then how could I feel shame? I was a brother, and my brother's brother. Forget, he tells me, but does he taste them in his tapwater, the savour of their hair and skin in his herbs? They too were brothers. Melbourne's in drought. The city a plain of dust and fire. The river hasn't water enough to wash the foreign matter out.

I have my work, and my garden, my mother in her glassy loneliness to attend. I have my mornings. Who knows if he'll come back? I have my dreams, too, which have come to seem coextensive with my memories. My sleep is shallow, and my dreams never seem to go all the way down. I step out of my night window and the river wipes the field before me, a smear of silver noise, the great fishes climbing the water by the plate-glass glint of their eyes, in their indigo and orange glows, mastering the dark. I am underneath, plunging as the grey scrim of surface blackens above me. Breathe, lungs, and let me time. We live our lives atop the body of emotion of which we're capable. I follow my dim thought-embryos, I see by my feeling, I sink with my words, for words are shadow, and shadow cannot explain light.

Where've you been.

You started a thought and you could end up anywhere. Like watching a fire: its false grabs and reachings, its licks and twists, you stared into the guts of it and came out in the nightlight glow of a shared childhood room, the cheap groan of a bunk bed, you're awake and listening to the breath snagging in your brother's nostrils, the low whistle of his open-mouthed sleep, the insideness of his life and its promise of protection from the harmful world outside.

Where've you been. You're late.

He's dragging a suitcase into the street. He makes it all the way out of the driveway, to the cherry tree, before I stop him. The air is full of pollen and sunscreen. He emerges from the concrete tunnel with a rueful smile on his face. He's bent over me on the couch—he rooted in his terrible motion and I in him.

I'm sorry I'm sorry I'm sorry.

I bite the red cushion. I feel his ribs on my ribs. My body an anvil and he's beating something upon it, shaping it into a truer shape, seeking to prove it, the strength, the ductility, the temper of his love.

ONE GOOD THING

Paddy O'Reilly

'If you were my sister,' I asked Klara Fuchs, 'do you think we'd still be best friends?'

'Oh, Natalie, of course we would,' she said, and I believed her.

We were in love, the way that primary school girls fall in love with each other. When I look back now I realise that Klara was thin and brittle like a bunch of sticks held together with cloth. But at that time I thought she was perfect. She wore bright striped dresses that her mother had made, and matching single-colour cardigans. She wore long white socks every day. She smelled different to everyone else, sour and spicy like an exotic fruit. The first night I had tea at her house and they served me sauerkraut I recognised the smell. Sometimes, in school, we held hands under the desk. I remember the sensation of her hot sticky fingers entwined in mine.

I was an only child. Klara had a sister and a brother. Her sister was nine years older than us, almost an adult. She only ever spoke to us to point out how annoying we were. Klara's brother, Dieter, was thirteen. As much as I wished Klara was my sister and could live with me at my house, I wished Dieter was not her brother and that I had never met him.

If Dieter found a drawing we had done, he ripped it up. If he caught us playing in the mud, he smeared the mud over our faces. At the swimming pool, he tried to hold us under. He might always be around a corner, so we had to speak softly. He might find the spell we had written to ward him off, so we ate the paper.

When I sat opposite him at the dinner table, smiling politely as I tried to chew my serve of sour cabbage and meaty sausage, Dieter watched me. He stared until my throat tightened and I couldn't swallow. He seemed to hate me for no other reason than the fact I was sitting opposite him at the dining table and had caught his eye. Klara sat next to me, hardly letting anything pass her lips, as if Dieter was controlling her food intake. She carried herself in a hunch, and she shivered easily. The temperature only had to be slightly cool and Klara would start shivering. Or if her brother was nearby. Then she shivered too.

The times Dieter was around were the only times I wondered if I could keep on being Klara's best friend.

One Sunday Klara's mother and father took us on a trip to the Caribbean Gardens in a suburb a long drive away. Klara, me, Dieter and his friend from school. Fibreglass statues of animals rose out of dry garden beds like we were in a museum, and the sun beat down over acres of brown dirt and colourless rides and stalls selling hot jam doughnuts and sausages in batter. The parents set up at a picnic table with a tablecloth. They brought baskets out of the car boot filled with bottles of beer for them and cordial for us, parcels of meat in pastry and thick, heavy cake smelling of honey. At the table Klara's father shook out a newspaper and held it in front of his face. Her mother stripped down to a pair of bathers, laid her towel on the dirt and settled down with a book and a sunhat.

'Why don't you go for a swim?' she said to us, nodding in the direction of the Caribbean lake, a large body of muddy water a few hundred yards away. A paddle-steamer ploughed through the water on the far side. Klara and I wandered around the statues of elephants and giraffes and crocodiles. Further along the shore a replica submarine rose out of the dust like a grey dinosaur. Dieter was on the deck trying to climb the periscope. Klara saw what I was looking at and she took hold of my hand and tugged me in the opposite direction.

'Let's play over there,' she said, pointing at a bare patch of earth further along the shore. I followed her and she picked up a big stick and started sketching something out on the ground.

'What are we playing?' I said.

Klara looked over my shoulder and whispered, 'Nothing.' She dropped the stick. She whispered again, 'Let's go and play over there,' and she pointed even further away, out into the field where even her parents couldn't see us.

'Are we allowed to go that far?' I asked. My parents would never let me wander that far. I glanced behind and saw Dieter coming towards us with his friend, red-faced and crying, staggering behind him.

'Okay,' I said to Klara and we started to walk quickly away.

'Hey,' Dieter shouted.

We bolted like startled deer, running till our breath was ragged and our chests sore. We ran past cages of monkeys and stands of poplar trees and enclosures of emus standing in the sun until finally Dieter gave up following us and we found ourselves in a small forest somewhere in the back of the Caribbean Gardens and we sat on the ground, cool earth covered in a dry carpet of leaves, and I felt as if I had travelled through some barrier to reach a place in another time or another dimension.

I had seen the trees as we ran towards them, a copse of trees next to a big shed made of corrugated iron. But now we were in the copse the trees seemed huge. I lay back on the fragrant eucalyptus leaves and looked up through the branches at the distant pale sky.

'Have we lost him?' Klara gasped, almost sobbing, trying to get breath into her skinny body. 'Is he behind us?'

I sat up. 'I can't see him,' I said.

She was doubled over, still sucking in air.

'He doesn't seem to be here,' I said. But that didn't mean he wasn't there.

•

He was there one day at their house when I rounded the corner, looking for Klara. He and another friend of his. His friends were always small boys, while he was big, solid, fleshy. His small friend was holding a dartboard and Dieter had a dart in his hand. They were in shorts, both of them bare-chested. I wore a pink spotted dress and my best sandals because Klara and I were going to practise walking with books on our heads.

I never saw the dart leave Dieter's hand, never saw it fly through the air. When the tip of the dart flew straight into the boy's chest, above the left nipple, and hung there, I was as silent and astonished as they were. We all stared at the dart standing straight out from the boy's chest as if it had hit a tree trunk or a pole. Four feathers, vanes quivering. A brass collar holding the dart tip to the shaft.

A drop of blood welled from the point where the dart had penetrated the boy's chest and dribbled down towards the dartboard he was still holding flat against his belly. When Dieter let out a sharp bark, a laugh of sorts, his friend's eyes widened as though he had only just realised that this dart was embedded in his own chest, and he shrieked. Long and high like a rabbit.

Dieter won't like that, I thought, my stomach starting to spin. The shriek went on and on. Dieter's mother came pelting out of the house. Klara's narrow frightened face appeared at her bedroom window.

'He moved,' Dieter called to his mother as she flew past. 'He shouldn't have moved.'

When she reached the boy, Dieter's mother took hold of the dartboard he was still pressing against himself like a target and flung it to the ground. The boy kept staring at the missile standing out from his breastbone. He pushed Klara's mother backwards when she reached for the dart. His mouth was wide open but no more sound came out. She stepped forward, grasped the dart, pulled, then covered the place it had come from with her hand.

A few weeks later I came to Klara's house and the boy was there with Dieter again. They were tying red crackers together and lighting the fuse before they threw the bundle into an empty oil drum in the vacant lot beside the house. The crackers hammered around the drum like a machine-gun. Dieter laughed and laughed, and the boy with a hole in his breastbone stood behind him and giggled, glancing around nervously as though the danger might come from somewhere else, not right in front of him.

'Go and get the catherine-wheels,' Dieter said.

'Okay,' the boy answered breathlessly, and as he raced past me to the house I wondered how Dieter could keep these people coming back.

•

When Klara and I were eleven, her family moved to a small farm in the country. The next summer holiday I went to spend a week at their new place. They lived in a fibro house. The property ended on the boundary of a flat scrubby national park. In the heat of the day Klara and I walked through the straggly bush and sat with our legs dangling in the creek. Or we lounged on her bed in her bedroom, batting away mosquitoes in the dense air and slurping fast-melting blocks of flavoured ice.

Klara sat with her arms wrapped around her legs, her chin resting on her knees. Sometimes she held her pillow like a shield pulled tight against her shins. She was so thin and could make herself so small that the pillow almost hid her from my view when I lay on the other end of the bed. When she was hidden away like that, she told me some of the dark thoughts that occupied her mind.

'I picture myself dead. Like I'm dreaming, it's so clear. My body lying bleeding on the floor, my head smashed in. My stomach split open like a supermarket bag. Do you ever have those dreams?'

'No,' I answered.

'Dieter will kill me one day. I'm sure of it.'

She turned the jam biscuit she had been holding for fifteen minutes around and around in the palm of her hand and finally took a tiny bite of the jam that had oozed out of the side of the biscuit. A red spot stuck to the corner of her mouth.

'I think he's insane,' she said.

Since she'd moved away Klara had sent me notes and cards. We'd talked on the phone but she had never mentioned Dieter.

'I haven't thought about your horrible brother all year,' I replied. 'Where is he?'

'He's been staying at a friend's place. He's back tonight. I don't want to see him. I don't want him to live here,' she whispered.

'Neither would I.'

We were silent for a moment. I picked at a mosquito bite on my shin and from the crater a trickle of thin red blood emerged. I blotted it with my hankie.

That evening Dieter arrived. The car dropping him off pulled up so fast at the front of the house that pebbles from the driveway flew up and pinged against the lounge room window. The car door slammed and the car backed away, tyres spinning and crunching on the gravel.

'Let's go to my room,' Klara said hurriedly. She took my hand and pulled me out of the lounge room and along the hall to her room. Behind us, the front door opened and a gust of fiery dusk wind burned down the hallway.

On my last day at their house I woke late. I was sleeping on a mattress on the floor of Klara's room. The night before, we had set the alarm to twelve for a secret midnight feast of chips and chocolate we'd been hoarding all week. Everything tasted extra salty and extra sweet by torchlight. We stifled our laughter by pressing the sheets against our mouths and fell asleep again at two.

'I think she's in the shed, darling,' her mother said when I came into the kitchen after my shower, so I skipped to the shed and pushed open the big door. Dieter and Klara were both inside in the gloom.

'Hi,' I said, still unable to see properly in the dim light. 'What's happening?'

Dieter giggled his high, unnatural giggle. My stomach leapt inside my ribcage and my skin prickled. As my eyes became accustomed to the dim light, I saw Klara standing against the wall, her arms held out horizontally, her face turned away from Dieter, who was standing a few metres back from the wall. Below her hemline Klara's legs were glistening and there was a puddle in the dust at her feet.

'Ready?' Dieter cried, and he giggled again.

Klara pressed her face harder against the wall as Dieter drew back his arm then flung a knife in her direction. The knife thudded into the wall above her left arm before clattering to the floor. Another was embedded in the wall near her face.

I tried to scream but no sound came out. Dieter was staring at me and giggling with such hysteria that he sounded like a neighing horse. I ran towards him and shoved as hard as I could, and he lurched backwards, dropping his handful of mismatched kitchen knives on the dirt floor. His laughter stopped. Instead, I could hear the furious rasping of his breath. He grabbed my arms and forced me back until I slammed into the shed door and it swung shut. The only light came in through the green translucent sheeting on the roof. Dieter's face above mine shone green like his eyes. Even his teeth, bared in a crazy grin, looked pale green. He forced me to the floor and started to pull at my jeans.

'Klara.' My voice came out like a long, high sigh.

Dieter pressed his forearm on my throat and leaned down hard while he wrestled with my jeans with his other hand. I was choking. I punched him with my fists until he slapped my face so hard I thought my head would fly off my body. As I lay stunned with my cheek against the dirt floor, he rocked back onto his heels. He took hold of my jeans and wrenched them off, dragging my sandals along with them. Then he pulled open his own jeans. Now I screamed. His hand came down so fast to cover my mouth that only a peep escaped.

He was too strong for me. I tried to throw myself to the side, but with one hand still over my mouth he caught my wrists and pinned them to the ground above my head. He used his knees to prise apart my thighs and he pushed and pushed until something broke and he was inside me. The pain split me in two. His green face was inches away from mine, sweaty and grimacing. His teeth, still bared, were tipped with foamy saliva like a dog's fangs.

As everything slowed down in my mind I rolled my eyes from side to side, trying to escape the face leering above me. When my eyes reached their lowest point of vision I saw Klara's corduroy sneakers. I looked up. She stood, with her arms hanging at her side, watching. She was watching me, my face, and she stared and stared and I stared back, our eyes locked, expressionless, as Dieter pounded into me, grunting and panting. Finally he shrieked and let go of my mouth and my hands. He pushed himself off me, stood up and walked out of the shed, doing up his jeans. The shed door stayed open a crack and suddenly nothing was green anymore, just dull grey, back to dull grey.

Klara stood above me and held out her hand to help me up, but I turned my face away from her.

'Go away,' I whispered, the tears starting. Pain in my face, my throat, between my legs, my wrists. Moisture dribbling from inside me onto the dirt floor. I felt the cold on my bare thighs, the goosebumps rising, the hairs standing on end.

Klara moved slowly to the door of the shed. She hesitated there, her hand curled around the edge of the door.

'Get out,' I whispered. My throat seemed to have closed. Words could barely escape.

She waited a few seconds more. Then she pulled open the shed door and the light savaged my naked skin.

'If you tell,' Klara said in a scratchy voice like an old vinyl record, 'he'll kill me. You know he will.' She pulled the door shut behind her.

•

Twenty years later that scratchy voice spoke behind me.

'There are seats at that table.'

A slim hand beside me pointed to a bench seat at my table which was littered with chip packets and a dozen glasses—half-empty, ringed with dried foam, lipsticked and smeared with greasy fingerprints—from the crowd that had headed out to the beer garden. The funeral was over. Everyone had moved on to the informal wake at the pub where the drinking and shouting was getting harder and louder.

'Natalie?' the voice said into my ear. Her fingers touched my wrist, light as fairy dust, and twenty years vanished. I was flung back to the days of Klara, the hot sunshine and tickly grass, our special jokes and the purse full of lucky white stones we collected from each corner of the playground, chanting as we went.

When I turned I half expected to see the old Klara, her earnest eyes gazing into mine, reedy brown hair wound into the tight plaits that boys at school felt compelled to twitch and pull at every opportunity. Instead there stood a woman with a blonde bob and smooth made-up skin. She shook her head and the hair followed in a perfect feathery swing.

'What are you doing here?' I said.

My chair rocked on its wobbly legs. Klara gave me some answer about a connection to my cousin's funeral as I tried to steady myself with my feet but found them jarring against the stubby carpet. A waiter came to collect the glasses and litter from the table. Once he had left, glasses in a ladder up his arm, the surface was still tacky with spilled beer and wine so that the underside of my arm peeled away from the table's veneer like a strip of contact paper.

'Natalie and I were at primary school together,' Klara explained to her husband. 'But my family moved to the country and we lost touch.'

I stared at her.

'We used to be best friends,' Klara said.

'I came to visit you after you moved.' I had to raise my voice against the clamour of the mourners. My glass was empty. Acid biting into my gut.

'Did you? I'd forgotten,' she said, tilting her head, still alert and birdy. She leaned sideways so that her shoulder rested against her husband's chest. 'Natalie was one of the smart ones at school. She's probably a doctor now, or a lawyer or something.'

'I stayed at your house for a week.'

She shook her head as if this was unbelievable to her. 'I've got a terrible memory,' she said. 'Haven't I, darling?'

'You always remember where the credit card lives,' her husband answered.

'That's because you let it live in my purse,' she replied smartly and laughed.

Of course she couldn't be like the old Klara. It was a kind of relief. This was not Klara. This person wouldn't know the answer to the elephant riddle that used to make us laugh until we got a stitch. She wouldn't know anything about us, or what happened.

•

On that day when we were twelve I eventually made my way back to the house. As I stumbled through the hot dry kitchen Klara's mother asked me what had happened. 'I fell over,' I told her and she asked if I was hurt and I said no, just a bruise. 'Are you sure, sweetheart?' she asked me and I said yes, I was sure. She told me I should change my clothes and have another shower because I had dirt all down my back and in my hair and she didn't want my mother thinking they hadn't taken care of me. The hot water of the shower hurt me in every place. Afterwards I sat on the bed in Klara's bedroom, wet hair dripping onto the eiderdown, waiting for my mother to arrive and take me home. Klara came and sat beside me. I was too exhausted to push her away. Klara's mother put her head around the doorway and saw us sitting there side by side.

'Oh, you darling girls are like a pair of beautiful dolls,' she exclaimed.

Until that day I'd thought Klara was like a doll made of porcelain, that she was the one who would be easily broken.

•

'I'm going to get another drink,' I said to Klara and her husband.

I wouldn't come back to the table. I would pretend to fall into conversation with someone on the way to the bar, then slip away home to try and gather everything close again.

'I'll have a G and T. Give Natalie some money, darling.'

'No!' I said too loudly. I pushed myself out of my seat and rushed into the crowd of people roaring and jostling elbows around the serving counter. Once I was surrounded by other people, I began to feel better. At the bar I ordered a shot of whisky and downed it on the spot. Above me, the racks of glasses jittered in time with the jukebox bass. I ordered another whisky and moved further along the bar, out of Klara's line of vision, holding onto the counter with my fingers resting on its damp sticky towel because my legs were still shaking.

'Natalie!' A man in a grey suit with his tie loosened and his sleeves pushed up emerged from the crowd. He leaned across the bar and ordered himself a beer and me another whisky. He looked me up and down as if he was appraising my value, as if I was a piece of real estate.

'You're looking good,' he said. He rigged his sleeves higher up his arms. Rolled his neck before he picked up his beer and drained the glass. He knew I was a likely chance.

Klara and her husband were waiting at the other end of the room for me to reappear with a gin and tonic and amnesia. My cousin was burning to ash and bone in the crematorium. As the noise around me pulsed in shouts and raucous laughter I sucked in fast desperate breaths, giddy with the unreality of it all. The only reality was Klara, sitting at a table in that room. Klara wearing peach silk. Klara all grown up. I didn't want her to be Klara, but she was.

On my way back from the bar with a gin and tonic and another whisky, the muscles in my neck tingled and released. The third shot was fanning through my bloodstream.

'We thought you'd run off,' Klara said, glancing at her husband.

I raised my fourth shot to my lips and swallowed. 'Not this time. How is everyone, anyway?' My voice rode the hubbub, a punchy voice filled with green light and dust.

'We've left Rhiannon with a babysitter. We hate parents who take their children to every inappropriate event, don't we, Squidge?'

Squidge—who had been introduced as Lawrence—nodded. He was nursing the same glass of wine he had first brought to the table. Klara nestled up to him again. He smiled as she turned back to me and lifted her glass. The straw bobbed up and down in the fizzy tonic and she followed it with her pursed lips like a baby seeking a nipple. At last she caught the straw between her lips and I saw the old Klara for a moment, focused intently on her drink, frowning. I would have recognised her anywhere, but I was surprised she had recognised me—it was as if she left little Klara behind on that dusty property.

'I meant the people I knew. Your family.'

Her face rippled, almost imperceptibly. It was the second sign of the Klara who had been my best friend so many years ago. I used to see that deep quiver when Dieter walked by, or when we heard his voice from another room.

'Oh, Mum and Dad have moved to Queensland. Dieter's married. Has his own salon now. Helen's still nursing.' Her eyes blinked, empty, while her hand travelled around her husband's lap like an animal searching for somewhere to hide. 'What about your family? I can't remember—did you have any brothers or sisters?'

'Salon?' I said. Did Klara remember our pretend salon? How I lay on the bed while she smeared my face with yoghurt and stained my lips purple with the juice of a cherry.

'He's a barber. He likes to call his shop a salon.'

A laugh hacked out of my chest. 'They let him near people with a razor? Does he still throw knives? I hope he got better at it if he does.'

Klara and Squidge stared at me. Then Klara dropped her gaze. She picked up her purse and began sorting through its contents.

'Sorry?' Squidge said, speaking directly to me for the first time.

'Dieter loved to throw things at people. Sharp things. Didn't he, Klara?'

She pressed her lips together and shook her head slowly, looking down at the table. Her blonde hair flared in the light. Both her hands had disappeared inside her purse now.

'Did he? He was a terrible teenager, I suppose. I told you I had a shocking memory.' She looked up at Squidge. 'Didn't I?'

'Dreadful,' he answered. 'Completely vague.'

I had to close my eyes because I couldn't stop staring at Klara's features, trying to find the child I had loved so deeply. We used to lie beside each other on the spongy surface of the playground and count each other's freckles. I would watch as Klara's bottom lip pressed briefly under her top teeth before she spoke. I thought it made her look like a mouse, a sweet, hesitant mouse. Sometimes I stood in front of the mirror trying it myself, but it never worked for me. I looked like a dumb rabbit. It was the shape of Klara's face and her mouth that had made her so loveable and vulnerable.

I rubbed my eyes till they stung, trying to superimpose one Klara on the other.

'I should get you home,' Squidge said to Klara.

'Yes,' she said. 'Yes, please.'

When I opened my left eye she was looking back at me. The blue of her eyes was like the sky shuddering behind a copse of wind-torn trees.

When I opened my right eye she was looking back at her lap.

I touched her arm. Her thin white arm.

'Klara,' I said. I didn't know what else needed to be said anymore. I tried our old call sign, one of the secret codes we used together. 'Time flies like an arrow.'

'Very nice to see you, Natalie,' she responded. She was supposed to reply, 'Fruit flies like a banana.'

Squidge stood and stretched, the bones in his back cracking.

I took Klara's hand in mine. I wanted to have the sensation of our damp childish hands clasped together under the desk one more time. But her hand was dry. Under the skin I could feel the tremor of her bones and muscles, a tremor that probably never left her.

'I'm glad you made it,' I told her softly, so her husband didn't hear, so there was one good thing left between us.

She stood. Her husband held out his hand to help her and she took her hand from mine and gave it to him like a princess taking the hand of the footman from the carriage step. He held her hand high as she edged her way out from the table.

'Goodbye,' I said.

'Goodbye,' she answered.

Once, we were like sisters. But we were not sisters. She has a real sister and a brother and they are her family. And she owes me nothing.

BLOOD

Tony Birch

Tommy Cole introduced himself to Nez and me wearing a pair of tight jeans, a black T-shirt, a felt cowboy hat sweat-stained around the brim, and a pair of R.M. Williams he spent half of his time spit polishing. The day he turned up we were living in a caravan on the beachfront in Adelaide. Gwen brought him home to the van from a club in town where she was working. The next morning he took a look around the van and told Gwen that a woman of her beauty and talent deserved better, which made Nez laugh; she had decided that Tommy was funny and that maybe he liked her.

We moved out of the van that day, into a motel further along the strip. Tommy booked two rooms, one for Nez and me to share, and the other for him and Gwen.

I didn't like the look of Tommy. He was way too friendly to be trusted. But I was happy with the move, as the motel had a swimming pool, cable TV and room service that let you order just about any meal you could think of.

The first night at the motel we watched a cop movie in our room while Gwen and Tommy went out drinking and dancing somewhere.

They got back late, long after the movie was over and I'd turned off the TV, put the lights out and gone to bed.

Only a paper-thin wall separated their room from ours and they kept me awake for most of the night. I could tell by the sound of Gwen's voice coming through the wall—she was just about singing—that she was drunk again. They played music and drank some more, while Tommy screamed out, 'Trick or treat, baby, trick or treat,' every five minutes or so, like they were having a Halloween party.

The next morning Gwen giggled that they were madly in love as she put her arm around Tommy's neck and chewed at his ear. And within a day or two she was talking about marriage, although I was pretty sure she hadn't discussed her plans with Tommy. While he was off doing some 'business' that Gwen would not elaborate on, she sat us at the breakfast table in the motel dining room and explained how Nez would be her flower girl, 'A pink satin dress, Nezzie, with fresh flowers through your hair,' while I would be giving the bride away.

Gwen then reached across the table and touched my cheek with the back of her hand. 'You could get yourself a suit, Jesse. With pinstripes and all. You'll look like a real man.'

I didn't like the idea of Tommy becoming stepfather to us, but I wasn't too worried about the prospect either. Gwen had announced that she was getting married about four or five times before and nothing came of it, so I wasn't expecting wedding bells in any hurry.

She and Tommy went hard at it day and night for the next week or so. After breakfast each morning he'd give me money to take Nez to see a movie and eat as much takeaway as we could stuff into ourselves. When we weren't at the movies or hanging around the beach we rode buses across the city, armed with a disposable camera that Tommy had given us to play with. We took pictures of other passengers on the buses or of people in the street when they weren't watching us. When Tommy handed me the camera he'd said it was a gift for us, and maybe it was, but I knew he hadn't paid a cent for it because I'd seen him steal the camera just the day before, from the 7-Eleven around the corner from where we were staying.

Nez and me came back to the motel one afternoon after a swim in the sea to find Gwen curled up on her bed, sobbing like a baby. She was wearing only her underwear, she had bruises all over her arms and legs, and her make-up was ruined, with mascara stains running down her cheeks.

I looked around the room, at the empty bottles, the overflowing ashtrays and coke foils, and the clothes and underwear lying on the floor. It was a mess. Nez was standing behind me, breathing heavily. I could tell by the rattling noise in her chest that her asthma was playing up, like it did whenever she was nervous.

I told Nez to leave the room and go next door and watch some TV, but she wouldn't. She ran past me, jumped onto the bed, lay down alongside Gwen and held onto her as tightly as she could.

It turned out that Cowboy Tommy had vanished just as quickly as he'd arrived. He left Gwen with a black eye and an unpaid bill for the rooms, as well as a bar tab fit for a football team on an end-of-season trip.

Tommy left us with no choice but to do a runner from the motel.

Later that night, after Gwen had put Nez to bed, I helped her load the boot of the car with two garbage bags stuffed with our clothes, her make-up case, and Nez's few toys. We then raided the housemaid's trolley, stealing packets of sweet biscuits, a cardboard box full of bottled water, blankets and pillows, some soap, and a toilet roll and towel.

The next morning we ate breakfast, took a final swim in the pool and ordered a lunch of roast chicken, baked potatoes and chocolate ice-cream. Gwen added the meal to our tab, along with a tip for the young waiter she'd flirted with over lunch. We then snuck away from the motel by the rear car park.

Our getaway car was a shit-coloured Commodore without a straight panel and tyres worn smooth as racing slicks. It was a bomb, for sure, but it had never broken down on us in the two years we'd had it, and kept us dry and more or less warm when it was the only place we had to sleep for the night.

After leaving Adelaide we drove to the border and crossed into the far west of Victoria. I sat in the back with Nez, who kicked me as she lay on the other side of the car, sulking over something she wouldn't talk about. I was pretty sure it would be over Tommy having abandoned us. He'd paid Nez a lot of attention that week and she'd lapped it up like a spoiled kitten.

The sky was big, blue and empty except for a ball of sun tracking us, while the land we drove through was as flat as an iron, and bone dry and brown.

I got thirsty just looking out of the car window at it.

There wasn't much we saw along the way that wasn't stone dead. We drove through one small town totally deserted and another just as empty except for an old man sitting in a rocker on the verandah of a rundown weatherboard house. He was wrapped in an old blanket and had shoulder-length white hair and grey skin. While he looked more like a ghost than a man and frightened me, I couldn't take my eyes off him as we drove by.

We also saw sheep and cows dotted here and there in the dry paddocks, and some farm machinery, most of which was rusted and looked like it hadn't been used in a long time.

It was a hot day on the highway. The air-conditioning in the car, which had never worked properly anyway, hummed and grunted so loudly I couldn't make out a single song on the radio, even though it was turned up full blast. Gwen made things worse by chain-smoking all the way with the car windows wound up.

I could hardly spot Nez through the smoke so I coughed a couple of times in the hope that Gwen would get the message and put her cigarette out. But she didn't, so I leaned over the seat, tapped her on the shoulder and yelled at her to turn the radio down and the air-conditioning off.

'What?' she screamed back at me.

'The radio. Can you turn it off? And the air?'

She eventually punched the 'off' button on the radio, but wouldn't touch the air-conditioning.

I started telling her about a science article I'd read in a magazine when we were back in Adelaide, in the laundromat at the caravan park. It was all about passive smoking and how it killed more people every year than the road toll and most known diseases combined.

'That's not true,' she interrupted, as she defiantly lit up another cigarette, turned around and blew smoke in my face.

'You always think you're a wealth of information, Jesse, but that story can't be true. What about cancer? Those numbers couldn't include cancer. They wouldn't have counted all them deaths, I bet. It's killed almost everyone I know over the age of fifty. It took your grandfather. He didn't even see his fortieth. Cancer's like a fucking plague.'

'The story is true. I read it in a magazine.'

'Makes no difference where you read it—it's bullshit.' She took another drag on the cigarette. 'Why you reading science magazines, anyway? Since when have you been interested in science? What did you get for the subject at that last school you were at? What was it? An F?'

'I wasn't there long enough to get a school report. Don't you remember?'

She wouldn't answer me, and only wound down her window and threw the lit cigarette from the car into the dry scrub when Nez started calling out from the back seat that we were all going to die of 'pastel smoking'.

'You'll start a bushfire doing that,' I complained, as I turned and looked out of the back window to the spot where she had just thrown the cigarette butt.

'Thank you, Fireman fucking Sam,' she screamed as she held the empty cigarette packet in her hand, crushed it into a ball and threw it out of the window as well.

'That should make the both of you happy. I'm all out of cigarettes now, and I've no money for another packet. So, it looks like we'll all have to live a bit longer.'

I tapped her on the shoulder again. 'You shouldn't litter. You can get a fine for that. I think it's thousands of dollars or something.'

It was dark before Gwen realised we had not much more than a drop of petrol in the tank. Her solution was to tap the petrol gauge in the hope that it might shift the needle. It didn't budge, of course. She pulled over to the side of the road, turned the engine off and rested her head on the steering wheel as she muttered and swore to herself.

When she finally lifted her head she told us we would have to stop when we got to the next town or the car might die on us on the side of the highway.

We drove back onto the road, took the next exit and headed for the lights of a small town not far off the highway. I wound down my window and looked out into the night. As far as I could see we'd arrived in the middle of nowhere anyway.

After doing a lap of the town Gwen pulled into a yard beside a wheat silo and railway siding. She got out of the car, went to the boot and grabbed the blankets and pillows that we'd nicked from the motel. She handed one of the blankets across the seat for Nez and me to share along with two packets of the sweet biscuits and a bottle of water each.

As soon as Gwen lay down across the front seat of the car, manoeuvring her arse around the floor shift, Nez started to cough and splutter. She had never got used to sleeping on the road and was afraid of the dark. It wouldn't take much for Nez to convince herself that a madman might come along in the night and kidnap her. Or cut our throats as we slept.

Nez pulled more than her share of our blanket over her head as she continued snivelling. Gwen tried to ignore her, pulling her own blanket over her head. Nez responded by crying a little louder, so Gwen told her to shut up. Nez didn't stop. Gwen eventually sat up, threw her blanket to the floor and climbed across into the back seat with us. She looked angry, like maybe she was about to slap Nez in the face. But she didn't. She squeezed in between us, put her arm around Nez and told her we were going to be okay.

We weren't going to be stuck here for too long, she explained. Although we hadn't seen one when we drove through the town, she was sure there'd be a pub around, and she'd get some work behind the bar for a couple of days. Then we'd be back out on the highway and heading for *home*, wherever that might be.

She was still going on about how things were going to pick up for us when I fell asleep.

Early the next morning the hackling grate of a bird and a dull tapping sound woke me. I sat up and looked out through the windscreen at a large blackbird perched on the end of the car bonnet, pecking at the duco. The bird tilted its head to one side to get a better look at me before lifting its wings and vanishing into the sky.

I looked over at Nez. She was still asleep.

I got out of the car, hobbled across the gravel yard in my bare feet and took a piss behind a tree. When I came back Gwen was sitting in the driver's seat with the car window wound down, puffing on a butt that she must have retrieved from the ashtray.

She looked out through the cracked windscreen at me as I walked by the car. Smoke hissed between a gap in her front teeth as she spoke. 'I've stuffed up this time, haven't I, Jesse?' She tried laughing.

I said nothing as I shrugged my shoulders. There'd been so many other times she'd got us into trouble there didn't seem to be a lot of difference *this time*.

Nez was awake. She rolled around inside her blanket a couple of times, sat up and looked around the car as she rubbed sleep from her eyes. She didn't have much of an idea about where she was. She complained that she had to go to the toilet. When Gwen told her she would have to do it behind the tree like I had, Nez looked at her in horror, which surprised me. Both Nez and me had been forced to take a piss in plenty of places worse than this one.

'The tree? I'm not going over there.'

'Yes you are, Nez. You'll go where I tell you to go.'

Nez screwed her face up. 'Well, I'm only going to pee then. That's all I'm going to do.'

Gwen held up her miserly butt and stared at it. 'Piss or don't piss then. See if I care.'

Nez got out of the car and slammed the door in protest. After she'd finished squatting behind the tree she ran back just as Gwen got out of the car herself and went to the boot. It sounded like she was rustling around in the garbage bags. After a couple of minutes she closed the boot and walked around to the side of the car.

Gwen had changed into what she liked to call her 'lucky dress'. It was sleeveless and a deep red colour with a low neckline. She smiled at us as she smoothed the creases of the dress with the palms of her hands. 'How do I look?'

Neither of us said a word. Me because I didn't care how she looked, and Nez because I could see that she was already worrying herself with the thought that Gwen might be about to shoot through on us. Gwen had done it before, and more than once—left us behind when things got so tight for her that all she could think to do was run away.

I looked along the stretch of highway leading away from the car. It would not have surprised me at all if Gwen walked away from the car and didn't come back. I also knew that if I didn't have Nez to look after I'd go too, as far away from Gwen as I could get.

Gwen told us we weren't to stray from the car, and if anyone came snooping around asking questions I was to tell them we'd broken down and that *our father* would be back soon with a mechanic from the town.

'What about the toilet?' Nez asked. 'What if I need to go? If I have to . . .'

Gwen ignored her. She was busy doing her lipstick in the side mirror. She then stood up, pointed the lipstick at Nez and jabbed the air with it as she spoke.

'Use your brains, Nez. Go where you have to. There's a toilet roll in the boot.'

As Nez got out to search through the boot Gwen took a final look at herself in the mirror, stood up and grabbed her bag from the floor of the car. She was about to walk off when Nez called out to her.

'Wait. I want to take your photo.'

Nez was holding the disposable camera in her hand. She walked towards Gwen, stopped about a metre in front of her, lifted the camera to her eye and looked through the lens.

'Smile.'

Gwen could never resist a photo opportunity. She draped the bag over her shoulder with one hand, rested the other on her hip and pouted her lips. She held her pose until Nez had taken the picture.

Before I knew what she was doing Gwen had grabbed hold of me and wrapped an arm tightly around my waist. 'Take this one, Nezzie, with my toy boy.'

Nez took the picture before I had wriggled free by elbowing Gwen in the ribs.

'Take it easy, Jesse, take it easy,' she yelled at me before posing again. 'Come on, love, another one of me.'

Nez examined the camera. 'No. There's only two pictures left—I'm saving them.'

Gwen appeared a little insulted. 'Suit yourself then. See you two later.' She dropped the bag to her side, turned around and walked off.

I strolled onto the road and watched as the red triangle of Gwen's dress grew smaller and smaller. It stopped for a moment and drifted in a haze coming off the hot tar on the road. While I could not make out her face I imagined that Gwen might be looking back at us and thinking about what she might do next.

The dress then moved forward and vanished.

I told Nez to stay with the car while I took a look around the yard, but I'd taken only a few steps when I heard the car door creak open, followed by Nez's footsteps scraping behind me in the gravel.

After circling the yard a couple of times I headed for a tin shed on one side of the wheat silo. When I opened the shed door I could hardly believe my luck: there was a toilet in one corner.

Nez waited in the doorway as I walked over to the toilet. What looked like the remains of a dead rat sat in the bowl. I would have to get rid of it before Nez saw it and started screaming. I pressed the button. Luckily the water was connected. After a few flushes the rat was gone and the bowl was clean enough.

I collected the toilet roll from the boot, then I wiped down the toilet seat with a few sheets of the roll before handing it to Nez.

She looked up at a cobweb in the corner of the corrugated-iron roof above the toilet seat and begged me to stay with her while she went.

'No, Nez. Jesus. I'm not going to wait here while you go to the toilet.'

Maybe it was because she was frightened, or just tired and hungry—I'm not sure—but she started to bawl and wouldn't stop until I promised I would stay with her while she sat on the toilet and that I would look out for any spiders that might come down from the roof.

After she'd finished I got her to scrub her hands as best she could in the murky water that came out of a tap on the wall across from the toilet.

We then left the shed and started to explore the paddocks beyond the silo.

We found a lot of junk lying around, bits and pieces of machinery mostly, and beer cans with what looked like bullet holes through them. Next to the hollow of a shallow dam in a paddock below the silo, we saw the flyblown carcass of a dead sheep. It reminded me of a story I'd seen on TV about the drought, and the pictures of dead sheep and cattle being pushed into a ditch by machines and then buried.

Shotgun shells lay on the ground near the sheep, so I guessed it had most likely been blasted to death rather than died of starvation.

Nez eventually got bored of trailing behind me. She complained that her feet were sore, that she was getting blisters, that she was hot, and she was thirsty. She sat down on the ground and wouldn't move.

I left her where she was and headed back to the car for a bottle of water. I closed the boot, opened the bottle and took a long drink as I looked across the yard to the railway siding. I could see a dirt road led away from the siding. It narrowed before disappearing into bushes.

I took another drink, put the top back on the bottle and walked across the yard to the track. I followed it into the bushes, where it ended suddenly. I was about to turn back when I heard a sound. It was running water. I forced my way through the bushes to a clearing on the other side. I could see a river below me.

'Nez. Nez! Come over here. Quick.'

The river water was the colour of weak tea and shimmered in the light. I stripped down to my underpants, ran across a muddy bank and plunged in. Nez wouldn't come all the way in. She took off her jeans and T-shirt, folded them neatly into a ball and sat them on a rock along with her camera. She walked slowly down to the water's edge and splashed around in the shallows in her undies and singlet while I swam.

Between swims I skipped stones across the surface of the water while Nez watched me from a rock she was perched on. Her job was to count the skips of the stones I threw in my attempt to break what I'd announced to her as the 'World Freshwater Tor Skipping Championship'.

'What's a tor, Jesse?' she asked, scratching the tip of her nose.

'It's a killer marble. An assassin. It's the prize you've got to capture if you're to have any chance of winning the game. Otherwise it will take you out. It's like the king in chess.'

She looked at the stone gripped between my fingers. 'A marble is round,' she said. 'The ones you're throwing are flat. They're not tors.'

'They are. At least this one will be. When I break the record, it will be this stone that clinches it for me.'

'But it won't be yours, Jesse. The stone will be at the bottom of the river somewhere.'

'Well, Nez, when you want something bad enough, there's a price to pay. Always.'

I threw my arm back, pitched the stone and watched as it skimmed across the water.

'Seven . . . eight . . . nine . . . ten . . . that's a new record, Jesse,' Nez squealed, clapping her hands together.

She picked up the camera and pointed it at me. 'Let me take a picture of the world champion.'

Although I wouldn't pose for her she took the picture anyway.

My arm was sore from all the throwing. I sat down next to Nez and poked at the bed of mud beneath my feet with the sharp end of a twig as our bodies dried in the sun. She'd taken her shoes off. I could see that she had mud caked between her toes.

I tapped her on the calf with my big toe. 'You'd better clean those feet before Gwen gets back. She won't want you putting that mud all over the back seat of the car.'

She wiggled her toes. One or two clumps of mud fell to the ground. She took the twig from me and started drawing something in the mud. It was a house.

'When will she, when will . . . Mum be back?'

I shrugged my shoulders. 'I don't know. Soon I hope. I'm starving. She'd better have something for us to eat.'

I dragged my foot across the rock and again tapped her on the side of the leg. 'And don't call her Mum, Nez. You know she don't like it.'

'But she is my mum. And she's your mum too, stupid.'

She finished drawing the house. She was now onto a girl, maybe a self-portrait?

'Yeah, I know she is. But you're wasting your time calling her that. She'll just ignore you. You know that. You might as well whistle her like a dog that doesn't want to come home.'

'But I like it, calling her Mum.'

'Well, she don't. Makes her feel old, she says. Makes her angry too. So don't do it. She'll be in a shitty mood already, and I don't want her starting on us.'

Nez ignored me as she busied herself with another drawing and whispered, 'Mum, Mum, Mum' under her breath. She drew another person, standing next to the house. I had no idea who it was.

When she had finished drawing Nez tossed the twig away and climbed up onto the rock. 'There's just one shot left in the camera. Will you take a picture of me?'

All the snooping around and swimming had made us hungry. We got dressed and walked back to the car, where we ate about six packets of biscuits each. My favourites were the Scotch Fingers, while Nez liked the Monte Carlos, so we did some swapping.

I munched on my last biscuit and looked across to the wheat silo. It had a metal staircase wrapped around the outside. I looked up at the sky and back down to the base of the silo. I decided to climb it. I walked across the yard towards the silo with Nez calling after me, 'What are you doing, Jesse?' as she stood up and followed.

I put my foot on the bottom step of the staircase. It shook from side to side and knocked against the silo, sending an echo across the yard. Some cockatoos perched high in the gum tree we had pissed against earlier in the day squawked and flew into the sky.

I began to climb the stairs.

'Are you sure it's safe?' Nez called out to me as she gripped the metal rail of the staircase while keeping both feet planted firmly on the bottom step.

'Probably not,' I called out as I kept on climbing, without looking back to see where she was.

As I moved quickly around the outside of the silo I could hear Nez calling, 'Jesse, hang on, will you? Hang on.'

I knew that if I didn't wait for her I would eventually have to go back anyway. I sat on a step and looked down at the ground, about fifty feet below me. When Nez finally reached me she was wheezing badly and her cheeks were the colour of beetroot. She had the camera around her neck.

I got her to sit down next to me and do the breathing exercises taught to her by a welfare nurse when we were in care together one time. As I counted each breath for her Nez looked across at the ugly scar on the side of my arm, just below my elbow.

'Tell me how you got that, Jesse.'

'What, now? We're supposed to be climbing. Anyway, you know how I got it. I've told you a thousand times already.'

'I know you have, lots of times. But tell me again, please. I'll count my breaths if you tell me the story about the scar. Please?'

The story was about how I'd fought off a vicious dog that had attacked me in the street one day, when I was about six or seven. As I'd done each time I'd gone over the story, I acted the scene where I'd poked the mongrel between the eyes, forcing it to release my mangled arm from its jaws of rotting yellow teeth. After the dog had retreated up the street, back to the junkyard it came from, I'd looked down at my arm, at the bloodied hunk of flesh that had been almost ripped away.

Nez leaned across to me and traced the jagged scar with a fingertip. She knew exactly what question to ask next.

'Did it hurt, Jesse? When the dog bit you?'

'Yeah. It hurt like hell. But not nearly as much as when they stitched me up at the hospital. They couldn't find no anaesthetic and no small needles, so they stitched my arm back together with something about the size of a knitting needle. It was all rusty and probably full of poison. The same needle had been used to stitch manure bags together. That hurt a lot more than the dog bite.'

'Is that a true story, Jesse?'

'What do you think?'

She lightly touched the scar again. 'I guess so. I guess so.'

I stood up. 'Come on. I'm going up to the top. You coming or not?'

As we climbed higher and the staircase wobbled and shook some more, Nez grabbed hold of my t-shirt.

When we finally reached the top I stood on a wooden platform surrounded by a wire frame. It was like being in a giant birdcage. I looked through a rotting gap in the floor to the ground, which was now maybe eighty or a hundred feet below where we were standing.

Nez looked up. 'It's beautiful up here. So close to the sky.'

I could see the ribbon of highway cutting through the scrub where we'd come from last night, and in the opposite direction, the town laid out as flat and empty as the land around it.

Nez pointed to the town. 'Can you see her, Jesse? Can you see Gwen?'

I looked down on the map of streets, and searched for Gwen's red dress. While there were one or two people moving about like ants, there was no sign of her.

'No. I can't see her.'

Nez slipped the camera over her head and clutched it in her hands. 'I've got us in here. Gwen and me and you.'

She looked through the wire cage and down at the ground for the first time. The colour faded from her face. She threw herself around me and held on tightly. I was not sure if it was the staircase shaking or just her body. Eventually she took a step back, but kept one hand wrapped tightly around my wrist.

'Jesse? Are we still blood brother and sister? Like you said we were, that time when we cut ourselves?'

'Of course we are. You can't undo that, Nez. It's like Holy Communion, sort of religious. Our blood is mixed together. It moves around our bodies. Forever.'

'Tell me about that day again.'

I looked at her white-knuckled grip around my wrist. 'I'll tell you, but only if you promise that we'll climb back down when I've finished. Promise?'

'I promise.'

Nez had just turned five when Gwen told her we didn't have the same father. She'd just got the sack from a job for taking days off, and would have upset Nez deliberately. When life was going poorly for Gwen she always hurt one of us. It was all she could think to do.

After telling Nez that we were not a 'legal' brother and sister, and that we could be separated forever if anything ever happened to her—'God forbid, Nezzie'—Gwen had gone out somewhere and left Nez alone in the flat. When I got home from the school I had been at for only two weeks I found her sitting on the landing out the front of the flat.

When I asked Nez what was wrong she asked me a question of her own; was it true that we did not have the same father? I couldn't think of a quick and convincing lie to tell her, so I said yeah it was true, 'but we have the good half, Nez'.

'But that's not right, Jesse. I want us to be the same, not half. I want us to be legal. That's what Mum said, *legal*.'

She then made fists out of her chubby soft hands and started banging them into her thighs. I knew I had to do something to fix the damage Gwen had done.

I took Nez into the flat and told her to sit at the kitchen table as I searched for a sharp knife in one of the drawers. I then put one hand over the sink and sliced across the top of my thumb with the knife, cutting myself deeper than I needed to.

A red line appeared across the top of my thumb, and then a stream of blood. It tracked along the outside of my thumb, down my arm, and onto the kitchen floor, where the splotches of blood made a pattern on the tiles.

I turned to Nez. 'Now it's your turn.'

She got up from the chair and came over to the sink. She couldn't take her eyes off my bloodied thumb. 'No, Jesse. I don't want to do it.'

'Nez, you just said that you want us to be whole. Do you want to be my full sister, or not? Look away, over at the telly.'

'It's not on. The telly's not on, Jesse.'

'Well, just pretend it is. Look away. Now.'

I wrapped one hand around her wrist, gripped it tightly and nicked the tip of her thumb with the knife before she had a chance to pull away. Although she could cry easily when she felt a need to, Nez did not shed a tear. She let out a yelp, like a puppy whose tail had just been trod on, but that was all.

I pressed my thumb against hers, and watched as our blood ran together.

'See. We're the same now, Nez. The same.'

'And will we always be together?' she quizzed me as she watched with fascination.

'Yes, we will always be together. Always.'

While Nez had been listening to me tell the story, I had been watching a large bird in the sky, maybe a falcon, or even an eagle. Its wingspan must have been ten feet across, maybe more. The bird glided above us then lifted into the air without making a sound or moving its wings at all.

'Is that the end, Jesse?'

When I looked around my sister was calm.

'Yeah, Nez. That's the end. We have to go now.'

She stood up and did a cautious three-sixty-degree turn as she looked out across the land. 'Do you think she'll come back for us?'

'Of course she will,' I answered, although I never felt sure that Gwen would be back.

'But if she didn't, if she didn't come, what would happen to us?'

'Nothing would happen to us, Nez. Nothing.'

'We wouldn't be separated again? Like the time she got sick and we were fostered?'

Her voice broke up a little as she spoke. I looked across to the horizon, and for the first time noticed a mountain range in the far distance. Behind the mountains was a band of dark cloud and what looked like heavy weather coming our way.

'No, we wouldn't be separated. Never again. We'd go. If Gwen didn't come back for us, then we'd go too.'

She squinted into the sharp light of the sun above the low cloud.

'But where to? Where would we go? Tell me that story too, Jesse. Tell me that one.'

THE DISCO AT THE END OF COMMUNISM

Christos Tsiolkas

It was Saverio's week to do the shopping. Trying to fit the key into the front door lock, with two full grocery bags under each arm, he noticed his wife's shadow looming towards him in the cloudy beer-bottle glass; she was rushing to open the door for him. He was about to kiss her, to ask her to help him unload the other bags from the car, but froze when he saw her expression. He didn't drop the bags, or cry out, but he could not speak.

'It's not the kids—they're fine.' Rachel grabbed two of the bags from him and ushered him into the house, leading him by the hand. When they got to the kitchen, she put down her bags, and took his hands. 'Julian rang while you were at the market. I'm so sorry, it's about Leo. He had a stroke this morning. He's dead. There's nothing anyone could have done, Sav. It must have been quick, he wouldn't have suffered.'

His first thought was to protect her, to banish the fear and confusion from her eyes. He did so by gripping her hand tighter. She started to cry. Almost immediately, he envied her ability to exhibit all the appropriate signs of grief. It had been well over a decade since she had last seen Leo.

'Julian's left a mobile number. He wants you to call him back straight away.'

'I'll unpack the groceries.'

She was shaking her head. 'I'll do that, baby. You call Julian.'

Julian answered on the first ring, his voice surprisingly youthful and clear. Saverio had always liked Julian, had considered him good for Leo and had been distressed when he'd heard that they had split up. But Julian had remained loyal to the friendship and Saverio was not surprised that he'd been the one there at Leo's end. Julian would be assuming all the responsibilities that, in the normal course of events, should now be Saverio's. But Leo had never been one for the normal course of events.

'Thank you.'

'What for?' Julian sounded astonished.

'For being there.'

There was silence, then a rapidly muttered, 'That's okay.'

'Rachel said that it was immediate, thank God.'

'Yes.' He could hear a match being struck, the long inhalation of smoke. 'He's been pretty crook, his liver has been giving him trouble for some time now.' Julian hesitated, then said quickly: 'I might as well be straight with you, Sav. He was pretty drunk when it happened—he was shooting up amphetamines.'

Saverio watched as Rachel methodically stacked the groceries on the kitchen table: toiletries for the bathroom, food and drinks for the kitchen and pantry, cat food and detergents for the laundry. Every now and then she would throw a quick glance over at him. Her eyes were still swollen and red.

He died shooting up speed, Rachel, he wanted to mouth at her. The dickhead was shooting up speed at fifty-two. The stupid, stupid fool.

'When did it happen?'

'Sometime last night.'

'Who found him?'

'There's a woman close by who keeps an eye on him. She's a good soul. She rang the police and then she rang me.'

'Are you there already?'

'Nah, nah, mate, I'm still in Sydney. I'm flying up tomorrow morning.'

'Does the coroner have to deal with it?'

'No. I've talked to the local cops and they say it's all straight-forward.'

That was it. Saverio was out of questions.

Julian cleared his throat. 'I'll arrange the funeral from Demons Creek. I've already got a copy of Leo's will and he wants to be buried up there. Sav, I want you to come up for it.'

Rachel wasn't concentrating. The dishwashing liquid was in the pile with the laundry stuff.

'Of course I'll come.'

Saverio caught the relief in her eyes, and felt it as well in Julian's affectionate farewell. He hung up, wanting to slam the phone against the wall, wanting to explode in anger like a child.

At that moment, shirtless, with his pyjama bottoms hanging half off his arse, Matthew shuffled into the kitchen, greeting his parents with a muffled grunt. Saverio checked the clock. It was just past noon.

The useless prick had been clubbing all night, wasting his money, probably doing the same stupid drugs that had just killed Leo.

'*Cazzo!* This is not a civilised hour to crawl out of bed, you lazy shit!'

Rachel's eyebrows arched and her mouth fell open—but she said nothing.

Matthew, who was peering into the fridge searching for the orange juice, swung around. 'What the fuck's wrong with you?'

Rachel came and stood beside Saverio, placing her hand on his shoulder. He wanted to shrug it off.

'Matty, we've just heard that your uncle Leo has died.'

There was a moment of incomprehension and then Matthew sheepishly hung his head. 'I'm sorry, Dad.'

Saverio couldn't speak. He felt wretched. He wasn't sorry that his brother was dead, he was just feeling relief. It was over.

•

In the end Rachel did not fly up north with him. She had been on higher duties since the beginning of the year, taking over the management of her unit from Gloria, who was on long-service leave. The extra money had been useful, allowed them to pay Matthew's university fees upfront, but it had meant Rachel working longer hours, bringing home work on the weekends and having to fly regularly to Canberra to assist the minister while parliament was sitting. Saverio felt as if he had hardly seen her over the last month; she had worked late every night organising an international conference on industrial relations. In response to his complaints she had booked a four-day retreat for them at Mount Hotham after the conference. Saverio was a keen skier but it was years since they had visited the snow. On the night they'd heard the news about Leo, she had come into the bedroom and announced that she was going to cancel the retreat.

'Why?'

'I'm sorry, darling, I can't go to both Leo's funeral and the snow. I just don't have the time.'

'I want to go to Mount Hotham with you.' He beckoned her over and pulled her onto the bed. Her hand was greasy from lotion she'd been rubbing into her arms. 'I really want this holiday. You don't have to come to the funeral. I just want to bury him, say my goodbyes and that's it. I'd rather go alone.'

Her eyes were searching his face. She didn't believe him. Or didn't want to believe him. 'I think I should be there.'

'Oh, for God's sake,' he groaned. 'As if Leo would have given a fuck if you were there or not.'

Her hand slipped out of his. Her eyes were cold, distant.

'More than anything,' he continued, lowering his voice, introducing a note of pleading, 'I want to be away with you, just you. That's what I'm going to need after the funeral.'

She gave no answer, just kissed him on the forehead and went back into the ensuite. In the mirror he watched her finish applying her creams, watched her floss and brush her teeth, grinned as she slid the door shut to take a pee, enjoying as he always did the fact that even after so many years she could still be shy with him. He'd also caught the hint of relief in her expression. She would have willingly come to say her farewell to Leo. He had always made her laugh. But Saverio knew she would have been dreading the idea of spending time with any of Leo's old friends.

•

As the plane began its descent into Coolangatta, Saverio took out his earphones and, ignoring the sleeping man next to him, looked down at the splendour of the Pacific and the ugly town thrusting out of the lush green landscape. Matthew had been rendered almost dumb by the news of his uncle's death—not from any personal shock or grief, for he had very few memories of Leo, but rather out of fear of having to communicate somehow with a supposedly mourning father. He had created a playlist on Saverio's MP3 player filled with uncomplicated rock and roll from the late seventies and early eighties. A tinny whisper of 'Brass in Pocket' still seeped softly from the earphones and an unsmiling stewardess leaned over to scold him.

'Please turn it off, sir, we are about to land.' Saverio settled back into his seat. He did appreciate Matty's clumsy effort at sympathy; it was a loving, masculine gesture. Words would have been impossible between them. Saverio didn't dare confess to his son his ambivalence about Leo's death. He had always been more comfortable with his daughter. On hearing the news, Adelaide had rushed to him, and clutched him tight, whispering, *I know it's difficult, I know it must be.* It had been exactly the right thing to say. He had marvelled at her innate wisdom: only two years older than her brother and, no matter how much Saverio still tried to deny it, undoubtedly an adult. He gritted his teeth and held tight to the armrests as the aeroplane surged. In a few seconds the wheels would touch earth, the moment he always feared, the point where the hubris of this mass of steel and wire defying gravity would end in calamity for all on board. The bronzed gentleman farmer sitting next to him, with the open-necked polo shirt and the clearly expensive Italian loafers, stifled a yawn. The wheels of the craft touched asphalt, the plane pogoed, swayed from side to side, then righted itself and screeched forward on the runway. They were safe.

The drive from Coolangatta to Mullumbimby cut through some of the loveliest forest in the country. Saverio could see that if one believed in deities, one could call it God's Country, could imagine that the hills and coves and vast open space were the garden and sky of Eden. From time to time, as the rental car climbed into the hinterland, he would catch sight of the ocean sparkling in the rear-view mirror, the silvery light of the sky touching the glimmer of the sea. It was beautiful. No wonder his brother had made this part of the world home. But as he veered off the highway onto Demons Creek Road, Saverio felt a knotting in his stomach. He tightened his grip on the wheel.

There had been money put into the communities that dotted the verdant hills. Eleven years ago the road had still been gravel. Now it was shiny black bitumen. Architect-designed holiday houses jutted out of the greenery, all with prominent verandahs overlooking the sea. When Leo had first moved here in the early nineties there still existed the remnants of a commune, the property itself owned by a septet of academics who were radicalised as students at universities in Sydney and Melbourne. The commune had disbanded soon after Leo had moved there with Julian but, nostalgically loyal to their old politics, the landlords had all agreed that Leo could live and paint there rent-free. Saverio and Rachel had urged him to buy some land when it was still going cheap, but Leo had scoffed at their capitalist avarice. To the end he had refused any of the money left to him by his parents. I don't believe in inheritance, he had brutally said to Rachel when she phoned after his father had finally died and they needed to know what to do with the portion of the estate left to Leo. But what do you want to do with the money? she persisted. The answer had come a week later in the form of a letter. Half of the money, it stated, was to go to the Aboriginal community centre in Redfern, the rest to an outreach centre in Kings Cross. The lawyer had raised her eyebrows on reading the letter and whistled out loud. 'Are you sure he's not a little mentally unbalanced, your brother?' It was intended as a joke but they did not miss the eagerness of her question. 'Just do whatever he says,' Saverio had replied. 'Just as long as I don't have to speak to the prick.'

The car nosed its way up the dirt drive to the cottage. Eleven years before there had been an immaculately maintained herb garden, a fig tree, and lime and lemon trees. The garden was now overrun by weeds, and rotting fruit covered the ground underneath the untamed foliage of the trees. Saverio wasn't surprised. The garden had been Julian's project and once he'd gone Leo wouldn't have had the gumption to keep it together. The chassis of the car scraped along the ground as the front left wheel sank into a pothole. Frigging Leo,

Saverio thought, he couldn't look after anything. Five or six cars were already parked haphazardly across the yard. There was music coming from the cottage and Saverio could see people standing and sitting on the wide verandah. He felt as though every eye was on him and his hand trembled as he turned off the ignition. The sun was setting behind the mountain and the crowd on the verandah was in shade. He was dreading the small talk, the hours to come. For a moment he contemplated simply turning back, weaving down the mountain back to the coast, to get the last plane home to Melbourne. The seatbelt was still buckled, his foot still rested on the accelerator.

He started at a tap on the window. Julian's cheery tanned face was smiling down at him—some grey stubble on the chin, the buzz-cut hair speckled salt-white at the temples, but his skin still smooth and his shining eyes still youthful. Julian opened the door and the two men hugged awkwardly. Saverio couldn't help thinking, What are we to each other? Not really friends—ex in-laws? Was there a new language, as yet undiscovered by himself and Rachel, that covered such relationships? He was relieved when Julian stepped back.

•

Within the first half hour Saverio deeply regretted that he had come. He was sure he wasn't imagining the suspicion and disapproval directed towards him. He wished only Julian was there—he alone seemed to bear him no ill-will. The others he had not seen for decades. Hannah Wiszler, who used to wear workers' overalls and shave her head, was now a journalist at the ABC; Siobhan F, who had dropped a surname in the late seventies when she was sixteen and was playing electric guitar in a three-piece called Penis Envy, was now a doctor with Médecins Sans Frontières. Dimitri Alexandropoulos he knew of, a playwright and scriptwriter; Ben Franks was a noted visual artist; Dawn Sallford was a parliamentary secretary, and Tom Jords was still a poet and still a drunk. They all had to be reminded of his name and none of them were the slightest bit interested in him or his life. Saverio took the wine offered to him by Julian and sat on the top step of the verandah listening in to them, their reminiscences of Leo. Leo at university, Leo at protests, Leo as an artist, Leo's jokes, Leo's witticisms, Leo's insults. 'Wasn't he fabulous?' That was Dawn Sallford, her voice raspy from the cigarettes she still chain-smoked. You'll be dead soon as well, Saverio couldn't help thinking. He hated himself for descending into the pettiness of the past, instantly transforming back into the unconfident, awkward older brother who never knew the right books to read, the right films to quote, the right music to have in his collection. They had all been so erudite, so opinionated, so intelligent. Even their father, who had detested the effeminacy and pretentiousness of Leo's university friends, had reluctantly granted them that: 'They're smart,' he used to spit out. 'That's all they are.'

Dawn was launching into another story about Leo, some political meeting which had bored them both and in which she had dared him to strip naked. It seemed that Leo had taken the dare, had stood up in the middle of the room and begun to undress. Dawn was elaborating on the story, the rollie in her hand swinging wildly as the tale unfolded.

'And I'm going, Dah-dah-DAH dah-dah-DAH Dah-dah-dah-DAH—you know, that frigging strippers' music—and Leo is down to his jocks and he pulls them off and throws them at the facilitator, who was this dumb-fuck po-faced Stalinist who bored you shitless with quotes from Lenin and deadshits like that.' Except for Saverio, everyone was laughing, Dawn so hard that she couldn't continue.

'And then? What else happened?' Julian's face was eager, expectant. For Christ's sake, Saverio thought, he must have heard this story, must have been bored by it a hundred times already. But no, he was like a child anticipating his favourite moment from a well-loved storybook. He was so young compared to them all, at least ten years younger than Leo.

'Come on, Dawn,' said Julian, 'tell us. What was so funny?'

Dawn straightened up, sniffed, took a breath. 'Now what was that prick's name? Nick? Nick Tate? No, that was the actor.' She looked triumphant. 'Nick Simmonds. Anyway, Leo's white jocks are flung over Nick's face, everyone is looking at him, so shocked, Leo's standing starkers in the middle of the circle—getting a stiffie I might add . . .'

'Always the fucking exhibitionist!' shrieked Tom Jords.

Dawn was coughing and chuckling again. 'He loved getting his bloody cock out, the silly old poof.' She took a swig of wine, finished the last puff from her cigarette, flicked it into the ashtray precariously perched on the bannister. 'So there's this silence and everyone is shocked and open-mouthed and I'm looking over at Nick and there's this big pair of white Y-fronts covering his head. So Leo, starkers, turns to me and announces, "Dawn, I think we're going to get purged."'

Dawn again collapsed into spasms of mirth. They all did, except Saverio. He threw back his wine and rose to his feet.

'Where am I sleeping?'

They were laughing so hard they couldn't hear him.

He cleared his throat and repeated the question.

Julian, still chuckling, smiled up at him. He pointed inside. 'You've got the main bedroom.'

'Thanks.' Saverio grabbed his bag off the verandah and walked into the house. They had all fallen back into laughter. He knew it was foolish, that it was not at all the case, but it felt like they were laughing at him.

•

'You think that's something to be proud of, do you? It's not. You should be fucking ashamed.'

It was at Leo's twenty-first birthday party and it had been Dawn who'd said it to him. Saverio had recently completed his engineering degree and that morning had received the call to say he'd been accepted as a graduate by Shell. He was just about to turn twenty-three and was excited at the prospect of his first professional job. Leo's birthday had been held in rooms above a popular vegetarian North Indian restaurant in Carlton. It attracted students and it was said that if you knew the staff they would let you onto the roof to smoke joints while surveying the skyline of Melbourne. Not that there had been much of a skyline to Melbourne back then. Just the forlorn apocalyptic Bauhaus towers of the housing commission.

Saverio couldn't wait to tell his brother about the job. Leo had already lived out of home for two years, having walked out after a final argument with their old man that had ended, as it usually did, with their father lashing out at Leo—but this time Leo had punched back. It was the night Leo had told them all that he was homosexual. '*Finocchio*,' their father kept repeating, confused. '*No, non lo sei!*'

'I am!'

'*No, no, no. Finocchio no!*' Saverio remembered the finality in his father's tone, the firm set of the distaste and denial on his face. He would not accept it. He would not have it.

'You know, Dad, you would have benefited from a good cock up your arse. It would have made you a better man. It would have made you a better husband.'

Saverio had not believed that his brother could say such things to their father. With a roar, their father had rushed over to Leo and started pummelling him with both fists. Saverio had been ready to leap up and defend his brother when Leo had raised a fist and struck back. It had been an ineffectual, weak, pansy hit, Saverio had thought, so fucking pansy, but it was enough to stop their father cold. A son had dared strike back.

'Go.' Their father pointed at the door. 'You don't live here no more.'

Leo smiled, a cruel, gloating smile that had been directly passed down to him from their father. 'I'm already gone, you ignorant shit. I've been gone for years.'

That, of course, had been Leo all over: throw a bomb, walk away and let someone else clean up the mess. It had always been that way; Leo and their father seemed to be born to battle. Leo refused to learn Italian, Leo wasn't interested in anything to do with soccer, all Leo wanted to do was get lost in books. At first it was their mother who intervened, protecting Leo from her husband's violence but also pleading, remonstrating, coaxing Leo into making his apologies. Then the cancer struck and she was dead within a year. Saverio had been fourteen and Leo just about to start high school. The younger boy disappeared deeper into his world of books and imagination and Saverio had become the go-between, even years later, after Leo had left home and immersed himself in the stimulating intellectual and political life of university, discovering the pleasures of drugs and sex. *Why can't you say something to him!* his father would roar. *What kind of older brother are you?* Ashamed, Saverio would try to broker a peace. It would be Leo's turn to scream at him. *I don't have to apologise to that patriarchal fascist shit!*

'You think that's something to be proud of, do you? It's not. You should be fucking ashamed!'

Dawn's voice was brutal and disapproving. Saverio had looked over to his brother, wanting Leo to save him from the ferocity of her contempt, but Leo had made no reply. It was a ghastly moment, one of those times when all other conversation had ceased and everyone seemed to be turned towards him. That could just be memory playing a trick, of course—probably no one else at the party really gave a damn. But he did not make up Leo's silence. Leo had *not* defended him.

'Dawn, I've been looking for work for ages, since completing my degree—'

She hadn't let him finish. It was what he remembered most about Leo's friends: the surety of their beliefs, the passion and the hostility.

'Shell supports the apartheid state in South Africa. You want to be part of that?'

No, I want a job. They interviewed me, have given me a graduate position—I've been trying for months. But that wouldn't do for Dawn and he had said nothing. She had stepped closer to him, and the vehemence in her eyes had startled him. She felt it so strongly. She wasn't even black.

'Don't take the job.'

'What?' He had been astounded. 'Of course I'm taking the job.'

He had thought she was going to spit on him but instead she had turned around and dismissed him with a guttural, vicious grunt of disgust.

From Leo there had been no word of congratulations, no questions about the job, what he would be doing, when he would be starting.

'She's right. You shouldn't take the job.' Then Leo had walked off to whisper and laugh and joke with his friends.

•

Saverio slammed his suitcase onto the bed. It had been over thirty years ago but the recollection of it still rankled, still filled him with impotent fury. He stared around the room. Every spare inch of wall seemed to be filled with canvases, and if not paintings, then photographs. Polaroids, cheap travel shots with florid colours, artistic black and white prints. Framed photos were crammed onto the bureau and bedside table. A stack of Leo's paintings was resting against the far wall, under a framed Aboriginal Land Rights poster that Saverio remembered from the early eighties. The photographs were of Leo and his friends. Leo in Hanoi and Paris and Mexico City. Leo and Dawn in Cuba. Leo and Tom Jords wearing pink T-shirts emblazoned with a black Women's Liberation fist at Mardi Gras. On the small table there was an old black and white photograph of their mother, when she was a young girl in Rome, her face sullen as she braved the camera. Of Saverio and their father there was nothing at all, not one snapshot. He shouldn't have come. Leo's true family had been the men and women now laughing and swapping reminiscences on the verandah outside.

There was a muffled, 'Can I come in?', and Saverio swung around. Julian was holding out a glass of wine with an apologetic smile. Saverio took it and gestured for Julian to come in.

'You should be the one sleeping in here,' Saverio said quietly.

Julian laughed and shook his head. 'It's fine. The old gang are going to sleep on mattresses and sleeping bags on the living-room floor. We'll probably keep you awake with our drunken raves.' Julian's brow suddenly squashed into a frown. 'Unless you prefer not to sleep in . . .'

'No, no, that's fine. Thanks—it's kind of you.'

Saverio was not frightened of Leo's ghost. They had that in common, brothers in their rationalism and atheism, their father's sons.

Julian walked around the bed and started flicking through the canvases against the wall.

'I'll have to sort through all of these before I head back to Sydney. Leo's named me executor of his estate.' Julian's voice had dropped to an anxious whisper.

'That's how it should be.'

Saverio glimpsed a corner of a painting, the strokes thick, the colours warm, fiery. A lavender-veined penis pushing through a glory hole. Julian let the canvases drop. He seemed to be searching the walls of the room and his gaze lighted on a small, vivid colour Polaroid. It was of a beaming Filipino woman holding a chuckling naked boy. Julian's features, his smile, his mischievous eyes, were unmistakable. Julian unpinned the Polaroid and put it in his shirt pocket.

'Leo was always meant to give that back. It's the only photo I have of me and Mum back in Manila.'

Saverio felt as if he were sinking. He had hoped that it would be cooler up in the hills but he had forgotten that it was impossible to escape the humidity in this part of the world. He wanted to be back in Melbourne, in less intense light, where he didn't feel that every corner and spare inch of space was illuminated. He didn't want to be sipping red wine. He wanted a beer. He didn't know how to make conversation with these people, even Julian who had always been kind to him and Rachel. There was the sound of smashing glass on the verandah and peals of laughter.

'It's probably going to be like this all night.'

Saverio searched his pockets, clasped the car keys. 'I'm going to go into town. Do we need anything?'

Julian, surprised, shook his head.

'I'll see you in a hour or two.'

'Sav, will you deliver a eulogy tomorrow?'

He felt snookered. No, he did not want to deliver a eulogy. There was absolutely nothing to say.

With a toss of his chin, Julian indicated the world outside. 'We'd all appreciate it.'

I thought you didn't believe in family. I thought you believed it was a patriarchal capitalist construct. But maybe they did now. Maybe now they believed in family and shares and television and parliamentary democracy. He just wanted to leave the room, the house, the unbearable heat. He nodded and Julian smiled.

Saverio almost ran to the verandah.

An old lime Volkswagen Beetle was coming up the drive. There was a noisy crunching of the gears, and then a small shudder before it came to a halt. Saverio looked through the flyscreen door to see everyone jump off the verandah and cluster around the white-haired woman who climbed out of the car. She wore faded bermuda shorts and a yellow singlet. A much younger woman stepped out from the driver's side. She looked like she was still shedding adolescence. She was wearing a pink see-through shirt and even from behind the screen Saverio could see the outline of the black bra beneath. Julian pushed past him through the door and Saverio almost fell out onto the verandah.

Everyone was talking, calling out, hugging and kissing the older woman. Only the young woman looked up, and smiled ruefully, as if to acknowledge him. She was not dressed for the weather at all. She had on a tight black miniskirt with embroidered white stockings. Her thick-soled black boots laced up past her ankles. Her hair was dyed a platinum blonde, set in curls that fell to her shoulders, and her face was heavily made-up with rouge, thick black eyeliner and scarlet lipstick. She reminded him of a young Marilyn Monroe. She seemed to know everyone, greeting them with kisses. Julian had placed a protective arm around her and was beckoning Saverio to come down. The older woman looked up as he descended the steps. He recognised her face—Margaret Cannon was a well-regarded fiction writer; Rachel had read all her books. Saverio had no recollection of meeting her before. But her smile was warm, inviting, and her grip tight as she shook his hand.

'It's Stephen, isn't it?'

'Saverio.'

'My apologies. That's a much better name, isn't it?' She turned to the younger woman. 'This is Leo's brother, Saverio. And this is Anna, my daughter and Leo's goddaughter.'

The young woman's hand was moist. She winced apologetically.

'I'm sorry. I'm so sweaty.'

'Of course you are, Anna. Look at what you're wearing.'

Anna's laugh was loud and deep-throated. 'You're a bitch, Dawn.'

'Yeah, shut up.' Julian's grip tightened around Anna's shoulders. 'I think you look gorgeous.'

'Thank you, Jules, so do you.'

Saverio now found himself at the edge of the circle. He jiggled the car keys in his pocket.

'I'm going into town. Anyone need anything?'

'Do we need more grog?'

'There's plenty. Even for us.'

Dawn wasn't satisfied. 'Is there whisky?'

Julian rubbed at his chin. 'I can go and have a look . . .'

'Get us a bottle of scotch,' she interrupted.

Give us some money, thought Saverio sourly.

But it was Anna who answered. 'Jesus, Dawn, what did your last slave die of?'

Dawn didn't miss a beat. 'Laziness.'

He couldn't help it, even he had to laugh. They were so fast, so sophisticated, so smart. He nodded and moved towards his car. He was surprised to find Anna following him.

She turned back to her mother. 'I'm going into town as well.'

'We just got here!'

Anna ignored her. She was waiting for Saverio to unlock the doors. She smiled across at him. 'It's alright with you, isn't it?'

'Of course.'

As they turned onto the Pacific Highway Anna let out a sigh of relief. 'Thank you. That was a bit too much.'

'What was?'

'Seeing everyone en masse. You know, that old libertarian femo crowd. They're lovely but it will be all the same stories, who slept with Germaine Greer, who sucked off Robert Hughes while they were all on acid.' She reminded Saverio of Adelaide, the affectation in her outburst. They were both young women, trying out accents, tones, registers. He wasn't at all shocked by her language. It just reminded him of how young she was.

'Tom looks awful.'

He didn't reply.

She shrugged her shoulders. 'I guess that's because of all the antiretroviral drugs he's on. And because he's a drunk.'

'He's always been an alcoholic.'

He felt her gaze fix on him. 'I didn't know Leo had a brother.'

'I didn't know he had a godchild.'

'He's got two. But Danny is in England or Poland or somewhere like that.'

They fell into silence. But something she'd said had made him curious. He couldn't help it. He felt a little embarrassed asking but ask he did: 'Who did Germaine Greer fuck?'

Anna grinned mischievously. 'Probably all of them.' She was searching through the glove box and underneath her seat. 'Do you have any music?'

'No. It's a hire car.'

She was examining the stereo unit. 'I should have brought along my iPod. There's a jack.' She turned to him eagerly. 'Do you have one?'

So that was what that attachment on the stereo was for. She, like his own kids, seemed to have a second sense for technology. He shook his head. 'I'm sorry, I left mine back at the house.'

Disappointed, she turned the radio on instead. She kept punching buttons, rapid sprays of music, country and western, pop, snatches of talkback. She settled on a familiar strained melancholic voice singing above a jangling melodious electric guitar.

'Do you like U2?'

They were a favourite, one of the few passions he shared with Matthew. 'I think I have every album,' he announced proudly.

'They're alright.' She sounded uncertain. Then with a derisive sniff, 'But that Bono is a sanctimonious cunt. He makes me want to hate them.' She was flicking through her purse and she placed a cigarette to her lips.

'This is a non-smoking car.'

'I thought you lot were all anarchists?'

'I'm not part of that lot and I don't want you to smoke in the car.'

She made a face, but returned the cigarette to its packet. Her fingers started tapping on the dashboard. 'How come I've never met you before?'

'Leo and I haven't seen each other for a while.'

'What's a while?'

'Eleven years.'

'Fuck!' There was awe as well as shock in her exclamation. 'You must be feeling awful.'

She was right. Probably not in the way she thought, but she was right nonetheless. He did feel awful. He was furious at himself. He had been cold and unfeeling for days and this was not the moment to experience the sting of tears in his eyes. He did not dare look at her.

'I'm sorry.' For the first time her voice had lost its brazen inflection. It sounded young and frightened. He did turn to her. She was looking out of the window at the lush landscape falling away from them. She continued to speak in that shy childlike tone. 'I loved Leo. He was amazing, wonderful. But he could be so mean.'

In town, she followed him confidently into the pub, as if they had known each other for years. The Demons Creek Hotel was a three-storey Victorian building with an ugly, box-like extension attached to the side of it which functioned as a bottleshop. It was blessedly cool inside the double-bricked walls of the building. All heads turned to look at them as they walked into the bar, then just as quickly everyone went back to contemplating their drinks. It was far from crowded. A few tradesmen who'd just knocked off work, two ferals with dreads, some elderly National Party types propped up on stools at the bar. The pub obviously catered with egalitarian ease to the long-established farmers, to the hippies and children of hippies who had laid claim to the hills over the last three decades, and also to the constant stream of local and international tourists who came through on their way south to Byron Bay. It was evident that they assumed Anna and Saverio were part of the latter group. No eyebrow was raised at Anna's aggressively urban attire. Saverio was conscious that if their entry had aroused any suspicions it had to do with what a middle-aged man like himself was doing in the company of such a young woman. She's my brother's goddaughter, he wanted to call out. She's got nothing to do with me. Instead he asked her if she wanted a beer and she said yes.

The three elderly blokes at the bar fell silent as he approached. He nodded to them and received a gruff 'g'day' in response. They all shared wrinkled ruddy skin and thin wisps of silver-yellow hair, and all wore open-necked white shirts that accentuated the burnt redness of their necks. Saverio looked around the bar as he waited for the beers to be poured. He wondered if his brother had spent much time in this pub; he couldn't really imagine Leo discussing Marxism with the farmers or anonymous gay sex with the hippies. He took a glass in each hand, nodded again to the old men, and found Anna at the rear of the pub. As part of the more recent extensions a small square dance area had been constructed against the back wall. On three sides mirrors ran from floor to ceiling reflecting the bar beyond. Anna was gazing at her reflection. A mirror ball hung from the ceiling. Some of the shingles of glass were missing.

'I guess this is where you come if you want to go clubbing.'

She laughed again, a deep resonant sound that came all the way up from her belly. 'I can see Leo here, he loved a bit of a dance.' She put on a mock accent, Leo at his most queenie, cruelly caricaturing other gay men. 'They're playing "I Will Survive", Brooce! They're playing "I Will Survive".' At the same time Anna was wiggling in such a close approximation of Leo's stilted dancing style that Saverio couldn't help laughing. Anna took the beer and indicated a door with a handwritten scrawl taped to it: *To the beer garden.*

'Am I allowed to smoke out there?'

I'm not your father, he almost snapped at her. Instead he opened the door for her and followed her out to the courtyard.

It was a stunning view. The gently sloping hill was immaculately mowed, with tall grey-limbed gum trees throwing shade on the tables and chairs set around the lawn. There were no fences and the ground disappeared abruptly to give way to the jutting tops of thick forest trees. Beyond the greenery and as far as the eye could see was the curve of the mighty Pacific Ocean. The garden was empty except for a blonde woman sitting on a bench at the end of the lawn, looking out over the view. She did not turn at the sound of their voices.

'So why did you and Leo stop talking to each other?'

He wished he had said nothing to her in the car. Tomorrow was the funeral and after that he would return to Melbourne. Then it was all over.

He took a mouthful of beer. 'It really doesn't matter now.'

She was searching his face again, her eyes inquisitive and excited. She drew ravenously on her cigarette.

'Your father was a fascist, wasn't he?'

He banged the beer glass on the table. 'That's nonsense. Did Leo tell you that?'

Anna was not at all perturbed. 'Yep. He said that your father supported Mussolini . . .'

'My father did not support Mussolini!' Saverio drew breath and looked out at the view. She was a child, she wasn't to blame. 'My father hated the Blackshirts, thought them thugs and criminals, but he respected some of what Mussolini was able to achieve for Italy and for poor people in Italy. He was not alone in that. Millions of Italian peasants were in agreement.'

'He did beat your mother, though, didn't he?'

And how the fuck is that your business? Saverio searched out to the horizon again. The sky and sea offered no assistance. The setting sun still had heat in it and he wished he had remembered his sunglasses.

'I think Leo might have exaggerated some of what occurred.' It was impossible to explain further. Yes, he had hit their mother, not very often, never bashed her, but yes, he hit her, three, possibly four times that he could recall, in front of him and Leo—smacks, slaps, always out of exasperation, driven almost senseless by her whining, her hypochondria, her almost bovine submissiveness. How to explain any of this to a young woman coming into adulthood at the dawn of this digital century? How to explain the behaviour of men and women from the end of a feudal millennium?

'If he wasn't so bad, why did Leo hate him so much?'

That question was so childish—as if there were any easy answers to it. Because Leo was unforgiving. Because Leo was stubborn. Because Leo was selfish. Because Leo relied upon their mother's support and when she died he felt betrayed. Because mothers always favoured the gay son. All of this was true, but to say any of it was to lead into an argument. He wished she hadn't come with him. He had wanted to forget Leo for a few hours, and her presence and her questions couldn't help but remind him of the duties he faced tomorrow. He couldn't do it, he just wasn't up to it. He would say so to Julian, and Julian would understand. I can't give a eulogy. I have nothing to say. I can't say what I want to say. I can't say that Leo was the kind of man who couldn't go and visit his dying father, the kind of man who didn't have it in him to ask after his niece and nephew. The rage seemed to flood through him, threatened to drown him. The heat, the humidity, the thickness of it, like a blanket over the world, was exhausting.

'Are you okay?' She was concerned now, biting her bottom lip. Her incisors were long and crooked. He wanted her to shut her mouth; the exposed teeth made her look crude, ugly.

'I have to go to the bathroom.'

It was blissful to be inside the cool anteroom of the toilets. They were part of the original hotel and the thick tiled walls were effective insulation against the heat. He was the only occupant of the male toilets and he unbuttoned his shirt to the navel and splashed water on his face, his neck, under his arms. He used his handkerchief to wipe himself dry. He examined his face critically in the mirror. He hadn't shaved that morning and across his chin and along his upper lip there had already formed a soft shadow of alternating white and black stubby bristles. He wished he'd had time for a haircut. His smoky-grey hair was shapeless, the harsh fluorescent light in the toilets seemed to shine directly above where his hair was thinnest. You idiot, he hissed to himself. You vain, stupid fuck, you want to impress that young girl.

The soft colourless scar above his left eyebrow was almost invisible. He should point that out to Anna. This is where my brother hit me with a hammer when I was ten. The reason for the argument was long forgotten. All he could remember was trying to squeeze the life out of Leo, his hands around his brother's neck, and how Leo would not submit, how he kicked and struck and scratched like a wild animal. The argument had started in their bedroom. They had punched and kicked each other into the kitchen and rolled into the laundry where Saverio's hands were around his brother's throat and Leo's hand had landed on a hammer and it was in raising this hammer to Saverio's face that the battle had ended. He had blood in his mouth and had fallen across the laundry door and Leo was on top of him, the hammer raised, ready to strike another blow. Don't, Saverio had screamed. Don't! Leo dropped the hammer, his lips were trembling. You're bleeding, he started to whimper. It's okay, I'm alright. His anger, his brother's anger, had disappeared in an instant.

When he got back to the table, the woman who had been at the end of the beer garden was sitting across from Anna. They were both smoking and looked up, smiling, as his shadow fell across them.

'Saverio, this is Melanie.'

'Call me Mel,' the woman said. Her voice was shockingly nasal and broad, almost a take-off of a rural Australian accent. Her grip was tight, firm. She wore sunglasses with big round lenses so he could not see her eyes but he guessed she was in her mid-forties. The skin around her mouth was wrinkled, her lips thin, and her hair was dyed a chemical yellow. She wore a black T-shirt a size too small for her full breasts and pot belly, and black jeans a size too small for her expanding arse and thick thighs. She was obviously what Matty and Adelaide would derisively call a *bogan*, and what his parents, with equal derision, would have called an *Australiana*. She was a woman who could not take root anywhere else but in this enormous infinite landscape. Unabashed, unashamed.

'He's better-looking than Leo.'

'Mel knew Leo,' Anna rushed to explain.

'Yeah, he was a good bloke, your brother.' Mel stubbed out her cigarette. 'I'm really sorry for your loss.' It was the expected phrase, it came from a stranger, but she had said it with unforced sincerity and they were the first words since hearing of Leo's death that brought home the finality of the event. His brother was no more. From now there would only be past.

'Thank you.'

'When I first left Brendan and began seeing Suzanne, Leo was the only one who I could talk to about things.' Mel was obviously continuing a conversation she had begun with Anna while he was in the toilet. 'Small towns are fucked. Everyone knows you and Brendan's really popular with everyone. He's done work on most people's pipes or plumbing so you can imagine what they thought of me when I took off with a woman.' Mel was shaking her head. 'I thought they were going to kill me. Kill both of us. Leo's was always a safe house; he'd let us come and stay, sleep over. Talk to us about gay rights and shit. Suzanne loved him. She's devastated he's gone.'

Saverio was horrified. Mel had started to cry.

'Fucking bitch, I hate her!'

Anna had wrapped her fingers around Mel's hand. Saverio, confused, looked away. A line of surfers, black and grey and silver strokes, was visible against the vast blue of the ocean. Mel blew her nose into a tissue one more time then glanced down guiltily at Anna's cigarettes.

Anna nodded.

'I shouldn't.'

'Today doesn't count.'

Mel laughed. 'Yeah, that's right.'

She was looking at Saverio. He couldn't smile, he didn't know what she wanted from him. All he could think was what an unlikely lesbian she seemed. He had thought she was a bikie's moll, an ex-stripper, a small-town mum. Of course it was possible she *was* all of those things. And a lesbian to boot. Though Dawn wouldn't find much communion with her. Just like him, Dawn wouldn't know what to say to Mel.

The woman was rising. 'Thank you for the smokes.'

Anna jumped to her feet and hugged her. 'You'll look after yourself?'

'Of course.' Mel seemed embarrassed by the spontaneous affection. She slipped out of Anna's embrace and held out her hand to Saverio, who had also risen.

'Mate, again, I'm really sorry. Your brother was a real good man.'

He couldn't speak. They watched in silence as Mel walked back into the pub. She was shaky on her feet.

'She shouldn't drive,' he said gruffly.

'I know, but her girlfriend's just left her for a younger woman so of course she's just going to do whatever she likes tonight. We'd all do that.' Anna pointed to the empty glasses. 'Another round?'

'One more.' He pointed to her empty chair. 'But you sit. I'm buying.'

'You bought the last round.'

'I work. I'm a corporate cocksucker, as my brother used to so fondly put it. You're young and a student. I'm paying.'

Anna looked as if she was about to protest again. Then, suddenly, she beamed. 'Sure. Thank you.'

At the bar, Mel was arguing with two men, one of them in a khaki uniform with an orange and yellow National Parks and Wildlife insignia stitched on the pocket, the other in football shorts and paint-splattered work singlet and Blundstones. She winked at him as he walked past. Saverio noticed that the painter had his right hand sitting flat against her wide buttocks.

'I hope our friend is alright in there,' he said to Anna as he delivered the new beer.

Anna shrugged and drank greedily. 'She looks like she can take care of herself.'

That was not his impression. She *looked* tough but Mel hadn't struck him as *being* tough.

The dying afternoon sun was still strong, but finally a breeze was coming off the darkening water.

'She really liked Leo.'

'Yes.' He would keep his answers short, non-committal, give nothing away.

'It's good to be reminded of what a wonderful man he could be. You could always talk to Leo about anything. He'd always listen.'

He sipped at his beer slowly.

'One of the things I loved about him was that he would never give you the standard adult answer, he'd always take you a little by surprise. When I was ten I found a stash of Julian's pornos in the house and wanted to read them but Leo asked me if I had started masturbating. I said no and he wouldn't let me have them, said it might dull my imagination. That was so unlike him—usually he let us watch and read anything we liked, no censorship whatsoever. But not this time. But he was right.' Anna sniggered. ''Course, once I started doing the old five-finger dance he let me have them.' She winked at Saverio. 'He was such a character. Was he always like that?'

'I guess so.'

Anna was frowning. For Christ's sake, what did she want from him?

She lit a cigarette, sat back in her chair and crossed her arms. 'Saverio, I think you should forgive him.'

Sin, Confession, Absolution. These children of communists and feminists and true believers were just as moralistic as the old believers.

'Anna, I'm sorry, but you're a child—you don't know what the fuck you are talking about.'

He had humiliated her. He could see that she was holding back tears and felt immediate regret. Again, she so reminded him of Adelaide. She was young, she had yet to learn how to hide her emotions from the world. He knew he should apologise but he was enjoying the relief of being harsh and uncompromising. There was a thrill to punishment, he had learned that raising his own children; the thrill of deflating them, confronting them with their own limitations, ignorance, powerlessness, foolishness, inadequacies. What did she know about him and Leo? She should just keep her fucking mouth shut.

Don't cry, please don't cry.

She wasn't crying. She was looking out to sea.

'Four years ago, for my seventeenth birthday, I came to stay here with Rowan, who was my boyfriend. I thought Rowan was going to be the love of my life. He was two years older, he played guitar in a band, he was at university, his mother was a feminist academic and his father was an actor. I thought he was so cool and so handsome and so wonderful and that I was going to be in love with him forever. I wanted Row to meet Leo and I wanted Leo to meet Row. I thought they were both the most fabulous men in the world and I wanted them to know each other.'

Her voice was detached, she stumbled a little over her words, but she sounded confident and deliberate. He was aware that a large part of it was a pose, that there was something theatrical in her delivery. She kept her eyes out to the horizon of sea and sky, but he knew that she was fully conscious of his stare. He wasn't sure why she was telling him all this, of how she was exacting her revenge.

'Rowan took to Leo immediately. He loved how funny he was and he loved all the gossip. We stayed up all that first night smoking ice while Leo told him the Germaine Greer story and the Sasha Soldatow story and the Jim Sharman story and who fucked whom and who blasted heroin with whom and who really should have taken the credit for what and of course Row was like a grateful child, just lapping it all up.'

Anna took a big breath. 'Do you want to hear all this?'

She was hesitating for effect. She would be crushed if he said no. He wanted to say no, that there was nothing that he could hear about Leo that would make his own heart feel any lighter.

'We all fall asleep at dawn, all in the big bed and I wake a few hours later and decide to take a walk in the forest. It's a beautiful day and I'm still feeling fantastic because of the drugs and I walk all the way to town to the bakery and pick up some croissants and rolls and I walk all the way back to Leo's. I get there and Leo is cooking in the kitchen and Rowan is playing his guitar on the porch and when I come up the steps and I'm smiling he looks at me and bursts into tears. He just keeps saying, We had sex, Anna, we fucked, Anna, I'm so sorry. I drop the bag of croissants and rolls and look up at the door where Leo is standing, a stupid apron on, a fork in one hand, and he just says, "Rowan wanted to tell you—he's still young and foolish. I told him you didn't have to know." Then he goes back into the kitchen and continues making us breakfast.'

Saverio couldn't believe how the bowerbirds continued their whispering song in the trees above, how the drumroll of the waves echoed off the coast below. He could barely control his voice as he asked: 'What did you do?'

'I cried and I asked them both how they could do it to me and Row was crying as well and he kept saying, "I'm sorry, I'm sorry, I'm sorry," and I ran after Leo and said, "Are you going to apologise, are you going to say you're sorry?" and he just said, "Anna, you know I am an anarchist and a libertarian. You don't possess Rowan and he doesn't possess you. There is nothing I have to apologise for."'

There was a burst of laughter. Mel and the two men had crashed through the door, into the beer garden, cigarettes in their mouths. Mel called out to them as they sat around a table but Saverio did not register the names of the men as they were introduced. He heard Mel whisper loudly to the man in the singlet, 'That's Leo's brother.'

'What did you say to him?'

Anna turned back to him, her face now unsmiling. 'I hit him. I hit him so hard I wanted to break him.'

'What did he do?'

'He kicked me out. He said he couldn't abide violence, that he had grown up in a violent house and he would not have it in a house of his own. He kicked me out and Row and I drove all the way back to Sydney, both of us crying all the way.' Anna shrugged her shoulders. 'Man, it was a miracle we weren't killed.'

Saverio stumbled out of his chair, across the lawn, bashed through the door, almost ran into the toilets. He wanted to put his fist through the mirror, kick down a cubicle door. If someone said the wrong word, offered the wrong look, made a move to stop him, he would gladly bring them down. He would gladly break their necks. But once again the toilets were empty. He breathed in deeply. Thankfully the toilets were empty.

•

'Do you think she'll be okay?'

He had been silent when he returned to the beer garden, had said nothing as they walked to the car, had been quiet for most of the drive. Anna, too, had said little.

As they'd been about to leave the pub Mel had rushed after them, taken Anna's arm and had tried to lead her onto the dance floor.

'I can't, we have to go.'

'Come on, just one dance, I love this song.'

The pub had begun to fill. The music was steak-and-three-veg Australian rock-and-roll, 'Cheap Wine' by Cold Chisel.

Anna pulled away from Mel. 'I can't dance to this.'

Mel, pouting, flung herself onto the dance floor. She danced on her own, claiming all of the small space, throwing herself into ugly jerks and spasms, singing along to the lyrics at the top of her lungs. Uncertain, Anna looked around the pub, at the tables of men laughing at the dancing woman.

'Maybe we should stay a little while longer?'

Saverio ignored her and walked outside. She could stay if she wanted. Mel was obviously going to be a messy drunk and he did not want the responsibility of looking after her. Anna would learn that life lesson soon enough. But Anna was running after him. Without a word they got into the car.

'She won't be okay. We should have stayed.'

He grunted again.

Anna crossed her arms. 'Why are you so angry?'

Maybe he should drive the car off the road, end it all in screeching tyres, smoke and fire and melting metal.

'Aren't you going to say a thing?'

His reply was to switch on the radio.

She turned it off immediately. 'If I have forgiven him, so can you.'

The petulant spoiled child. This broke his silence.

'You have not forgiven him. How could you forgive him?'

'I have. I really have.' Her tone was urgent, pleading. But he didn't believe her. His brother did not deserve forgiveness.

'What you told me just confirms that he was indeed an animal.'

'That's not true.' She was stumbling for the right words. 'He was just, you know . . . uncompromising . . .'

'For fuck's sake, Anna, he was a cunt. I'm glad he is dead.'

The words appeared to strike her with the force of a punch. Her body shrank into itself. When she spoke next, she was timid, barely audible. 'Leo never lied. He loved sex. Sex was his politics. I always knew that about him.'

Politics? This wasn't politics, this was delusion. Thank God it was over, thank God what they called politics—Leo, Dawn, Tom, the whole damn lot of them—thank God the world no longer listened to such rubbish. Thank God it was all going to die with them.

'Nothing can excuse what he did to you.'

'You're so hard. Just like him, just like all of them. Why the fuck is your generation so hard?'

His foot slammed on the brake and the car swerved onto the side of the road.

Anna jolted forward. She screamed.

He turned on her. 'I am not like them. I'm not anything like them. Do you understand?'

She was terrified now. He was mortified. It didn't matter that Leo was dead. He'd always do this to him, always lay bare a rage he had thought long buried. Alive or dead, the memories and scars wrought on him by Leo were there forever. She had just seen it, that childish selfish annihilating hate. She cowered away from him.

'I'm sorry. I didn't mean to scare you.'

'What the fuck did Leo do to you?'

He tried to explain. He told her of their father's cancer, how it began in the stomach, then spread to the pancreas and how it reached the lungs, how the old man, a skeleton in his bed, the folds of flesh hanging off his bones, how he had succumbed to a delirium in which the past and the present were one. Where is my son, Saverio, where is your brother? Has he forgiven me? He told her about his countless calls to Leo, pleading with him, begging him to come home one last time. He told her what Leo had said to him: Good, the old bastard deserves to die in pain, he deserves to suffer. You can't mean that, Leo. Don't you get it, Sav? That man means nothing to me. He then told her how the fury had gripped him, how he had made the call and organised the plane ticket and flown to Coolangatta and hired the car and driven down the coast and up through the hills to force Leo to return. He told her how they had screamed at one another, slapped and punched one another, how he had gripped Leo's hair and pulled him onto the porch, down the steps, dragged him through the gravel, Leo shrieking, biting him, scratching him, how it was only Julian who stilled their frenzy, Julian crying, howling at them to stop. Don't, please, don't. They were the words that had broken him. He'd left Leo in the dirt and had walked back to the car. *Fuck off! You're just like him*. And still, he explained, to this day he did not know if they were Leo's last words to him or his last words to Leo.

When he finished speaking, Anna was sobbing. Saverio, his eyes dry, his hands steady, eased the car back onto the road and drove them back to the house.

It was dusk when they arrived. The party was still in force on the verandah.

'Have you got my bloody whisky?' Dawn called out to them.

'We forgot,' Anna yelled back. She was looking at her face in the rear-view mirror. She took a compact from her purse and applied powder to her face.

'How do I look?'

Like a child, he wanted to answer, you look like a child. 'You look fine.'

He didn't acknowledge anyone on his way to the bedroom. He closed the door behind him, shutting out the laughter and jokes and talk. On the bed lay a small square canvas. It was of his own children when they were toddlers on the beach. Matty was naked, plonked down in the sand, Adelaide standing next to her brother in pink undies. The colours were intense, garish blues and greens, flaming reds and yellows. His children's faces were elongated, distorted but recognisable nevertheless. Adelaide looked bored, impatient. Matty's dough-like baby face stared blankly out at him. Leo had painted them that first year that he and Julian had moved up to the coast. Saverio, Rachel and the kids had spent a week with them over the summer holidays, a week in which Leo had cooked for them every night and had entertained Rachel with his wild stories, the gossip and slander from the past, extravagant narratives of sexual escapades and orgies. During the day Leo and Julian would take the kids swimming or into town while Rachel and Saverio took long walks in the bushland, found near-empty coves to swim in, read books, had sex and did crosswords.

There was a knock on the door and Julian entered.

'Dawn's all good. I found a bottle of Jameson's in one of the kitchen cupboards.' Julian looked at the canvas in Saverio's hands. 'I thought you might want to keep it.'

Saverio wanted to say, I don't want to talk tomorrow, there is nothing I can say. 'Thank you.'

'Come out for a drink. Our bark is worse than our bite.'

Saverio shook his head. 'Nah, I want to ring Rachel, I want to check on home.'

•

The service began with a recording of Maria Callas singing an aria from *Tosca*, and then it was Dawn who first stepped onto the platform.

Before she spoke she walked to the back of the dais and took down the Australian flag. There was a burst of applause. Leo wouldn't have wanted it, she explained to the shocked civil celebrant. This time there were no outlandish stories, no off-colour jokes or declarations. She told the assembled mourners of how she had first met Leo when they were volunteers at the Aboriginal Legal Centre in Fitzroy, of how frightened she had been of the Aboriginal men, of how Leo had never succumbed to white guilt, how one youth had hurled a barrage of abuse at them one afternoon to which Leo had stood his ground and answered, 'You pay me and you can call me a white cunt—but if I am a volunteer and you insult me then you're a black cunt.'

Tom Jords spoke next, about Leo's work and activism in those first terrible years of the AIDS epidemic, Leo's sense of humour, how his flat in the Cross was always left open in case any of the working girls or boys needed a safe house to escape to. Margaret Cannon got up after Tom and read Leo's favourite poem, 'To Posterity' by Bertolt Brecht.

Then it was Saverio's turn to speak. He scanned the crowd. Mel was there in the back, in a black dress, a chunky silver crucifix around her neck, holding hands with an Islander woman who wore black jeans and a black T-shirt. His eyes came to rest on Anna. He spoke to her. To her and to Julian. He began by telling them that Leo's real name was Luigi, how Leo had hated that name because it was yelled at him with such derision and spite by the Aussie boys. 'Once he started university, Luigi became Leo. You're his family, you were the ones he learned with and experimented with and found so much joy with. You looked after him, you protected him, you understood him. Thank you for that.'

The room had fallen quiet except for the merry screams of the birds, the steady hum of the distant ocean.

'I'm not going to speak about Leo but about Luigi, my younger brother. When he first started school Dad made sure I understood that I had to walk with him every day, that I was not to let him out of my sight. "He's your brother," he said to me, "you will always have to look after him. Do you understand?" But from the second day of school Luigi was determined to walk on his own. I guess he was an anarchist from birth.'

There was a ripple of laughter.

'I knew I couldn't change his mind. I knew it even back then. So I said, yes you can walk ahead of me. That's my favourite memory of him, his walking ahead, a hundred metres in the distance, but every now and then turning back to look at me to make sure I was still there. That was what he was like, always wanting to be independent, free, not reliant on anyone. But I have to believe that from time to time he was still turning back, searching for me.' At this Saverio's voice cracked. 'I have to believe he never forgot me.'

The applause that followed him back to his seat was warm and generous. Anna's claps were the last to die out. Saverio looked over at Julian, who was walking onto the dais. Thank you, the younger man mouthed. It was Julian who spoke at the end and he spoke simply about love. There were no hymns, there was no religion, no prayers. The service finished with Lou Reed's voice singing 'Perfect Day'.

•

Rachel was waiting for him at the airport and as she folded him into her arms he submitted to the sweet calmness of their life together.

At home, as he unpacked, she sat on their bed, took Leo's painting of their kids and scrutinised it critically.

'I always liked this painting.' She took it and walked out of their bedroom.

He followed her into the lounge where she held up the canvas against a stretch of blank wall above the stereo.

'Here,' she said with pleased finality. 'I think it will be perfect here.'

BIOGRAPHIES

TEGAN BENNETT DAYLIGHT was born in Sydney in 1969. She is the author of the novels *Bombora* (1996), *What Falls Away* (2001) and *Safety* (2006).

TONY BIRCH has published widely in short fiction, both in Australia and internationally. His linked collection of short stories *Shadowboxing* (Scribe Publications) was shortlisted for the Queensland Premier's Literary Award in 2006. Tony's collection of short stories, *Fathers Day*, was published by Hunter Publishers in 2009. Tony teaches in the School of Culture and Communication at the University of Melbourne.

ROBERT DREWE grew up on the West Australian coast, the setting for his best-selling memoir *The Shark Net*. His other work includes many novels and short stories. *The Drowner* won the premiers' literary awards in every state, as well as the Adelaide Festival Prize and *The Australian* Book of the Year Award, and was named one of the ten best international novels of the last decade. His most recent book is the short-story collection *The Rip*. After twenty-five years constantly in print, his story anthology *The Bodysurfers* has recently been made a Penguin Classic.

ASHLEY HAY is the author of four books of non-fiction, *The Secret*, *Gum*, *Herbarium* and *Museum* (with the visual artist Robyn Stacey). A former literary editor of *The Bulletin*, her words have also appeared in journals and anthologies including *The Monthly*, *Best Australian Essays*, *Heat* and the *Griffith Review*. Her first novel, *The Body in the Clouds*, will be published by Allen & Unwin in 2010. Currently based in Brisbane, she is a happily siblingless and happily resolute mother of one.

CATE KENNEDY is the author of the short-story collection *Dark Roots* (Scribe); the memoir *Sing*; and *Don't Cry: A Mexican Journal* (Transit Lounge); and two collections of poetry, *Signs of Other Fires* (Five Islands Press) and *Joyflight* (Interactive Press). Her novel *The World Beneath* will be published by Scribe in late 2009. Her short stories have been published widely, appearing everywhere from *The New Yorker* to *The Big Issue*. She lives in Victoria's northeast with her partner and daughter, fitting in as much writing and reading as possible.

NAM LE'S debut collection of short stories, *The Boat*, was published in 2008 and has since been translated into twelve languages. Its honours include the Anisfield-Wolf Book Award, the Dylan Thomas Prize, the New South Wales Premier's Literary Award for

Book of the Year, the UTS Glenda Adams Award, the Pushcart Prize, and selections in *The Sydney Morning Herald* Best Young Novelists and US National Book Foundation '5 Under 35' awards. It was also selected as a *New York Times* Notable Book, *New York Magazine*'s best book debut of 2008, and a book of the year by *The Age*, *The Australian*, *The Sydney Morning Herald*, the *Herald Sun*, *The Monthly* and other sources around the world. Le is currently the fiction editor of the *Harvard Review*.

ROGER McDONALD is the author of seven novels, *1915*, *Slipstream*, *Rough Wallaby*, *Water Man*, *The Slap*, *Mr Darwin's Shooter*, *The Ballad of Desmond Kale*, and of two books of non-fiction, *Shearers' Motel* and *The Tree in Changing Light*. His work has been awarded *The Age* Book of the Year Award, the New South Wales Premier's Literary Award, the Victorian Premier's Literary Award, the South Australian Premier's Literary Award, the Adelaide Festival Book of the Year, the Miles Franklin Literary Award, and the O. Henry Prize (USA).

PADDY O'REILLY is the author of a collection of award-winning stories, *The End of the World*; a novel, *The Factory*; and a novella, 'Deep Water', in the novella anthology *Love and Desire*, edited by Cate Kennedy.

VIRGINIA PETERS is currently working on her first book, a creative non-fiction project focused on the area of crime. She is enrolled in the research program at Newcastle University. To date, her short stories have appeared in the *Sleepers Almanac*, *New Australian*

Stories and UTS anthologies. Virginia lives in the Northern Rivers region with her partner and three children in a place called Coorabell, not far from Byron Bay.

MICHAEL SALA was born in the Netherlands, and emigrated to Australia twice with his family; the first time as a five-year-old, and again when he was ten. He has experimented with various careers, including law, medicine and teaching. He still really likes teaching. In 2007, he was shortlisted for *The Australian*/Vogel Literary Award, and also awarded a mentorship with the Australian Society of Authors. He is currently working on his first novel while completing a PhD at the University of Newcastle.

CHRISTOS TSIOLKAS is the author of four novels: *The Slap*, which won the Commonwealth Writers' Prize for Overall Best Book, the Australian Literature Society Gold Medal, the Booksellers' Choice Award and the ABIA Book of the Year and was shortlisted for the Miles Franklin Literary Award and the Victorian Premier's Literary Award; *Loaded*, which was made into the feature film *Head-On*; *The Jesus Man*; and *Dead Europe*, which won the 2006 *Age* Fiction Prize and the 2006 Melbourne Best Writing Award. Christos also collaborated with Sasha Soldatow on *Jump Cuts* and is the author of a monograph on Fred Schepisi's *The Devil's Playground*. He is also a playwright, essayist and screenwriter. He lives in Melbourne.

CHARLOTTE WOOD is the editor of this collection and author of *The Children*, *The Submerged Cathedral* and *Pieces of a Girl*. Her novels have been shortlisted for various prizes including the Miles Franklin Literary Award and the regional Commonwealth Writers' Prize. She is a proud member of PEN, the human rights group working to protect freedom of expression around the world. Charlotte has four siblings and lives in Sydney with her husband Sean.

ACKNOWLEDGEMENTS

The editor wishes to thank all the contributors to this collection, not only for their stunning writing, but their receptiveness and enthusiasm for the project. Sincere thanks also to Jane Palfreyman for suggesting the book, to Jenny Darling and Donica Bettanin, to editors Ali Lavau, Siobhán Cantrill and Clara Finlay, to Andy Palmer and Felicity McLean, and to Gayna Murphy.